Praise for

HENNING MANKELL

and

Faceless Killers

"An excellent thriller.... A terrific novel."
—*The Independent* (London)

"[Mankell is] one of my new favorites.... **Beautifully constructed plots.**" —Otto Penzler, *New York Post*

"It is Wallander's ... voice ... that **captures us.**"
—*The New York Times Book Review*

"Intelligent, moving and topical, this is **a thriller of the very best kind.**" —*The Times* (London)

"[Mankell] keeps things at **a high level of suspense.**"
—*Detroit Free-Press*

"Inspector Wallander has established himself as one of the best of recent detectives.... **Tightly plotted.**"
—*The Times Literary Supplement* (London)

HENNING MANKELL

Faceless Killers

Henning Mankell's Kurt Wallander mysteries
have been published in thirty-three countries
and consistently top the bestseller lists. He di-
vides his time between Sweden and Maputo,
Mozambique, where he has worked as the director of Teatro Avenida since 1985.

www.henningmankell.com

BOOKS BY HENNING MANKELL

Kurt Wallander Mysteries
Faceless Killers
The Dogs of Riga
The White Lioness
The Man Who Smiled
Sidetracked
The Fifth Woman
One Step Behind
Firewall
The Pyramid
The Troubled Man

A Kurt and Linda Wallander Mystery
Before the Frost

Novels
Chronicler of the Winds
Depths
The Eye of the Leopard
Italian Shoes

Other Mysteries
The Return of the Dancing Master
Kennedy's Brain
The Man from Beijing

Faceless Killers

R

Faceless Killers

HENNING MANKELL

Translated from the Swedish by
STEVEN T. MURRAY

VINTAGE CRIME/BLACK LIZARD
Vintage Books
A Division of Random House, Inc.
New York

FIRST VINTAGE CRIME/BLACK LIZARD MASS-MARKET EDITION, JANUARY 2011

English translation copyright © 1997 by Steven T. Murray
Excerpt from The Troubled Man *English translation copyright © 2011 by Laurie Thompson*

Library of Congress Cataloging-in-Publication Data
Mankell, Henning, 1948–
[Mördare utan ansikte. English]
Faceless killers : a mystery / Henning Mankell; translated from the Swedish by Steven T. Murray.
p. cm.
ISBN: 978-0-307-74285-8
Originally published: [Stockholm]: Ordfront, c1991.
I. Title.
PT9876.23.A49M6713 2003
839.7'374—dc21
2002028805

Map by Reginald Piggot

www.blacklizardcrime.com

Printed in the United States of America
10 9 8 7 6 5 4 3 2 1

Faceless Killers

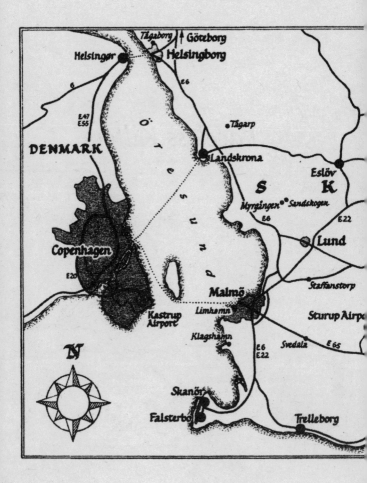

CHAPTER 1

He has forgotten something, he knows that for sure when he wakes up. Something he dreamt during the night. Something he ought to remember. He tries to remember. But sleep is like a black hole. A well that reveals nothing of its contents.

At least I didn't dream about the bulls, he thinks. Then I would have been hot and sweaty, as if I had suffered through a fever during the night. This time the bulls left me in peace.

He lies still in the darkness and listens. His wife's breathing at his side is so faint that he can scarcely hear it. One of these mornings she'll be lying dead beside me and I won't even notice, he thinks. Or maybe it'll be me. Daybreak will reveal that one of us has been left all alone. He checks the clock on the table next to the bed. The hands glow and register 4:45 a.m.

Why did I wake up? he asks himself. Usually I sleep till 5:30. I've done that for more than forty years. Why did I wake now? He listens to the darkness and suddenly he is wide-awake. Something is different.

Something has changed. He stretches out one hand tentatively until he touches his wife's face. With his fingertips he can feel that she's warm. So she's not dead. Neither of them has been left alone yet. He listens intently to the darkness.

The horse, he thinks. She's not neighing. That's why I woke up. Normally the mare whinnies at night. I hear it without waking up, and in my subconscious I know that I can keep on sleeping. Carefully he gets up from the creaky bed. For forty years they've owned it. It was the only piece of furniture they bought when they got married. It's also the only bed they'll ever have. He can feel his left knee aching as he crosses the wooden floor to the window.

I'm old, he thinks. Old and worn out. Every morning when I wake up I'm surprised all over again that I'm seventy years old. He looks out into the winter night. It's January 7, 1990, and no snow has fallen in Skåne this winter. The lamp outside the kitchen door casts its glow across the yard, the bare chestnut tree, and the fields beyond. He squints towards the neighbouring farm where the Lövgrens live. The long, low, white house is dark. The stable in the corner against the farmhouse has a pale yellow lamp above its black door. That's where the mare stands in her stall, and that's where she whinnies uneasily at night when something disturbs her. He listens to the darkness. The bed creaks behind him.

"What are you doing?" mutters his wife.

"Go back to sleep," he replies. "I'm just stretching my legs."

"Is your knee hurting again?"

"No."

"Then come back to bed. Don't stand there freezing, you'll catch cold."

He hears her turn over onto her side. Once we loved each other, he thinks. But he shields himself from his own thought. That's too noble a word. Love. It's not for the likes of us. Someone who has been a farmer for more than forty years, who has worked every day bowed over the heavy Scanian clay, does not use the word "love" when he talks about his wife. In our lives, love has always been something totally different.

He looks at the neighbour's house, peering, trying to penetrate the darkness of the winter night. Whinny, he thinks. Whinny in your stall so I know that everything's all right. So I can lie down under the quilt for a little while longer. A retired, crippled farmer's day is long and dreary enough as it is.

He realises that he's looking at the kitchen window of the neighbour's house. All these years he has cast an occasional glance at his neighbour's window. Now something looks different. Or is it just the darkness that's confusing him? He blinks and counts to twenty to rest his eyes. Then he looks at the window again, and now he's sure that it's open. A window that has always been closed at night is open. And the mare hasn't whinnied at all.

The mare hasn't whinnied because Lövgren hasn't

taken his usual nightly walk to the stable when his prostate acts up and drives him out of his warm bed.

I'm just imagining things, he says to himself. My eyes are cloudy. Everything is as it always is. After all, what could happen here? In the village of Lunnarp, just north of Kade Lake, on the way to beautiful Krageholm Lake, right in the heart of Skåne? Nothing ever happens here. Time stands still in this village where life flows along like a creek without vigour or intent. The only people who live here are a few old farmers who have sold or leased out their land to someone else. We live here and wait for the inevitable.

He looks at the kitchen window once more, and thinks that neither Maria nor Johannes Lövgren would fail to close it. With age comes a sense of dread; there are more and more locks, and no one forgets to close a window before nightfall. To grow old is to live in fear. The dread of something menacing that you felt when you were a child returns when you get old.

I could get dressed and go out, he thinks. Hobble through the yard with the winter wind in my face, up to the fence that separates our properties. I could see close to that I'm just imagining things.

But he doesn't move. Soon Johannes will be getting out of bed to make coffee. First he'll turn on the light in the bathroom, then the light in the kitchen. Everything will be the way it always is.

He stands by the window and realises that he's freezing. He thinks about Maria and Johannes. We've had a marriage with them too, he thinks, as neighbours and as farmers. We've helped each other, shared the hardships and the bad years. But we've shared the good times too. Together we've celebrated Midsummer and eaten Christmas dinner. Our children ran back and forth between the two farms as if they belonged to both. And now we're sharing the long-drawn-out years of old age.

Without knowing why, he opens the window, carefully so as not to wake Hanna. He holds on tight to the latch so that the gusty winter wind won't tear it out of his hand. But the night is completely calm, and he recalls that the weather report on the radio had said nothing about a storm approaching over the Scanian plain.

The starry sky is clear, and it is very cold. He is just about to close the window again when he thinks he hears a sound. He listens and turns, with his left ear towards the open window. His good ear, not his right that was damaged by all the time he spent cooped up in stuffy, rumbling tractors.

A bird, he thinks. A night bird calling. Suddenly he is afraid. Out of nowhere fear appears and seizes him. It sounds like somebody shouting. In despair, trying to be heard. A voice that knows it has to penetrate thick stone walls to catch the attention of the neighbours.

I'm imagining things, he thinks. There's nobody shouting. Who would it be? He shuts the window so hard that it makes a flowerpot jump, and Hanna wakes up.

"What are you doing?" she says, and he can hear that she's annoyed.

As he replies, he feels sure. The terror is real.

"The mare isn't whinnying," he says, sitting down on the edge of the bed. "And the Lövgrens' kitchen window is wide open. And someone is shouting."

She sits up in bed.

"What did you say?"

He doesn't want to answer, but now he's sure that it wasn't a bird that he heard.

"It's Johannes or Maria," he says. "One of them is calling for help."

She gets out of bed and goes over to the window. Big and wide, she stands there in her white nightgown and looks out into the dark.

"The kitchen window isn't open," she whispers. "It's smashed."

He goes over to her, and now he's so cold that he's shaking.

"There's someone shouting for help," she says, and her voice quavers.

"What should we do?"

"Go over there," she replies. "Hurry up!"

"But what if it's dangerous?"

"Aren't we going to help our best friends?"

He dresses quickly, takes the torch from the kitchen cupboard next to the corks and coffee cans. Outside, the clay is frozen under his feet. When he turns around he catches a glimpse of Hanna in the window. At the fence he stops. Everything is quiet. Now he can see that the kitchen window is broken. Cautiously he climbs over the low fence and approaches the white house. But no voice calls to him.

I am just imagining things, he thinks. I'm an old man who can't figure out what's really happening anymore. Maybe I did dream about the bulls last night. The bulls that I would dream were charging towards me when I was a boy, making me realise that someday I would die.

Then he hears the cry. It's weak, more like a moan. It's Maria. He goes over to the bedroom window and peeks cautiously through the gap between the curtain and the window frame.

Suddenly he knows that Johannes is dead. He shines his torch inside and blinks hard before he forces himself to look. Maria is crumpled up on the floor, tied to a chair. Her face is bloody and her false teeth lie broken on her spattered nightgown. All he can see of Johannes is a foot. The rest of his body is hidden by the curtain.

He limps back and climbs over the fence again. His knee aches as he stumbles desperately across the frozen clay. First he calls the police. Then he takes his crowbar from a closet that smells of mothballs.

"Wait here," he tells Hanna. "You don't need to see this."

"What happened?" she asks with tears of fright in her eyes.

"I don't know," he says. "But I woke up because the mare wasn't neighing in the night. I know that for sure."

It is January 7, 1990. Not yet dawn.

CHAPTER 2

The incoming call was logged by the Ystad police at 5:13 a.m. It was taken by an exhausted officer who had been on duty almost without a break since New Year's Eve. He listened to the stammering voice on the phone and thought at first that it was just a deranged senior citizen. But something sparked his attention nevertheless. He started asking questions. When the conversation was over, he hesitated for just a moment before lifting the receiver again and dialling a number he knew by heart.

Kurt Wallander was asleep. He had stayed up far too long the night before, listening to recordings of Maria Callas that a good friend had sent him from Bulgaria. Again and again he had played her *Traviata*, and it was close to 2 a.m. before he finally went to bed. When the telephone roused him, he was deep in an intense, erotic dream. As if to assure himself that he had only been dreaming, he reached out and felt next to him. But he was alone in the bed. Neither his wife, who had left him three months ago, nor the black woman with whom he had just been making fierce love in his dream, was there.

He looked at the clock as he reached for the phone. A car crash, he thought instantly. Treacherous ice and someone driving too fast and then spinning off the E65. Or trouble with refugees arriving from Poland on the morning ferry.

He sat up in bed and pressed the receiver to his cheek, feeling the sting of his unshaven skin.

"Wallander."

"I hope I didn't wake you."

"No, damn it. I'm awake."

Why do I lie? he thought. Why don't I just tell the truth? That all I want is to go back to sleep and recapture in a fleeting dream the form of a naked woman.

"I thought I should call you."

"Traffic accident?"

"No, not exactly. An elderly farmer called and said his name was Nyström. Lives in Lunnarp. He claimed that the woman next door was tied up on the floor and that someone was dead."

Wallander thought rapidly about where Lunnarp was. Not so far from Marsvinsholm, in a region that was unusually hilly for Skåne.

"It sounded serious. I thought it best to call you at home."

"Who have you got at the station right now?"

"Peters and Norén are out trying to find someone who broke a window at the Continental. Shall I call them?"

"Tell them to drive to the crossroads between Kade Lake and Katslösa and wait till I get there. Give them the address. When did the call come in?"

"A few minutes ago."

"Sure it wasn't just some drunk calling?"

"Didn't sound like it."

"Huh. All right then."

Wallander dressed quickly without showering, poured himself a cup of the lukewarm coffee that was still in the thermos, and looked out the window. He lived on Mariagatan in central Ystad, and the façade of the building across from him was cracked and grey. He wondered fleetingly whether there would be any snow in Skåne this winter. He hoped not. Scanian snowstorms always brought periods of uninterrupted drudgery. Car wrecks, snowbound women going into labour, isolated old people, and downed power lines. With the snowstorms came chaos, and he felt ill-equipped to deal with chaos this winter. Anxiety at his wife's departure still burned inside him.

He drove down Regementsgatan until he came out onto Österleden. At Dragongatan he stopped at a red light, and he turned on the car radio to listen to the news. An excited voice was talking about a plane that had crashed on a far-off continent.

A time to live and a time to die, he thought as he rubbed the sleep from his eyes. He had adopted this incantation many years ago, when he was a young policeman cruising the streets of Malmö, his hometown.

A drunk had pulled out a big butcher's knife as he and his partner were trying to take him away in the squad car from Pildamm Park. Wallander was stabbed deep, right next to his heart. A few millimetres were all that saved him from an untimely death. He had been twenty-three then, suddenly profoundly aware of what it meant to be a policeman. The incantation was his way of fending off the memories.

He drove out of the city, passing the newly built furniture warehouse at the edge of town, and caught a glimpse of the sea in the distance. It was grey but oddly quiet for the middle of the Scanian winter. Far off towards the horizon was the silhouette of a ship heading east.

The snowstorms are on their way, he thought. Sooner or later they'll be upon us. He shut off the car radio and tried to concentrate on what was in store for him. What did he actually know? An old woman tied up on the floor? A man who claimed he saw her through a window? Wallander accelerated after he passed the turn-off to Bjäre Lake, thinking that it was undoubtedly an old man who was struck by a flare-up of senility. In his many years on the force he had seen more than once how old, lonely people would call the police as a desperate cry for help.

The squad car was waiting for him at the side road towards Kade Lake. Peters had climbed out and was watching a hare bounding back and forth out in a field. When he saw Wallander approaching in his blue

Peugeot, he raised his hand in greeting and got in behind the wheel.

Wallander followed the police car, the frozen gravel
crunching under the tyres. They passed the turn-off
towards Trunnerup and continued up a number of
steep hills until they came to Lunnarp. They swung
onto a narrow dirt road that was hardly more than
a tractor rut. After a kilometre they were there. Two
farms next to each other, two whitewashed farm-
houses, and neatly tended gardens.

An elderly man came hurrying towards them. Wallander saw that he was limping, as if one knee was hurting him. When Wallander got out of the car he noticed
that the wind had started to blow. Maybe snow was on
the way after all. As soon as he saw the old man he knew
that something truly unpleasant awaited him. In the
man's eyes shone a horror that could not be imaginary.

"I broke open the door," he repeated feverishly, over
and over. "I broke open the door because I had to see.
But she'll be dead soon too."

They went in through the damaged door frame.
Wallander was met by a pungent old-man smell. The
wallpaper was fusty, and he was forced to squint to be
able to see anything in the dim light.

"So what happened here?" he asked.

"In there," replied the old man. Then he started
to cry.

The three policemen looked at each other. Wallander pushed open the door with one foot. It was worse than he had expected. Much worse. Later he would say that it was the worst he had ever seen. And he had seen plenty.

The couple's bedroom was covered in blood. It had even splashed onto the porcelain lamp hanging from the ceiling. Prostrate across the bed lay an old man with no shirt on and his long underwear pulled down. His face was crushed beyond recognition. It looked as though someone had tried to cut off his nose. His hands were tied behind his back and his left thigh was shattered. The white bone shone against all that red.

"Oh shit," he heard Norén moan behind him, and Wallander felt nauseated himself.

"Ambulance," he said, swallowing. "And make it quick."

Then they bent over the woman, half-lying on the floor, tied to a chair. Whoever had tied her up had rigged a noose around her scrawny neck. She was breathing feebly, and Wallander yelled at Peters to find a knife. They cut the thin rope that was digging deep into her wrists and neck, and laid her gently on the floor. Wallander held her head on his knee.

He looked at Peters and realised that they were both thinking the same thing. Who could have been cruel enough to do this? Tying a noose on a helpless old woman.

"Wait outside," said Wallander to the old man

sobbing in the doorway. "Wait outside and don't touch anything."

He could hear that his voice sounded like a roar. I'm yelling because I'm scared, he thought. What kind of world are we living in? Almost twenty minutes passed before the ambulance arrived. The woman's breathing grew more and more irregular, and Wallander began to worry that it might come too late.

He recognised the ambulance driver, a man called Antonson. His assistant was a young man he had never seen before.

"Good morning," said Wallander. "He's dead. But the woman here is alive. Try to keep her that way."

"What happened?" asked Antonson.

"I hope she'll be able to tell us, if she makes it. Hurry up now!"

When the ambulance had vanished down the road, Wallander and Peters went outside. Norén was wiping his face with a handkerchief. The dawn was approaching. Wallander looked at his wristwatch. It was 7:28 a.m.

"It's a slaughterhouse in there," said Peters.

"Worse," replied Wallander. "Call in and request a full team. Tell Norén to seal off the area. I'm going to talk to the old man."

Just as he said that, he heard something that sounded like a scream. He jumped, and then the scream came again. It was a horse whinnying. They went over to the stable and opened the door. Inside in the dark a horse was rustling in its stall. The place smelled of warm manure and urine.

"Give the horse some water and hay," said Wallander. "Maybe there are other animals here too."

When he emerged from the stable he gave a shudder. Crows were screeching in a lone tree far out in a field. He sucked the cold air into his throat and noted that the wind was picking up.

"Your name is Nyström," he said to the man, who by now had stopped weeping. "You have to help me. If I understand correctly, you live next door."

The man nodded. "What happened here?" he asked in a quavering voice.

"That's what I'm hoping you can tell me," said Wallander. "Maybe we could go to your house."

In the kitchen a woman in an old-fashioned dressing gown sat slumped in a chair crying. But as soon as Wallander introduced himself she got up and started to make coffee. The men sat down at the kitchen table. Wallander noticed Christmas decorations still hanging in the window. An old cat lay on the windowsill, staring at him without blinking. He reached out his hand to pat it.

"He bites," said Nyström. "He's not used to people. Except for Hanna and me."

Wallander thought of his own wife, who had left him, and wondered where to begin. A bestial murder, he thought. And if we're really unlucky, it'll be a double murder. Something occurred to him. He knocked on the kitchen window to get Norén's attention.

"Excuse me for a moment," he said, getting up.

"The horse had both water and hay," said Norén. "There aren't any other animals."

"See that someone goes over to the hospital," said Wallander. "In case she wakes up and says something. She must have seen everything."

Norén nodded.

"Send somebody with good ears," said Wallander. "Preferably someone who can lip-read."

When he came back into the kitchen he took off his overcoat and laid it on the sofa.

"Now tell me," he said. "Tell me, and leave nothing out. Take your time."

After two cups of weak coffee he could see that neither Nyström nor his wife had anything significant to tell. He got the chronology of events, and the life story of the couple who had been attacked. He had two questions left to ask them.

"Do you know if they kept any large sums of money in the house?" he asked.

"No," said Nyström. "They put everything in the bank. Their pensions too. And they weren't rich. When they sold off the fields and the animals and the machinery, they gave the money to their children."

The second question seemed futile. But he asked it anyway. In this situation he had no choice.

"Do you know if they had any enemies?" he asked.

"Enemies?"

"Anybody who might possibly have done this?"

They didn't seem to understand the question. He repeated it. The two old people looked at each other, bewildered.

"People like us don't have enemies," the man replied, sounding offended. "Sometimes we quarrel with each other. About the upkeep of a wagon path, or the location of the field boundaries. But we don't kill each other."

Wallander nodded.

"I'll be in touch again soon," he said, getting up and taking his coat. "If you think of anything else, don't hesitate to call the police. Ask for me, Inspector Wallander."

"What if they come back...?" asked the old woman.

Wallander shook his head.

"They won't," he said. "It was probably robbers. They never come back. There's nothing for you to worry about."

He thought that he ought to say something more to reassure them. But what? What security could he offer to people who had just seen their close neighbour brutally murdered? Who had to wait and see whether his wife was also going to die?

"The horse," he said. "Who will feed it?"

"We will," replied the old man. "We'll see that she gets what she needs."

Wallander went outside into the cold dawn. The wind was stronger, and he hunched his shoulders as he walked towards his car. He knew he ought to remain and give the crime-scene technicians a hand. But he was freezing and feeling lousy and didn't want to stay any longer. Besides, he saw through the window that it was Rydberg who had come with the team's car. That meant that the technicians wouldn't finish their work until they had turned over and inspected every lump of clay. Rydberg, who was supposed to retire in a couple of years, was a passionate policeman. He might appear pedantic and slow, but his presence was a guarantee that a crime scene would be treated the way it should be.

Rydberg had rheumatism and used a cane. Now he came limping across the yard towards Wallander.

"It's not pretty," Rydberg said. "It looks like a slaughterhouse in there."

"You're not the first to say that," said Wallander.

Rydberg looked serious. "Have we got any leads?"

Wallander shook his head.

"Nothing at all?" There was something of an entreaty in Rydberg's voice.

"The neighbours didn't hear or see anything. I think it was ordinary robbers."

"You call this insane brutality ordinary?"

Rydberg was upset, and Wallander regretted his choice of words. "I meant, of course, that it was particularly fiendish individuals who did this last night.

The kind who make their living picking out farms in isolated locations where lonely old people live."

"We have to find these people," said Rydberg. "Before they strike again."

"You're right," said Wallander. "Even if we don't catch anyone else this year."

He got into his car and drove off. On the narrow farm road he almost collided with a car coming around a curve towards him at high speed. He recognised the man driving. It was a reporter for one of the big national papers, who always showed up when something of more than local interest happened in the Ystad area.

Wallander drove back and forth through Lunnarp a few times. There were lights in the windows, but no one was out and about. What were they going to think when they found out?

He was feeling uneasy. Being confronted with the old woman with the noose around her neck had shaken him. The cruelty of it was unthinkable. Who would do something like that? Why not hit her over the head with an axe so it would all be over in an instant? Why torture her?

He tried to plan the investigation in his head as he drove slowly through the village. At the crossroads towards Blentarp he stopped, turned up the heat in the car because he was cold, and then sat motionless, gazing off towards the horizon.

He was the one who would have to lead the investigation, he knew that. No one else was even possible.

After Rydberg, he was the criminal detective in Ystad who had the most experience, despite the fact that he was only forty-two years old.

Much of the investigative work would be routine. Examining the scene of the crime, questioning people in Lunnarp and along the escape routes the robbers might have taken. Had anyone seen anything suspicious? Anything unusual? The questions were already running through his mind. But Wallander knew from experience that farm robberies were often difficult to solve. What he could hope for was that the old woman would survive. She had seen what happened. She knew. But if she died, a double murder would be even harder to solve.

He felt uneasy. Under normal circumstances this unease would have spurred him to greater energy and activity. Since these were the prerequisites for all police work, he had imagined that he was a good policeman. But right now he felt uncertain and tired. He forced himself to shift into first gear. The car rolled a few metres. Then he stopped again. It was as if he only now realised what he had witnessed on that frozen winter morning.

The senselessness and savagery of the attack on the helpless couple scared him. Something had happened that shouldn't have, not here. He looked out of the car window. The wind was rushing and whistling around the doors. I have to get started, he thought. It's as if Rydberg said: we've got to find whoever did this.

He drove directly to the hospital in Ystad and took the lift up to the intensive care unit. In the corridor he immediately recognised the young police cadet Martinsson sitting on a chair outside one of the rooms. Wallander could feel himself getting annoyed. Was there really no one else available to send to the hospital but a young, inexperienced cadet? And why was he sitting outside the door? Why wasn't he sitting at the bedside, ready to catch the slightest whisper from the brutalised woman?

"Hello," said Wallander, "how is she?"

"She's unconscious," replied Martinsson. "The doctors don't seem too hopeful."

"Why are you sitting out here? Why aren't you in the room?"

"They said they'd tell me if anything happened."

Wallander noticed that Martinsson was starting to feel unsure of himself.

I sound like a grumpy schoolteacher, he thought. Carefully he pushed open the door and looked in. Various machines were sucking and pumping in death's waiting room. Tubes undulated like transparent worms along the walls. A nurse was standing there reading a chart.

"You can't come in here," she said sharply.

"I'm a police inspector," replied Wallander feebly. "I just wanted to hear how she's doing."

"You've been asked to wait outside," said the nurse. Before he could answer, a doctor came rushing into the room. Wallander thought he looked surprisingly young.

"We would prefer not to have any unauthorised persons in here," said the doctor when he caught sight of Wallander.

"I'm leaving. But I just wanted to hear how she's doing. My name is Wallander, and I'm a police inspector. Homicide," he added, not sure whether that made any difference. "I'm heading the investigation into the person or persons who did this. How is she?"

"It's amazing that she's still alive," said the doctor, nodding to Wallander to step over to the bed. "We can't tell yet the extent of the internal injuries she may have suffered. First we have to see whether she survives. But her windpipe has been severely traumatised. As if someone had tried to strangle her."

"That's exactly what happened," said Wallander, looking at the thin face visible among the sheets and tubes.

"She should have died," said the doctor.

"I hope she survives," said Wallander. "She's the only witness we've got."

"We hope all our patients survive," replied the doctor sternly, studying a monitor where green lines moved in uninterrupted waves.

Wallander left the room after the doctor insisted that he could tell him nothing more. The prognosis was uncertain. Maria Lövgren might die without regaining consciousness. There was no way to know.

"Can you lip-read?" Wallander asked the cadet.

"No," Martinsson replied in surprise.

"That's too bad," said Wallander, and left.

From the hospital he drove to the brown police station that lay on the road out towards the east end of town. He sat down at his desk and looked out of the window, over at the old red water tower.

Maybe the times require another kind of policeman, he thought. Policemen who aren't distressed when they're forced to go into a human slaughterhouse in the Swedish countryside early on a January morning. Policemen who don't suffer from my uncertainty and anguish.

His thoughts were interrupted by the telephone. The hospital, he thought at once. They're calling to say that Maria Lövgren is dead. But did she wake up? Did she say anything? He stared at the ringing telephone. Damn, he thought. Damn. Anything but that.

But when he picked up the receiver, it was his daughter. He gave a start and almost dropped the phone on the floor.

"Papa," she said, and he heard the coin dropping into the pay phone.

"Hello," he said. "Where are you calling from?"

Just so long as it's not Lima, he thought. Or Katmandu. Or Kinshasa.

"I'm here in Ystad."

He felt happy. That meant he'd get to see her.

"I came to visit you," she said. "But I've changed my

plans. I'm at the train station. I'm leaving now. I just wanted to tell you that at least I thought about seeing you."

Then the conversation was cut off, and he was left sitting there with the receiver in his hand. It was like holding something dead, something hacked off. That damned kid, he thought. Why does she do things like this?

His daughter Linda was nineteen. Until she was fifteen their relationship had been good. She came to him rather than to her mother when she had a problem or when there was something she really wanted to do but didn't quite dare. He had seen her metamorphose from a chubby little girl to a young woman with a defiant beauty. Before she was fifteen, she never gave any hint that she was carrying around secret demons that one day would drive her into a precarious and inscrutable landscape.

One spring day, soon after her fifteenth birthday, Linda had without warning tried to commit suicide. It happened on a Saturday afternoon. Wallander had been fixing one of the garden chairs and his wife was washing the windows. He had put down his hammer and gone into the house, driven by a sudden unease. Linda was lying on the bed in her room. She had used a razor to cut her wrists and her throat. Afterwards, when it was all over, the doctor told Wallander that she would have died if he hadn't come in when he did and had the presence of mind to apply pressure bandages.

He couldn't get over the shock. All contact between

him and Linda was broken off. She pulled away, and he never managed to understand what had driven her to attempt suicide. When she finished school she took a string of odd jobs, and would abruptly disappear for long periods of time. Twice his wife had pressed him to report her missing. His colleagues had seen his pain when Linda became the subject of his own investigation. But then she would reappear, and the only way he could follow her travels was to go through her pockets and leaf through her passport on the sly.

Hell, he thought. Why didn't you stay? Why did you change your mind?

The telephone rang again and he snatched up the receiver.

"This is Papa," said Wallander without thinking.

"What do you mean?" said his father. "What do you mean by picking up the phone and saying Papa? I thought you were a policeman."

"I don't have time to talk to you right now. Can I call you later?"

"No, you can't. What's so important?"

"Something serious happened this morning. I'll call later."

"So what happened?"

His elderly father called him almost every day. On several occasions Wallander had told the switchboard not to put through any calls from him. But then his father saw through his ruse and started giving false names and disguising his voice to fool the operators.

Wallander saw only one possibility of evading him.

"I'll come out and see you tonight," he said. "Then we can talk."

His father reluctantly let himself be persuaded. "Come at seven. I'll have time to see you then."

"I'll be there at seven. See you."

Wallander hung up and pushed the button to block incoming calls. For a moment he considered taking the car and driving down to the train station to try and find his daughter. Talk to her, try to rekindle the contact that had been lost so mysteriously. But he knew that he wouldn't do it. He didn't want to risk her running away from him for good.

The door opened and Näslund stuck his head in.

"Hello," he said. "Should I show him in?"

"Show who in?"

Näslund looked at his watch.

"It's nine o'clock. You told me yesterday that you wanted Klas Månson here for an interview at nine."

"Who's Klas Månson?"

Näslund looked at him quizzically. "The guy who robbed the shop on Österleden. Have you forgotten about him?"

It came back to Wallander, and at the same time he realised that Näslund obviously hadn't heard about the murder that had been committed in the night.

"You deal with Månson," he said. "We had a murder last night out in Lunnarp. Maybe a double murder.

An elderly couple. You can take over Månson. But put it off for a while. The thing we have to do first is plan the investigation at Lunnarp."

"Månson's lawyer is already here," said Näslund. "If I send him away, he's going to raise hell."

"Do a preliminary questioning," said Wallander. "If the lawyer makes a fuss later, it can't be helped. Set up a case meeting in my office for ten o'clock. Make sure everyone comes."

Now he was in motion. He was a policeman again. His anxiety about his daughter and his wife would have to wait. Right now he had to begin the arduous hunt for a murderer. He removed the piles of paper from his desk, tore up a football lottery form he wouldn't get around to filling out anyway, and went out to the canteen and poured himself a cup of coffee.

At 10 a.m. everyone gathered in his office. Rydberg had been called in from the scene of the crime and was sitting in a chair by the window. Seven police officers in all, sitting and standing, filled the room. Wallander phoned the hospital and managed to ascertain that Mrs. Lövgren's condition was still critical. Then he told them what had happened.

"It was worse than you could imagine," he said. "Wouldn't you say so, Rydberg?"

"You're right," replied Rydberg. "Like an American movie. It even smelt like blood. That doesn't usually happen."

"We have to find whoever did this," said Wallander,

concluding his presentation. "We can't leave maniacs like this on the loose."

The policemen fell silent. Rydberg was drumming his fingertips on the arm of his chair. A woman could be heard laughing in the corridor outside. Wallander looked around the room. All of them were his colleagues. None of them was his close friend. And yet they were a team.

"Well," he said, "what are we waiting for? Let's get started."

It was 10:40 a.m.

CHAPTER 3

At 4 p.m. that afternoon Wallander discovered that he was hungry. He hadn't had a chance to eat lunch. After the case meeting in the morning he had spent his time organising the hunt for the murderers in Lunnarp. He found himself thinking about them in the plural. He had a hard time imagining that one person could have been responsible for that bloodbath.

It was dark outside when he sank into the chair behind his desk to try and put together a statement for the press. There was a pile of messages, left by one of the women from the switchboard. After searching in vain for his daughter's name among the slips, he placed them all in his in-tray. To escape the unpleasantness of standing in front of the TV cameras of News South and telling them that at present the police had no leads on the criminal or criminals who had carried out the heinous murder of Johannes Lövgren, Wallander had appealed to Rydberg to take on that task. But he had to write and give the press release himself. He took a sheet of paper from a desk drawer. But what would he write? The day's work had involved little more than collecting a large number of questions.

It had been a day of waiting. In the intensive care unit the old woman who had survived the noose was fighting for her life. Would they ever find out what she had witnessed on that appalling night in the lonely farmhouse? Or would she die before she could tell them anything?

Wallander looked out of the window, into the darkness. Instead of a press release he started writing a summary of what had been done that day and what the police actually had to go on. Nothing, he thought, when he was finished. Two elderly people with no enemies, no hidden cash, were brutally attacked and tortured. The neighbours heard nothing. Not until the attackers were gone had they noticed that a window had been broken and heard the old woman's cry for help. Rydberg had so far found no clues. That was it.

Old people in the countryside have always been targets for robbery. They have been bound, beaten, and sometimes killed. But this is different, thought Wallander. The noose tells a gruesome story of viciousness or hate, maybe even revenge. Something about this attack doesn't add up.

All they could do now was hope. All day long police patrols had been talking to the inhabitants of Lunnarp. Perhaps someone had seen something? In crimes of this nature those responsible had often cased the place in advance. Maybe Rydberg would find some clues at the farmhouse after all.

Wallander looked at the clock. How long since he'd last called the hospital? Forty-five minutes? An hour? He decided to wait until after he had written his press release. He popped a cassette of Jussi Björling into his Walkman and put on the headphones. The scratchy sound of the 1930s recording could not detract from the magnificence of the music from *Rigoletto*.

The press release ran to eight lines. Wallander took it to one of the clerks to type up and make copies. While this was being done he read through a questionnaire that was to be mailed to everyone living in the area around Lunnarp. Had anyone seen anything out of the ordinary? Anything that could be connected to the brutal attack? He didn't have much confidence that the questionnaire would produce anything but inconvenience. The telephones would ring incessantly and two officers would need to be assigned to listen to useless reports.

Still, it has to be done, he thought. At least we can satisfy ourselves that no one saw anything. He went back to his office and phoned the hospital. Nothing had changed. Mrs. Lövgren was still fighting for her life. Just as he put down the phone, Näslund came in.

"I was right," he said.

"What about?"

"Månson's lawyer hit the roof."

Wallander shrugged. "We'll just have to live with that."

Näslund scratched his forehead and asked how the investigation was going.

"Not a thing so far. We've started. That's about it."

"I noticed that the preliminary forensic report came in."

Wallander raised an eyebrow. "Why didn't I get it?"

"It was in Hansson's office."

"That's not where it's supposed to be, damn it!"

Wallander got up and went out into the corridor. Always the same, he thought. Papers never end up where they're supposed to. More and more police work was recorded on computers, but even so there was a tendency for important papers to get lost.

Wallander knocked and went into Hansson's office. Hansson was talking on the phone. He saw that Hansson's desk had strewn all over it, hardly concealed, betting slips and form guides from racetracks around the country. It was common knowledge at the station that he spent the best part of his working day calling various horse trainers begging for tips. Then he spent his evenings figuring out all manner of betting systems that would guarantee him the maximum winnings. It was also rumoured that Hansson had hit it big on one occasion, but no one knew this for certain. And Hansson wasn't exactly living the highlife.

When Wallander came in, Hansson put his hand over the mouthpiece.

"The forensic report," said Wallander. "Have you got it?"

Hansson pushed aside a form guide from Jägersrö. "I was just about to bring it over to you."

"Number four in the seventh race is a sure thing," said Wallander, taking the plastic folder from the desk.

"What do you mean by that?"

"I mean it's a sure thing."

Wallander walked out, leaving Hansson gaping. He saw by the clock in the corridor that there was half an hour left until the press conference. He went back to his office and read carefully through the doctor's report.

The brutal nature of the murder of Johannes Lövgren was thrown into even sharper relief, if possible, than when he had arrived in Lunnarp that morning. In the preliminary examination of the body, the doctor had not been able to determine the actual cause of death. There were too many to choose from.

The body had received eight deep stab wounds with a sharp, serrated implement. The report suggested a compass saw. In addition, the right femur was broken, as were the left upper arm and wrist. The body showed signs of burn wounds, the scrotum was swollen, and the forehead was bashed in.

The doctor had made a note beside the official report. "An act of madness," he had written. "This man was subjected to injuries sufficient to kill him four or five times over."

Wallander put down the report. He was feeling worse and worse. Something here was beyond reason. Robbers who attacked old people weren't full of hate.

They were after money. Why this insane degree of violence?

When Wallander realised that he couldn't come up with a satisfactory answer, he read again through the summary he had written. Had he forgotten something? Had he overlooked some detail that would later turn out to have been significant? Even though police work was mostly a matter of patiently searching for clues that could then be combined, he had also learnt from experience that the initial impression of the scene of a crime was important. More so when the officer was one of the first there after the crime had been committed.

There was something in his summary that puzzled him. Had he left out an important detail? He sat for a long time without managing to think what it might be.

A woman opened the door and handed him the typed press release and the copies. On the way to the press conference he went to the men's room and looked in the mirror. He saw that he needed a haircut. His brown hair was sticking out round his ears. And he ought to lose some weight too. In the three months since his wife had left him, he had put on seven kilos. In his apathetic loneliness he had eaten nothing but takeaways and pizza, greasy hamburgers and pastries.

"You flabby piece of shit," he said out loud. "Do you really want to look like a pitiful old man?"

He made a decision to change his eating habits at once. If it would help him lose weight, he might even consider taking up smoking again. He wondered why almost every policeman was divorced. Why their wives left them. Sometimes, when he read a crime novel, he discovered with a sigh that things were just as bad in fiction. Policemen were divorced. That's all there was to it.

The room where the press conference was to be held was full. He recognised most of the reporters. But there were a few unfamiliar faces too, including a young girl with a pimply face, who seemed to be casting amorous glances at him as she adjusted her tape recorder.

Wallander passed out the press release and sat down on the little dais at one end of the room. The Ystad chief of police should have been there too, but he was on his winter holiday in Spain. If Rydberg managed to finish with the TV crews, he had promised to attend. But otherwise Wallander was on his own.

"You've received the press release," he began. "I don't have anything to add at present."

"Can we ask questions?" said a reporter Wallander recognised as the local stringer for *The Worker*.

"That's why I'm here," replied Wallander.

"If you don't mind my saying so, this is an unusually poor press release," said the reporter. "You must be able to tell us more than this."

"We have no leads on the offenders," said Wallander.

"So there were more than one?"

"Possibly."

"Why do you think so?"

"We think there were. But we don't know."

The reporter made a face, and Wallander nodded to another reporter he recognised.

"How was Mr. Lövgren killed?"

"By external force."

"That can mean a lot of different things!"

"Well, we don't know yet. The doctors haven't finished the forensic examination. It'll take a couple of days."

The reporter had more questions, but he was interrupted by the pimply girl with the tape recorder. Wallander could see by the letters on the lid that she was from the local radio station.

"What did the robbers take?"

"We don't know," replied Wallander. "We don't even know if it was a robbery."

"What else could it be?"

"We don't know."

"Is there anything that encourages you to believe that it wasn't a robbery?"

"No."

Wallander could feel that he was sweating in the overheated room. He remembered how as a young policeman he had dreamt of holding press conferences. But they had never been stuffy and sweaty in his dreams.

"I asked a question," he heard one of the reporters say from the back of the room.

"I didn't hear it," said Wallander.

"Do the police regard this as an important crime?" asked the reporter.

Wallander was surprised at the question.

"Naturally it's important that we solve this murder," he said. "Why shouldn't it be?"

"Will you be needing extra resources?"

"It's too early to comment on that. Of course we're hoping for a quick solution. I don't understand your question."

A very young reporter with the thick glasses pushed his way forwards. Wallander had never seen him before.

"In my opinion, no one in Sweden cares about the elderly these days."

"*We* do," replied Wallander. "We will do everything we can to ensure that we arrest those responsible. In Skåne there are many elderly people living alone on isolated farms. We would like, above all, to reassure them that we are doing everything possible."

He stood up. "We'll let you know when we have more to report," he said. "Thank you for coming."

The young woman from the local radio station blocked his path as he was leaving the room.

"I have nothing more to say," he told her.

"I know your daughter Linda," she said.

Wallander stopped. "You do? How?"

"We've met a few times. Here and there."

Wallander tried to think whether he knew her. Had the girls been classmates?

She shook her head as if reading his mind.

"You and I have never met," she said. "You don't know me. Linda and I ran into each other in Malmö."

"I see," said Wallander. "That's nice."

"I think she's great. Could I ask you some questions now?"

Wallander repeated into her microphone what he had said earlier. Most of all he wanted to talk about Linda, but he didn't have a chance.

"Say hello to her," she said, packing up her tape recorder. "Say hello from Cathrin. Or Cattis."

"I will," said Wallander. "I promise."

When he went back to his office he could feel a gnawing in his stomach. But was it hunger or anxiety? I've got to stop this, he thought. I've got to accept that my wife has left me. I've got to admit that all I can do is wait for Linda to contact me herself. I've got to take life as it comes...

Just before 6 p.m. the investigative team gathered for another meeting. There was no news from the hospital. Wallander quickly drew up a roster for the night.

"Is that necessary?" wondered Hansson. "Just put a tape recorder in the room, then any nurse can turn it on if the old lady wakes up."

"It is necessary," said Wallander. "I can take midnight to six myself. Any volunteers until midnight?"

Rydberg nodded. "I can sit at the hospital just as well as anywhere," he said.

Wallander looked around. Everyone seemed pale in the glare from the fluorescent lights.

"Did we get anywhere?" he asked.

"We've checked out Lunnarp," said Peters, who had led the door-to-door inquiry. "Everybody says they didn't see a thing. But it usually takes a few days before people really think. People are pretty scared up there. It's damned unpleasant. Almost everyone is old. Except for a terrified young Polish family, who are probably here illegally. But I didn't bother them. We'll have to keep trying tomorrow."

Wallander nodded and looked at Rydberg.

"There were plenty of fingerprints at the scene," he said. "Maybe that will produce something. But I doubt it. It's mostly the knot that interests me."

Wallander gave him a searching look. "What knot?"

"The knot on the noose."

"What about it?"

"It's unusual. I've never seen a knot like it."

"Have you ever seen a noose before?" interrupted Hansson, who was standing in the doorway, itching to leave.

"Yes, I have," replied Rydberg. "We'll see what this knot can tell us."

Wallander knew that Rydberg didn't want to say more. But if the knot interested him, it might be important.

"I'm driving back out to see the neighbours tomorrow morning," said Wallander. "Has anyone tracked down the Lövgrens' children yet, by the way?"

"Martinsson is working on it," said Hansson.

"I thought Martinsson was at the hospital," said Wallander, surprised.

"He traded with Svedberg."

"So where the hell is he now?"

No one knew where Martinsson was. Wallander called the switchboard and found out that he had left an hour earlier.

"Call him at home," said Wallander.

Then he looked at his watch.

"We'll meet again in the morning at ten o'clock," he said. "Thanks for coming, see you then."

Everyone else had left by the time the switchboard connected him with Martinsson.

"Sorry," said Martinsson. "I forgot we had a meeting."

"How are you getting on with the children?"

"Damned if Rickard doesn't have chicken pox."

"I mean the Lövgrens' children. The two daughters."

Martinsson sounded surprised when he answered. "Didn't you get my message?"

"I didn't get any message."

"I gave it to one of the girls at the switchboard."

"I'll take a look. But tell me first."

"One daughter, who's fifty, lives in Canada. Winnipeg,

wherever that is. I completely forgot that it was the middle of the night over there when I called. She refused to believe what I was saying. It didn't sink in until her husband came to the phone. He's a policeman, by the way. A genuine Canadian Mountie. I'm going to call them back tomorrow. But she's flying over, of course. The other daughter was harder to reach, even though she lives in Sweden. She's forty-seven, the manager of the buffet at the Ruby Hotel in Göteborg. Evidently she's away coaching a handball team in Skien, in Norway. But they promised that they'd get word to her. I gave the switchboard a list of the Lövgrens' other relatives. There are lots of them. Most of them live in Skåne. Some of them will probably call tomorrow when they see the story in the papers."

"Good work," said Wallander. "Can you relieve me at the hospital tomorrow morning at six? If she doesn't die by then."

"I'll be there," said Martinsson. "But is it such a good idea for you to take that shift?"

"Why not?"

"You're the one heading the investigation. You ought to get some sleep."

"I can handle it for one night," replied Wallander and hung up.

He sat completely still and stared into space. Are we going to get to the bottom of this? he thought. Or do they already have too much of a head start? He put on his overcoat, turned off the desk lamp, and left his office. The corridor leading to the reception area was deserted. He stuck his head in the glass cubicle where the operator on duty sat leafing through a magazine. He noticed that it was a form guide. Was everyone playing the horses these days?

"Martinsson should have left some papers for me," he said.

The operator, who was named Ebba and had been with the police department for more than thirty years, gave a friendly nod and pointed at the counter.

"We have a girl here from the youth employment bureau," she said, smiling. "Sweet and nice but completely incompetent. Maybe she forgot to give them to you."

Wallander nodded. "I'm leaving now," he said. "I'll probably be home in a couple of hours. If anything happens before then, call me at my father's place."

"You're thinking of poor Mrs. Lövgren," said Ebba.

Wallander nodded.

"It's terrible."

"Yes, it is," said Wallander. "Sometimes I wonder what's happening to this country."

When he went out through the glass doors of the police station the wind hit him in the face. It was cold and biting, and he hunched his shoulders as he hurried to the car park. As long as it doesn't snow, he thought. Not until we catch whoever paid the visit to Lunnarp.

He clambered into his car and spent a long time looking through the cassettes he kept in the glove compartment. Without really making a decision, he shoved Verdi's *Requiem* into the tape deck. He had expensive speakers in the car, and the magnificent sounds surged in his ears. He set off, turning right, down Dragongatan towards Österleden. A few leaves whirled across the road, and a cyclist strained against the wind. Hunger gnawed at him again, and he crossed the main road and turned in at OK's Cafeteria. I'll change my eating habits tomorrow, he thought. If I get to Dad's place a minute past 7 p.m., he'll accuse me of abandoning him.

He ate a hamburger special. He ate it so fast that it gave him diarrhea. As he sat on the toilet he noticed that he ought to change his underwear. He realised how exhausted he was. He didn't get up until someone banged on the door.

He filled the petrol tank, and drove east, through Sandskogen, turning off onto the road to Kåseberga. His father lived in a little farmhouse that seemed to have been flung onto a field between Löderup and the sea. It was just before 7 p.m. when he swung onto the gravel drive in front of the house. The drive had been the cause of the latest and most drawn out of his arguments with his father. It had been a lovely cobblestone courtyard as old as the farmhouse itself. One day his father had got the idea of covering it with gravel. When Wallander had protested, he was outraged.

"I don't need a guardian!" he had shouted.

"Why do you have to destroy the beautiful cobblestone courtyard?" Wallander had asked.

Then they had quarrelled. And now the courtyard was covered with grey gravel that crunched under the car's tyres. He could see that a light was on in the shed. Next time it could be my father, he thought. The nighttime killers might pick him out as a suitable old man to rob, maybe even to murder.

No one would hear him scream for help. Not in this wind, half a kilometre from the nearest neighbour, an old man himself.

He listened to the end of "Dies Irae" before he climbed out of the car and stretched. He went over to the shed, which was his father's studio where he painted his pictures, as he had always done. This was one of Wallander's earliest childhood memories. The way his father had smelled of turpentine and oil. And the way he stood in front of his sticky easel in his dark-blue overalls and cut-off rubber boots.

Not until Wallander was five or six years old did he realise that his father wasn't working on the same painting year after year. It was just that the motif never changed. He painted a melancholy autumn landscape, with a shiny mirror of a lake, a crooked tree with bare branches in the foreground, and, far off on the horizon, mountain ranges surrounded by clouds that shimmered in an improbably colourful sunset. Now and then he would add a grouse standing on a stump at the far left edge of the painting.

At regular intervals men in silk suits with heavy gold rings on their fingers would visit the house. They came in rusty vans or shiny American gas-guzzlers, and they bought the paintings, with or without the grouse.

His father had been painting that same motif all his life. The family had lived off the sale of his paintings, which were sold at fairs and auctions. They had lived in Klagshamm outside Malmö, in a converted smithy. Wallander had grown up there with his sister Kristina, and their childhood had been wrapped in the pungent odour of turpentine.

When his father was widowed he sold the smithy and moved out to the country. Wallander had never really understood why since his father was continually complaining about the loneliness.

He opened the door to the shed and saw that his father was working on a painting without the grouse. Just now he was painting the tree in the foreground. He muttered a greeting and continued dabbing with his brush. Wallander poured a cup of coffee from a dirty pot that stood on a smoking spirit stove.

He looked at his father, who was almost eighty, short and stooped, but still radiating energy and strength of will. Am I going to look like him when I'm old? he thought. As a boy I took after my mother. Now I look like my grandfather. Maybe I'll be like my father when I get old.

"Have a cup of coffee," said his father. "I'll be ready in a minute."

"I've got one," said Wallander.

"Then have another," said his father.

He's in a bad mood, thought Wallander. He's a tyrant with his changeable moods. What does he want with me, anyway?

"I've got a lot to do," said Wallander. "Actually I have to work all night. I thought there was something you wanted."

"Why do you have to work all night?"

"I have to sit at the hospital."

"How come? Who's sick?"

Wallander sighed. Even though he had carried out hundreds of interrogations himself, he would never be able to match his father's persistence in questioning him. And his father didn't even give a damn about his career. Wallander knew that his father had been deeply disappointed when he had decided, at eighteen, to become a policeman. But he was never able to find out what aspirations his father had actually had for him. He had tried to talk to him about it, but without success.

On the few occasions that he had spent time with his sister Kristina, who lived in Stockholm and owned a beauty salon, he had tried to ask her, since he knew that she and his father were close. But even she had no idea. He drank the lukewarm coffee, wondering whether his father had wanted him to take up the brush and continue to paint the same motif for another generation.

His father put down his brush and wiped his hands on a dirty rag. When he came over to him and poured a cup of coffee, Wallander could smell the stink of dirty clothes and his father's unwashed body.

How do you tell your father that he smells bad? he thought. Maybe he can't take care of himself any longer. And then what do I do? I can't have him at my place, that would never work. We'd murder each other. He watched his father rub his nose with one hand as he slurped his coffee.

"You haven't come out to see me in a long time," his father said reproachfully.

"I was here the day before yesterday, wasn't I?"

"For half an hour!"

"Well, I was here, anyway."

"Why don't you want to visit me?"

"I do! It's just that I have a lot to do sometimes."

His father sat down on a rickety, ancient toboggan that creaked under his weight.

"I just wanted to tell you that your daughter came to visit me yesterday."

Wallander was astounded.

"Linda was here?"

"Aren't you listening to what I'm telling you?"

"Why did she come?"

"She wanted a painting."

"A painting?"

"Unlike you, she actually appreciates what I do."

Wallander had a hard time believing what he was hearing. Linda had never shown any interest in her grandfather, except when she was very small.

"What did she want?"

"A painting, I told you! You're not listening!"

"I am listening! Where did she come from? Where was she going? How the hell did she get out here? Do I have to drag everything out of you?"

"She came in a car," said his father. "A young man with a black face drove her."

"What do you mean by black?"

"Haven't you heard of Negroes? He was very polite and spoke excellent Swedish. I gave her the painting and then they left. I thought you'd like to know, since you have so little contact with each other."

"Where did they go?"

"How should I know?"

Wallander realised that neither of them knew where Linda actually lived. Occasionally she slept at her mother's house. But then she would quickly disappear again, off on her own mysterious paths. I've got to talk to Mona, he thought. Separated or not, we have to talk to each other. I can't stand this anymore.

"Do you want a drink?" his father asked.

The last thing Wallander wanted was a drink. But he knew it was useless to say no.

"All right, thanks," he said.

A path connected the shed with the house, which was low-ceilinged and sparsely furnished. Wallander noticed at once that it was messy and dirty. He doesn't even see the mess, he thought. And why didn't I notice it before? I've got to talk to Kristina about it. He can't keep living alone like this. At that moment the telephone rang. His father picked it up.

"It's for you," he said, making no attempt to hide his annoyance.

Linda, he thought. It's got to be her. But it was Rydberg calling from the hospital.

"She's dead," he said.

"Did she wake up?"

"As a matter of fact, she did. For ten minutes. The doctors thought the crisis was over. Then she died."

"Did she say anything?"

Rydberg sounded thoughtful when he answered. "I think you'd better come back to town."

"What did she say?"

"Something you won't want to hear."

"I'll come to the hospital."

"It's better if you go to the station. She's dead, I told you."

Wallander hung up. "I've got to go," he said.

His father glared at him. "You don't like me," he said.

"I'll be back tomorrow," replied Wallander, wondering what to do about the squalor his father was living in. "I'll come tomorrow for sure. We can sit and talk. We can make dinner. We can play poker if you want."

Even though Wallander was a wretched card player, he knew that a game would mollify his father. "I'll be here at seven," he said.

Then he drove back to Ystad. He walked back

through the same glass doors that he had walked out of not much earlier. Ebba nodded at him.

"Rydberg is waiting in the canteen," she said.

He was there, hunched over a cup of coffee. When Wallander saw the other man's face, he knew that something unpleasant was in store for him.

CHAPTER 4

Wallander and Rydberg were alone in the canteen. In the distance they could hear the ruckus a drunk was making, loudly protesting at his arrest. Otherwise it was quiet. Only the faint whine of the radiator could be heard.

Wallander sat down across from Rydberg.

"Take off your overcoat," said Rydberg. "Or else you'll freeze when you go back out in the wind again."

"First I want to hear what you have to say. Then I'll decide whether or not to take off my coat."

Rydberg shrugged. "She died," he said.

"So I understand."

"But she woke up for a while right before she died."

"And she spoke?"

"That may be putting it too strongly. She whispered. Or wheezed."

"Did you get it on tape?"

Rydberg shook his head. "It wouldn't have worked anyway," he said. "It was almost impossible to hear what she was saying. Most of it was just raving. But I wrote down what I'm sure I understood."

Rydberg took a battered notebook out of his pocket. It was held together by a wide rubber band, and a pencil was stuck in between the pages.

"She said her husband's name," Rydberg began. "I think she was trying to find out how he was. Then she mumbled something I couldn't understand. That's when I tried to ask her, 'Who was it that came in the night? Did you know them? What did they look like?' Those were my questions. I repeated them for as long as she was conscious. And I actually think she understood what I was saying."

"So what did she answer?"

"I only managed to catch one word. 'Foreign.' "

"'Foreign'?"

"That's right. 'Foreign.' "

"Did she mean that the people who attacked her and her husband were foreigners?"

Rydberg nodded.

"Are you sure?"

"Do I usually say I'm sure if I'm not?"

"No."

"Well then. So now we know that her last message to the world was the word 'foreign.' In answer to the question: Who committed this insane crime?"

Wallander took off his coat and got himself a cup of coffee.

"What the hell could she have meant?" he muttered.

"I've been sitting here thinking about that while I was waiting for you," replied Rydberg. "Maybe they looked un-Swedish. Maybe they spoke a foreign language. Maybe they spoke poor Swedish. There are lots of possibilities."

"What does an 'un-Swedish' person look like?" asked Wallander. "You know what I mean," said Rydberg. "Or rather, you can guess what she thought."

"So it could have been her imagination?"

Rydberg nodded. "That's quite possible."

"But not particularly likely?"

"Why should she use the last minutes of her life to say something that wasn't true? Elderly people don't usually lie."

Wallander took a sip of his lukewarm coffee.

"This means we have to start looking for one or more foreigners," he said. "I wish she'd said something different."

"It's damned unpleasant, all right."

They sat in silence for a moment, lost in their own thoughts. They could no longer hear the drunk out in the corridor.

"You can just picture it," Wallander said after a while. "The only clue the police have to the double murder in Lunnarp is that those responsible are probably foreigners."

"I can think of something much worse," replied Rydberg.

Wallander knew what he meant. Just twenty

kilometres from Lunnarp there was a big refugee camp that had been the focus of attacks against foreigners on several occasions. Crosses had been burned at night in the courtyard, rocks had been thrown through windows, buildings had been spray-painted with slogans. The camp, in the old castle of Hageholm, had been established despite vigorous protests from the surrounding communities. And the protests had continued. Hostility to refugees was flaring up.

But Wallander and Rydberg knew something else that the general public did not know. Some of the asylum seekers being housed at Hageholm had been caught red-handed breaking into a business that rented out farm machinery. Fortunately the owner was not one of those most fiercely opposed to taking in refugees, so it was possible to keep the whole affair quiet. The two men who had committed the break-in were no longer in Sweden either, since they had been denied asylum. Wallander and Rydberg had discussed what might have happened if the incident had been made public on several occasions.

"I have a hard time believing that refugees seeking asylum could commit murder," said Wallander.

Rydberg gave Wallander a quizzical look. "You remember what I told you about the noose?"

"Something about the knot?"

"I didn't recognise it. And I know quite a bit about knots, because I spent my summers sailing when I was young."

Wallander looked at Rydberg attentively. "What are you saying?" he asked.

"What I'm saying is that this knot wasn't tied by someone who was a member of the Swedish Boy Scouts."

"What the hell do you mean by that?"

"The knot was made by a foreigner."

Before Wallander could reply, Ebba came into the canteen to get some coffee.

"Go home and get some rest if you can," she said. "By the way, reporters keep calling and saying that they want you to make a statement."

"About what?" asked Wallander. "About the weather?"

"They seem to have found out that the woman died."

Wallander looked at Rydberg, who shook his head.

"We're not making a statement tonight," he said. "We're waiting till tomorrow."

Wallander got up and went over to the window. The wind was blowing hard, but the sky was still cloudless. It was going to be another cold night.

"We can hardly avoid mentioning what happened," he said. "That she managed to say something before she died. And if we say that much, then we'll have to tell them what she said. And then all hell will break loose."

"We could try to keep it internal," said Rydberg, getting up and putting on his hat. "For investigative reasons."

Wallander looked at him in surprise.

"And risk having it come out later that we withheld

important information from the press? That we were shielding foreign criminals?"

"It's going to affect so many innocent people," said Rydberg. "What do you think will happen at the refugee camp when it gets out that the police are looking for some foreigners?"

Wallander knew that Rydberg was right. Suddenly he was full of doubt.

"Let's sleep on it," he said. "We'll have a meeting, just you and me, tomorrow morning at eight. We'll decide then."

Rydberg nodded and limped towards the door. There he stopped and turned to Wallander again.

"There is one possibility we shouldn't overlook," he said. "That it really was refugees who did it."

Wallander rinsed out his coffee cup and put it in the dish rack.

Actually I hope it was, he thought. I really hope that the killers are at that refugee camp. Then maybe it'll put an end to this arbitrary, lax policy that allows anyone at all, for any reason at all, to cross the border into Sweden. But of course he couldn't say that to Rydberg. It was an opinion he intended to keep to himself.

He fought his way through the strong wind out to his car. Even though he was tired, he had no desire to drive home. In the evenings the loneliness hit him. He turned on the ignition and changed the cassette. The overture to *Fidelio* filled the darkness inside the car.

His wife's departure had come as a complete surprise.

But deep inside he knew, even though he still had a hard time accepting it, that he should have sensed the danger long before it happened. That he was living in a marriage that was slowly breaking apart because of its own dreariness. They had married when they were very young, and far too late realised that they were growing apart. Of the three of them, maybe it was Linda who had reacted most openly to the emptiness surrounding them.

On that night in October when Mona had said that she wanted a divorce, he realised that he had seen it coming; but the thought had been too painful for him and he had repeatedly pushed it aside, blaming it on the fact that he was working so hard. Too late, he saw that she had prepared her departure down to the smallest detail. One Friday evening she had talked about wanting a divorce, and by Sunday she had left him and moved into the flat in Malmö, which she had rented in advance. The feeling of being abandoned had filled him with both shame and anger. In an impotent rage he had slapped her face.

Afterwards there was only silence. She had picked up some of her things during the daytime when he wasn't home. But she left most of her belongings behind, and he had been deeply hurt that she seemed prepared to trade her entire past for a life that did not include him, even as a memory.

He had telephoned her. Late in the evenings they had spoken. Devastated by jealousy, he had asked whether she had left him for another man.

"Another life," she had replied. "Another life, before it's too late."

He had appealed to her. He had tried to give the impression that he was indifferent. He had begged her forgiveness for all the attention he had failed to give. But nothing he said changed her mind.

Two days before Christmas Eve the divorce papers had arrived in the post. When he opened the envelope and realised that it was all over, something had cracked inside him. As if in an attempt to flee, he had called in sick over the Christmas holidays and had set off on an aimless trip that had taken him to Denmark. In northern Sjælland a sudden storm had left him snowbound, and he had spent Christmas in Gilleleje, in a freezing room at a pension near the beach. There he had written her long letters, which he had later torn to pieces and strewn out over the sea in a symbolic gesture, demonstrating that in spite of everything he had begun to accept what had happened.

Two days before New Year's he had returned to Ystad and gone back to work. He spent New Year's Eve working on a serious case involving spousal abuse in Svarte, and he had a terrifying revelation that he could just as easily have physically abused Mona.

The music from *Fidelio* broke off with a screech. The machine had swallowed the tape. The radio came on automatically, and he heard the commentary of an ice hockey game.

He pulled out of the car park, intending to drive

towards home. But he drove in the opposite direction instead, out along the coast road heading west to Trelleborg and Skanör. When he passed the old prison he accelerated. Driving had always distracted his thoughts...

He realised that he had driven almost all the way to Trelleborg. A big ferry was just entering the harbour, and on an impulse he decided to stay for a while. He knew that a number of former policemen from Ystad had become immigration officers at the ferry dock in Trelleborg. He thought some of them might be on duty tonight.

He walked across the harbour area, which was bathed in pale yellow light. A large lorry came roaring towards him like a ghostly prehistoric beast.

When he walked through the door with the sign "Authorised Personnel Only," he found he didn't know either of the officers. Wallander introduced himself. The older of the two had a grey beard and a scar across his forehead.

"That's a nasty business you've got in Ystad," he said. "Did you catch them?"

"Not yet," replied Wallander.

The conversation was interrupted as the passengers from the ferry approached passport control. The majority of them were Swedes returning from celebrating the New Year's holiday in Berlin. There were also some East Germans exercising their newly won freedom by taking a trip to Sweden.

After twenty minutes there were only nine passengers left. All of them were trying in various ways to make it clear that they were seeking asylum in Sweden.

"It's pretty quiet tonight," said the younger of the two officers. "Sometimes up to a hundred asylum seekers arrive on one ferry. You can imagine what it's like."

Five belonged to the same Ethiopian family. Only one of them had a passport, and Wallander wondered how they had managed to make the long journey and cross all those borders with a single passport. Besides the Ethiopian family, two Lebanese and two Iranians were waiting at passport control.

Wallander found it difficult to decide whether the nine refugees looked hopeful or whether they were simply scared.

"What happens now?" he asked.

"Malmö will come and pick them up," replied the older officer. "It's their turn tonight. We get word over the radio when there are a lot of people without passports on the ferries. Sometimes we have to call for extra manpower."

"What happens in Malmö?" asked Wallander.

"They're put on one of the ships anchored out in the Oil Harbour. They have to stay there until they're moved on. If they're allowed to stay in Sweden, that is."

"What do you think about these people here?"

The policeman shrugged.

"They'll probably get in," he answered. "Do you want some coffee? It'll be a while before the next ferry."

Wallander shook his head. "Some other time. I have to get going."

"Hope you catch them."

"Right," said Wallander. "So do I."

On the way back to Ystad he ran over a hare. When he saw it in the beam of his headlights he hit the brakes, but it struck the left front wheel with a soft thud. He didn't stop to check whether the hare was still alive.

What's wrong with me? he thought.

That night Wallander slept uneasily. Just after 5 a.m. he awoke with a start. His mouth was dry, and he had dreamt that somebody was trying to strangle him. When he realised that he wouldn't be able to go back to sleep, he got up and made some coffee.

The thermometer outside the kitchen window showed −6° C. The light that hung on a wire suspended across the street was swaying in the wind. He sat down at the kitchen table and thought about his conversation with Rydberg the night before. What he had feared had happened. Mrs. Lövgren had revealed nothing before she died that could give them a lead. Her mention of something "foreign" was just too vague. They didn't have a single clue to go on.

He got dressed, searching for a long time before finding the heavy sweater he wanted. He went outside, feeling the wind tearing and biting at him, drove out Österleden, and turned onto the main road towards Malmö. Before he met Rydberg, he had to pay a return visit to the Nyströms. He couldn't shake the feeling that something didn't quite add up. Attacks like this one usually weren't random, but were preceded by rumours of money stashed away. And even though they could be brutal, they were hardly characterised by the methodical violence that he had witnessed at this murder scene.

People in the country get up early in the morning, he thought as he swung onto the narrow road that led to the Nyströms' house. Maybe they've had time to mull things over.

He stopped in front of the house and turned off the engine. At the same moment the light in the kitchen went out. They're scared, he thought. They probably think it's the killers coming back. He left the lights on as he got out of the car and walked across the gravel to the steps.

He sensed rather than saw the flash coming from a bush beside the house. The ear-splitting noise made him dive for the ground. A pebble slashed his cheek, and for an instant he thought he had been hit.

"Police!" he yelled. "Don't shoot! Damn it, don't shoot!"

A torch shone on his face. The hand holding the torch was shaking, and the beam wobbled back and forth. Nyström was standing in front of him, an ancient shotgun in his hand.

"Is it you?" he asked.

Wallander got up and brushed off the gravel. "What were you aiming at?"

"I shot straight up in the air," said Nyström.

"Do you have a permit for that gun?" Wallander asked. "Otherwise there could be trouble."

"I've been up all night, keeping watch," said Nyström. Wallander could hear how upset he was.

"I have to turn off my lights," said Wallander. "Then we'll talk, you and I."

Two boxes of shotgun shells lay on the kitchen table. On the sofa lay a crowbar and a big sledgehammer. The black cat was in the window, and stared menacingly at Wallander as he came in. Hanna Nyström stood at the stove stirring a pot of coffee.

"I had no idea that it was the police," said Nyström, sounding apologetic. "And so early."

Wallander moved the sledgehammer and sat down.

"Mrs. Lövgren died last night," he said. "I thought I'd come out and tell you myself."

Every time Wallander was forced to notify someone of a death, he had the same unreal feeling. To tell strangers that a child or a relative had died, and to do it with dignity, was impossible. The deaths that the police informed people of were always unexpected, and often violent and gruesome. Somebody drives off to buy something at the shops and dies. A child on a bicycle is run over on the way home from the playground. Someone is abused or robbed, commits suicide or drowns. When the police are standing in the doorway, people refuse to accept the news.

The couple were silent. The woman stirred the coffee

with a spoon. The man fidgeted with his shotgun, and Wallander discreetly moved out of the line of fire.

"So, Maria is gone," Nyström said slowly.

"The doctors did everything they could."

"Maybe it was just as well," said Hanna Nyström, unexpectedly forceful. "What did she have left to live for after he was dead?"

The man put the shotgun down on the kitchen table and stood up. Wallander noticed that he put his weight on one knee.

"I'll go out and give the horse some hay," he said, putting on a tattered cap.

"Do you mind if I come with you?" asked Wallander.

"Why would I mind?" said the man, opening the door.

From her stall the mare whinnied as they entered the stable. With a practised hand Nyström flung an armload of hay into the stall.

"I'll muck out later," he said, stroking the horse's mane.

"Why did they keep a horse?" Wallander wondered.

"To a retired dairy farmer an empty stable is like a morgue," replied Nyström. "The horse was company."

Wallander thought that he might just as well start asking his questions here in the stable.

"You stayed up to keep watch last night," he said. "You're scared, and I can understand that. You must have thought to yourself: 'Why were they the ones who were attacked?' You must have thought: 'Why them? Why not us?'"

"They didn't have any money," said Nyström. "Or anything else that was especially valuable. Anyway, nothing was stolen, as I told one of the policemen here yesterday. The only thing that might have been stolen was a wall clock."

"Might have been?"

"One of their daughters might have taken it. I can't remember everything."

"No money," said Wallander. "And no enemies."

Something occurred to him.

"Do you keep any money in the house?" he asked. "Could it be that whoever did this got the wrong house?"

"All that we have is in the bank," replied Nyström. "And we don't have any enemies either."

They went back to the house and drank coffee. Wallander saw that Hanna Nyström was red-eyed, as if she had been careful to cry while they were out in the stable.

"Have you noticed anything unusual recently?" he asked the couple. "Anyone visiting the Lövgrens you didn't recognise?"

They looked at each other and then shook their heads.

"When was the last time you talked to them?"

"We were over there for coffee the day before yes-

terday," said Hanna. "As always. We drank coffee together every day. For over forty years."

"Did they seem frightened of anything?" asked
Wallander. "Worried?"

"Johannes had a cold," Hanna replied. "But otherwise everything was normal."

It seemed hopeless. Wallander didn't know what
else to ask them. Each reply he got was like a door
slamming shut.

"Did they have any acquaintances who were foreigners?" he asked.

The man raised his eyebrows in surprise.

"Foreigners?"

"Anyone who wasn't Swedish," Wallander ventured.

"One Midsummer a few years ago some Danes
camped on their field."

Wallander looked at the clock. At 8 a.m. he was supposed to meet Rydberg, and he didn't want to be late.

"Try and think," he said. "Anything you can come
up with may help."

Nyström walked out to the car with him.

"I have a permit for the shotgun," he said. "And I
didn't aim at you. I just wanted to scare you."

"You did a good job," replied Wallander. "But I
think you ought to get some sleep tonight. Whoever
did this isn't coming back."

"Would you be able to sleep?" asked Nyström.
"Would you be able to sleep if your neighbours had
been slaughtered like dumb animals?"

Since Wallander couldn't think of a good answer, he said nothing.

"Thanks for the coffee," he said, got in his car, and drove away.

This is all going to hell, he thought. Not one clue, nothing. Only Rydberg's strange knot, and the word "foreign." Two old people with no money under the bed, no antique furniture, are murdered in such a way that there seems to be something more than robbery behind it. A murder of hate or revenge.

There must be something out of the ordinary about them, he thought. If only the horse could talk! He had an uneasy feeling about that horse. It was just a vague hunch. But he was too experienced a policeman to ignore his unease.

Just before 8 a.m. he braked to a halt outside the police station in Ystad. The wind was down to light gusts. Still, it felt a few degrees warmer today. Just so long as we don't get snow, he thought.

He nodded to Ebba at the switchboard. "Did Rydberg show up yet?"

"He's in his office," replied Ebba. "They're calling already. TV, radio, and the newspapers. And the county police commissioner."

"Stall them awhile," said Wallander. "I have to talk with Rydberg first."

He hung up his jacket in his office before he went in to see Rydberg, whose office was a few doors down the corridor. He knocked and heard a grunt in reply.

Rydberg was standing looking out the window when Wallander entered. It was obvious that he hadn't had enough sleep.

"Good morning," said Wallander. "Shall I bring in some coffee?"

"Sure. But no sugar. I've cut it out."

Wallander went out to get two coffees in plastic mugs and then went back to Rydberg's office. Outside the door he stopped. What's my plan, anyway? he thought. Should we keep her last words from the press for "investigative reasons"? Or should we release them?

I don't have a plan, he thought, annoyed, and pushed open the door with his foot. Rydberg was sitting behind his desk combing his sparse hair. Wallander sank into a visitor's chair with worn-out springs.

"You ought to get a new chair," he said.

"There's no money for one," said Rydberg, putting away his comb in a desk drawer.

Wallander set his cup on the floor beside his chair.

"I woke up so damned early this morning," he said. "I drove out and talked to the Nyströms. The old man was waiting in a bush and took a shot at me with a shotgun."

Rydberg pointed at his cheek.

"Not from buckshot," said Wallander. "I hit the deck. He claimed he had a permit for the gun. Who the hell knows?"

"Did they have anything new to say?"

"Not one thing. Nothing out of the ordinary. No money, nothing. Provided they're not lying, of course."

"Why would they be lying?"

"No, why would they?"

Rydberg took a slurp of coffee and made a face.

"Did you know that policemen are unusually susceptible to stomach cancer?" he asked.

"I didn't know that."

"If it's true, it's because of all the lousy coffee we drink."

"But we solve our cases over our mugs of coffee."

"Like now?"

Wallander shook his head. "What do we really have to go on? Nothing."

"You're too impatient, Kurt." Rydberg looked at him while he stroked his nose. "You'll have to excuse me if I seem like a schoolteacher," he went on. "But in this case I think we have to be patient."

They went over the progress of the investigation again. The technicians had taken fingerprints from the scene of the crime and were checking them against the national centralised records. Hansson was busy investigating the location of all known criminals with records of assault on old people, to find out whether they were in prison or had alibis. They would continue questioning the residents of Lunnarp, and perhaps the questionnaire they sent out would produce something. Both Rydberg and Wallander knew that the police in

Ystad carried out their work precisely and methodically. Sooner or later something would turn up. A trace, a clue. It was just a matter of waiting. Of working methodically and waiting.

"The motive," Wallander persisted. "If the motive isn't money, or the rumour of money hidden away, then what is it? The noose? You must have thought the same thing I did. This crime has revenge or hate in it. Or both."

"Let's imagine a pair of suitably desperate robbers," said Rydberg. "Let's assume that they were convinced that Lövgren had money squirrelled away. Let's assume that they were sufficiently indifferent to human life. Then torture isn't out of the question."

"Who would be that desperate?"

"You know as well as I do that there are plenty of drugs that create such a dependency that people are ready to do anything."

Wallander did know that. He had seen the accelerating violence firsthand, and narcotics trafficking and drug dependency almost always lurked in the background. Even though Ystad's police district was seldom hit by this increasing violence, he harboured no illusions: it was steadily creeping up on them.

There were no protected zones anymore. An insignificant little village like Lunnarp was confirmation of that fact. He sat up straight in the uncomfortable chair.

"What are we going to do?" he said.

"You're the boss," replied Rydberg.

"I want to hear what you think."

Rydberg got up and went over to the window. With one finger he felt the soil in a flowerpot. It was dry.

"If you want to know what I think, I'll tell you. But you should know that I'm by no means sure that I'm on the right track. I think that no matter what we decide to do, there's going to be a big fuss. But maybe it would be a good idea to keep quiet for a few days anyway. There are plenty of things to investigate."

"Like what?"

"Did the Lövgrens have any foreign acquaintances?"

"I asked about that this morning. They may have known some Danes."

"There, you see."

"It couldn't have been Danish campers, could it?"

"Why not? No matter what, we'll have to check it out. And there are more people than just the neighbours to question. If I understood you correctly yesterday, the Lövgrens had a big family."

Wallander realised that Rydberg was right. There were investigative reasons to keep quiet about the fact that the police were searching for a person or persons with foreign connections.

"What do we know about foreigners who have committed crimes in Sweden?" he asked. "Do the national police have special files on that?"

"There are files on everything," Rydberg replied. "Put someone in front of a computer and link up to the central criminal database, and maybe we'll find something."

Wallander stood up.

Rydberg looked at him quizzically. "Aren't you going to ask about the noose?"

"I forgot."

"There's supposed to be an old sail maker in Limhamn who knows all about knots. I read about him in a newspaper sometime last year. I thought I'd try to track him down. Not because I'm confident anything will come of it. But just in case."

"I want you to come to the meeting first," said Wallander. "Then you can drive over to Limhamn."

At 10 a.m. they were all gathered in Wallander's office.

The run through was very brief. Wallander told them what the woman had said before she died. For the time being, this piece of information was not to be disclosed. No one seemed to have any objections.

Martinsson was put on the computer to search for foreign criminals. The officers who were going to continue with the questioning in Lunnarp went on their way. Wallander assigned Svedberg to concentrate on the young Polish family, who were presumably in the country illegally. He wanted to know why they were living in Lunnarp. Rydberg left for Limhamn to look for the sail maker.

When Wallander was alone in his office, he stood for a while looking at the map on the wall. Where had the killers come from? Which way did they go afterwards?

He sat down at his desk and asked Ebba to start putting through calls. For more than an hour he spoke with various reporters. But there was no word from the girl from the local radio station.

A while later Norén knocked on the door.

"I thought you were going to Lunnarp," Wallander said, surprised.

"I was," said Norén. "But I just thought of something."

Norén sat on the edge of a chair, since he was wet. It had started to rain. The temperature had now risen to 1° C.

"This might not mean anything," said Norén. "It just crossed my mind."

"Most things mean something," said Wallander.

"You remember that horse?" asked Norén.

"Sure."

"You told me to give it some hay."

"And water."

"Hay and water. But I never did."

Wallander wrinkled his brow. "Why not?"

"The horse already had hay. Water too." Wallander sat in silence for a moment, looking at Norén.

"Go on," he said. "You're getting at something."

Norén shrugged his shoulders.

"We had a horse when I was growing up," he said. "When the horse was in its stall and was given hay, it would eat all of it. I mean that someone must have given the horse some hay. Maybe just an hour or so before we got there."

Wallander reached for the phone.

"If you're thinking of calling Nyström, don't bother," said Norén.

Wallander let his hand drop.

"I talked to him before I came here. And he hadn't given the horse any hay."

"Dead men don't feed their horses," said Wallander. "Who did?" Norén stood up. "It seems weird," he said. "First they kill a man. Then they put a noose on somebody else. And then they go out to the stable and give the horse some hay. Who the hell would do anything that weird?"

"You're right," said Wallander. "Who would do that?"

"It might not mean anything," said Norén.

"Or maybe it does," replied Wallander. "It was good of you to tell me."

Norén said goodbye and left.

Wallander sat and thought about what he had just heard.

His hunch had been correct. There *was* something about that horse.

His thoughts were interrupted by the telephone. Another reporter who wanted to talk with him. At 12:45 he left the police station. He had to visit a friend he hadn't seen in many, many years.

CHAPTER 5

Kurt Wallander turned off the E65 where a sign pointed towards the ruins of Stjärnsund Castle. He got out of the car and unzipped to have a leak. Through the roar of the wind he could hear the sound of accelerating jet engines at Sturup airport. Before he got back in the car, he scraped the mud from his shoes. The change in the weather had been abrupt. The thermometer in his car showed −5° C. Ragged clouds were racing across the sky as he drove on.

Beyond the castle ruin the gravel road forked, and he kept to the left. He had never come this way before, but he was positive it was the right road. Despite the fact that almost ten years had passed since it had been described to him, he remembered the route in detail. He had a mind that seemed programmed for landscapes and roads.

After about a kilometre the surface deteriorated. He went slowly forwards, wondering how large lorries ever managed to negotiate it. The road sloped sharply downwards, and a large farm with long wings of stables lay spread out before him. He drove into the yard and stopped. A flock of crows cawed overhead as he climbed out of the car.

The farm seemed oddly deserted. A stable door flapped in the wind. For a moment he wondered whether he had taken the wrong road after all.

What desolation, he thought. The Scanian winter with its screeching flocks of crows. The clay that sticks to the soles of your shoes.

A young, fair-haired girl emerged from one of the stables. How like Linda she looked, he thought. She had the same blond hair, the same thin body, the same ungainly movements as she walked. He watched her closely.

The girl started tugging at a ladder that led to the stable loft. When she caught sight of him she let go of the ladder and wiped her hands on her grey breeches.

"Hello," said Wallander. "I'm looking for Sten Widén. Is this the right place?"

"Are you a policeman?" asked the girl.

"Yes," Wallander replied, surprised. "How could you tell?"

"I could hear it in your voice," said the girl, once more pulling at the ladder, which seemed to be stuck.

"Is he at home?" asked Wallander.

"Help me with the ladder," the girl said.

He saw that one of the rungs had caught on the cladding of the stable wall. He grabbed hold of the ladder and twisted it until the rung came free.

"Thanks," said the girl. "Sten is probably in his office." She pointed to a red brick building a short distance from the stable.

"Do you work here?" asked Wallander.

"Yes," said the girl, climbing quickly up the ladder. "Now I'd move away if I were you!"

With surprisingly strong arms she began heaving bales of hay through the loft doors. Wallander walked over towards the office. Just as he was about to knock on the heavy door, a man came walking around the end of the building.

It was more than ten years since Wallander had seen Sten Widén, but he didn't seem to have changed. The same tousled hair, the same thin face, the same red eczema near his lower lip.

"Well, this is a surprise," said the man with a nervous laugh. "I thought it was the blacksmith. But it's you. How long has it been, anyway?"

"Nearly eleven years," said Wallander. "Summer of '79."

"The summer all our dreams fell apart," said Sten Widén. "Would you like some coffee?"

They went into the red brick building. Wallander noticed the smell of oil emanating from the walls. A rusty combine harvester stood inside in the darkness. Widén opened another door. A cat ran out as Wallander entered a room that seemed to be a combination of office and living quarters. An unmade bed stood along one wall. There was a TV and a VCR, and a microwave on a table. An old armchair was piled high with clothes. Most of the rest of the space was taken up by a large desk. Widén poured coffee from a thermos next to a fax machine in one of the wide window recesses.

Wallander was thinking about Widén's lost dream of becoming an opera singer. About how in the late 1970s the two of them had imagined a future for themselves that neither of them could achieve. Wallander was supposed to become an impresario, and Widén's tenor would resound from the opera stages of the world.

Wallander had been a policeman back then. And he still was.

When Widén realised that his voice wasn't good enough, he had taken over his father's run-down racing stables. Their earlier friendship had not been able to withstand the shared disappointment. At one time they had seen each other every day, but now eleven years had passed since their last meeting. Even though they lived no more than fifty kilometres apart.

"You've put on weight," said Widén, moving a stack of newspapers from a wooden chair.

"And you haven't," said Wallander, conscious of his own irritation.

"Racehorse trainers seldom get fat," said Widén, laughing nervously again. "Skinny legs, skinny wallets. Except for the big time trainers, of course. Khan or Strasser. They can afford it."

"So how's it going?" asked Wallander, sitting down on the chair.

"So so," said Widén. "I get by. I've always got one horse in training that does well. I get in a few new colts and manage to keep the place going. But actually—" He broke off.

Then he stretched, opened a drawer in his desk, and pulled out a half-empty bottle of whisky.

"Want some?" he asked.

Wallander shook his head. "It wouldn't look good if a policeman got caught for being drunk in charge," he replied. "Though it happens once in a while."

"Well, *skål*, anyway," said Widén, drinking from the bottle.

He extracted a cigarette from a crumpled pack and rummaged through the papers and form guides before he found a lighter.

"How's Mona doing?" he asked. "And Linda? And your dad? And your sister, what's her name, Kerstin?"

"Kristina."

"That's it. Kristina. I've never had a particularly good memory, you know that."

"You never forgot the music."

"I didn't?"

He drank from the bottle again, and Wallander could see that something was troubling him. Maybe he shouldn't have dropped by. Maybe Sten didn't want to be reminded of what once had been.

"Mona and I have split up," Wallander said, "and

Linda's got her own place. Dad is the same as ever. He keeps painting that picture of his. But I think he's becoming a little senile. I don't really know what to do with him."

"Did you know that I got married?" said Widén.

Wallander wondered whether he'd heard a word he'd said. "I didn't know that."

"I took over these damned stables, after all. When Dad finally realised that he was too old to take care of the horses, he started doing some serious drinking. Before, he always had control over how much he put away. I realised that I couldn't handle him and his drinking mates. So I married one of the girls who worked here, mainly because she was so good with Dad. She treated him like an old horse. Didn't try to change his habits, but set limits for him. Took the hose and rinsed him off when he got too filthy. But when Dad died, it seemed to me as if she started to smell like him. So I got a divorce."

He took a swig from the bottle, and Wallander could see that he was beginning to get drunk.

"Every day I think about selling this place," he said. "I own the farm itself. I could probably get a million for the whole thing. After the mortgage is paid off, I might have 400,000 kronor left over. Then I'll buy a camper and hit the road."

"Where to?"

"That's just it. I don't know. There's nowhere I want to go."

Wallander felt uncomfortable listening to this. Even though Widén was outwardly no different, on the inside he had gone through some big changes. It was the voice of a ghost talking to him, cracked and despairing. Ten years ago Sten Widén had been happy and high-spirited, the first to invite you to a party. Now his love of life seemed gone.

The girl who had asked if Wallander was a policeman rode past the window.

"Who's she?" he asked. "She could tell I was police."

"Her name is Louise," said Widén. "She could probably smell it. She's been in and out of institutions since she was twelve. I'm her guardian. She's good with the horses. But she hates policemen. She claims that she was raped by one once."

He took another swig and gestured towards the unmade bed.

"She sleeps with me sometimes," he said. "That's how it feels at any rate. That she's taking me to bed, not the other way around. I suppose that's against the law, right?"

"Why should it be? She isn't a minor, is she?"

"She's nineteen. But are guardians allowed to sleep with their wards?"

Wallander thought he caught a hint of aggression in Widén's voice. He was sorry he had come. Even though he did have a reason for the visit that was connected with the investigation, he now wasn't sure whether it had been more than an excuse. Had he come to see Widén to talk about Mona? To seek out some sort of consolation? He no longer knew.

"I came here to ask you about horses," he said. "Maybe you saw in the paper that there was a double murder in Lunnarp?"

"I don't read newspapers," said Widén. "I read form guides and starting price lists. That's all. I don't give a damn about what's happening in the world."

"An old couple have been killed," Wallander continued. "And they had a horse."

"Was it killed too?"

"No. But I think the killers gave it some hay before they left. And that's what I wanted to talk to you about. How fast does a horse eat an armload of hay?"

Widén emptied the bottle and lit another cigarette.

"Are you kidding?" he asked. "You came all the way out here to ask me how long it takes a horse to eat an armload of hay?"

"As it happens, I was thinking about asking you to come with me and take a look at the horse," said Wallander, making a quick decision. He could feel himself starting to get angry.

"I don't have time," said Widén. "The blacksmith is coming today. I've got sixteen horses that need vitamin jabs."

"Tomorrow, then?"

Widén gave him a glazed look. "Is there money involved?"

"You'll be paid."

Widén wrote his telephone number on a dirty scrap of paper.

"Maybe," he said. "Call me in the morning."

When they stepped outside, Wallander noticed that the wind had picked up.

The girl came riding up on her horse.

"Nice horse," he said.

"Masquerade Queen," said Widén. "She'll never win a race in her life. The rich widow of a Trelleborg contractor owns her. I was actually honest enough to suggest that she sell the horse to a riding school. But she thinks it can win. And I get my training fee. But there's no way in hell this horse will ever win a race."

They said goodbye at the car.

"You know how my dad died?" asked Widén suddenly.

"No."

"He wandered off to the castle ruin one autumn night. He used to sit up there and drink. He stumbled into the moat and drowned. The algae are so thick there that you can't see a thing. But his cap floated to the surface. 'Live Life' the legend said on the cap. It was an ad for a travel bureau that sells sex holidays in Bangkok."

"It was nice to see you," said Wallander. "I'll call you tomorrow."

"Whatever," said Widén and went off towards the stable.

Wallander drove away. In the rearview mirror he could see Widén talking to the girl on the horse.

Why did I come here? he thought again. Once, a long time ago, we were friends. We shared an impossible dream. When the dream evaporated like a phantom there was nothing left. It may be true that we both loved opera. But perhaps that was just a fantasy too.

He drove fast, as if he were letting his agitation dictate the pressure he put on the accelerator. Just as he braked for the stop sign at the main road, his car phone rang. The connection was so bad he could hardly make out that it was Hansson.

"You'd better come in," the voice yelled. "Can you hear what I'm saying?"

"What happened?" Wallander yelled back.

"There's a farmer from Hagestad here who says he knows who killed them," Hansson shouted.

Wallander felt his heart beating quicker.

"Who?" he shouted. "Who?"

The connection abruptly died. The receiver hissed and squawked.

"Damn," he said out loud.

He drove back into Ystad. Much too fast, he thought. If Norén and Peters had been on traffic duty today, I'd have been in real trouble.

Just as he was going down the hill into the centre of town, the engine started coughing. He had run out of petrol. The warning light was obviously on the blink.

He managed to make it to the petrol station across

from the hospital before the engine died completely. Getting out to put some money in the pump, he discovered that he didn't have any cash on him. He went next door to the locksmith in the same building and borrowed 20 kronor from the owner, who recognised him from an investigation of a break-in a few years back.

He parked and hurried into the station. Ebba tried to tell him something, but he dismissed her with a wave.

The door to Hansson's office was ajar, and Wallander went in without knocking. It was empty. In the corridor he found Martinsson, who was holding a handful of printouts.

"Just the man I'm looking for," said Martinsson. "I dug up some stuff that might be interesting. I'll be damned if some Finns might not be behind this."

"When we don't have a lead, we usually say it's Finns," said Wallander. "I haven't time now. You know where Hansson is?"

"He never leaves his office, you know that."

"Then we'll have to put out an APB on him, because he's not there now."

He poked his head into the canteen, but there was only an office clerk there making an omelette. Where the hell is that Hansson? he thought, flinging open the door to his own office. Nobody there either. He called Ebba at the switchboard.

"Where's Hansson?" he asked.

"If you hadn't been in such a rush, I could have told you when you came in," said Ebba. "He told me he had to go down to the Union Bank."

"What was he going there for? Was anyone with him?"

"Yes. But I don't know who it was."

Wallander slammed down the phone. What the hell was he up to? He picked up the phone again.

"Can you get Hansson on the phone for me?" he asked Ebba.

"At the Union Bank?"

"If that's where he is."

He very rarely asked Ebba for help tracking people down. If he needed something done, he did it himself. In the past he'd put it down to his upbringing. Only rich, arrogant people sent others out to do their footwork. Not being able to look up a number in the phone book and pick up a receiver was indefensible laziness.

The telephone rang, interrupting his thoughts. It was Hansson calling from the Union Bank.

"I thought I'd get back before you did," said Hansson. "You're probably wondering what I'm doing here."

"You could say that."

"We're taking a look at Lövgren's bank account."

"Who's we?"

"His name is Herdin. But you'd better talk to him yourself. We'll be back in half an hour."

Wallander finally met the man called Herdin an

hour and a half later. He was almost six foot six, thin and wiry, and Wallander felt like he was shaking hands with a giant.

"It took a while," said Hansson. "But we got results. You have to hear what Herdin has to say. And what we've discovered."

Herdin was sitting erect and silent on a wooden chair. Wallander guessed that the man had put on his Sunday best before coming to the police station. Even if it was only a worn suit and a shirt with a frayed collar.

"We'd better start at the beginning," said Wallander, picking up a pad.

Herdin gave Hansson a bewildered look.

"Should I start all over again?" he asked.

"That would probably be best," said Hansson.

"It's a long story," Herdin began hesitantly.

"What's your name?" asked Wallander. "Let's start with that."

"Lars Herdin. I have a farm of forty acres near Hagestad. I'm trying to make ends meet raising livestock. But things are pretty tight."

"I've got all his personal data," Hansson interrupted, and Wallander guessed that Hansson was in a hurry to get back to his form guides.

"If I understand correctly, you came here because you think you may have information relating to the murder of Mr. and Mrs. Lövgren," said Wallander, wishing he had expressed himself more simply.

"It's obvious that it was the money," Lars Herdin said.

"What money?"

"All the money they had!"

"Could you clarify that a little?"

"The German money."

Wallander looked at Hansson, who shrugged slightly. Wallander took this to mean that he had to be patient.

"I think we're going to need a little more detail on this," he said. "Do you think you could be more specific?"

"Lövgren and his father made money during the war," said Herdin. "They kept livestock in secret on some forest pastures up in Småland. And they bought up worn-out old horses. Then they sold them on the black market to Germany. They made an obscene amount of money on the meat. And nobody ever caught them. Lövgren was both greedy and clever. He invested the money, and it's been growing over the years."

"You mean Lövgren's father?"

"His father died straight after the war. I mean Lövgren himself."

"So you're telling me that the Lövgrens were wealthy?"

"Not the family. Just Lövgren. She didn't know a thing about the money."

"Would he have kept his fortune a secret from his own wife?"

Herdin nodded. "Nobody has ever been as foully cheated as my sister."

Wallander raised his eyebrows in surprise.

"Maria Lövgren was my sister. She was killed because he had stashed away a fortune."

Wallander heard the barely concealed bitterness. So maybe it *was* a hate crime, he thought.

"And this money was kept at home?"

"Only sometimes," replied Herdin.

"Sometimes?"

"When he made the large withdrawals."

"Could you give me a little more detail?"

Suddenly something seemed to boil over inside the man in the worn-out suit.

"Johannes Lövgren was a brute," he said. "It's better now that he's gone. But that Maria had to die, that I can never forgive."

Lars Herdin's outburst came so suddenly that neither Hansson nor Wallander had time to react. He grabbed a solid glass ashtray from the table beside him and flung it full force at the wall, where it smashed close to Wallander's head. Splinters of glass flew in every direction, and Wallander felt a shard strike his upper lip.

The silence after the outburst was deafening.

Hansson had sprung out of his chair and seemed ready to throw himself at the rangy Herdin, but Wallander raised his hand to stop him, and Hansson sat back down.

"I beg your pardon," said Herdin. "If you have a broom and dustpan I'll clean up the glass. I'll pay for it."

"The cleaners will take care of it," said Wallander. "I think we should go on with our talk."

Herdin now seemed perfectly calm.

"Johannes Lövgren was a beast," he repeated. "He pretended to be like everybody else. But the only thing he thought about was the money he and his father made from the war. He complained that everything was so expensive, and the farmers so poor. But he had his money, and it kept on growing and growing."

"And he kept this money in the bank?"

Herdin shrugged. "In the bank, in shares and bonds, who knows what else."

"Why did he keep the money at home sometimes?"

"Lövgren had a mistress," said Herdin. "There was a woman in Kristianstad whom he had a son with in the 1950s. Maria knew nothing about that either—not the woman, not the child. He gave his mistress more money every year than he spent on Maria in her whole life."

"How much money are we talking about?"

"Two or three times a year he gave her twenty-five or thirty thousand. He withdrew the money in cash. Then he would think up some excuse and go to Kristianstad."

Wallander thought for a moment about what he had heard. He tried to decide which questions were the most important. It would take hours to work out all the details.

"What did they say at the bank?" he asked Hansson.

"If you don't have the search warrants all in order, the bank doesn't say anything," said Hansson. "They wouldn't let me look at his bank statements. But I did get the answer to one question: Had he been to the bank recently?"

"Well?"

Hansson nodded. "Last Thursday. Three days before he was killed."

"Are they sure?"

"One of the clerks recognised him."

"And he withdrew a large sum of money?"

"They wouldn't say exactly. But the clerk nodded when the bank manager turned his back."

"We'll have to talk to the prosecutor when we have written up this statement," said Wallander. "Then we can look into his assets and see where we are."

"Blood money," said Herdin.

Wallander wondered whether he was going to start throwing things again.

"There are plenty of questions left," he said. "But one is more important than all the others right now. How do you know about all this? You say that Lövgren kept it secret from his wife. So how come you know?"

Herdin didn't answer the question. He stared mutely at the floor.

Wallander looked at Hansson, who shook his head.

"You really have to answer the question," said Wallander.

"I don't have to answer at all," said Herdin. "I'm not the one who killed them. Would I murder my own sister?"

Wallander tried to approach the question from another angle. "How many other people know what you just told us?"

Herdin didn't answer.

"Whatever you say won't go beyond this room," Wallander said.

Herdin stared at the floor. Wallander knew instinctively that he must wait.

"Would you get us some coffee?" he asked Hansson. "And see if you can find some pastries."

While Hansson was gone, Herdin kept staring at the floor, and Wallander waited. Hansson brought in the coffee, and Herdin ate a stale pastry.

Wallander thought it was time to ask the question again. "Sooner or later you'll have no choice but to answer," he said.

Herdin raised his head and looked him straight in the eye.

"When they got married I already had a feeling that there was another person behind Johannes Lövgren's friendly yet taciturn exterior. I thought there was something fishy about him. Maria was my little sister. I wanted the best for her. I was suspicious of Lövgren from the first time he came to our parents' house to court her. It took me thirty years to work out who he was. How I did it is my business."

"Did you tell your sister what you found out?"

"Never. Not a word."

"Did you tell anyone else? Your own wife?"

"I'm not married."

Wallander looked at the man sitting in front of him. There was something hard and dogged about him. Like a man who had been brought up eating gravel.

"One last question," said Wallander. "Now we know that Lövgren had plenty of money. Maybe he also had a large sum of money at home the night he was murdered. We'll have to find that out. But who would have known about it? Besides you."

Herdin looked at him. Wallander saw a glint of fear in his eyes.

"I didn't know about it," said Herdin.

Wallander nodded.

"We'll stop here," he said, shoving aside the pad on which he had been taking notes. "But we're going to be needing your help again."

"Can I go now?" said Herdin, getting up.

"You can go," replied Wallander. "But don't leave the district without talking to us first. And if you think of anything else, we'd like to hear from you."

As he was leaving, Herdin hesitated as if there was something more he wanted to say. Then he pushed open the door and was gone.

"Tell Martinsson to run a check on him," said Wallander. "Probably we won't find anything. But it's best to make sure."

"What do you think about what he said?" Hansson wondered.

Wallander thought before replying.

"There was something convincing about him. I don't think he was lying or making things up. I believe he did discover that Johannes Lövgren was living a double life. I think he was protecting his sister."

"Do you think he could have been involved?"

Wallander was certain when he answered. "Herdin didn't kill them. Nor do I think he knows who did. I believe he came to us for two reasons. He wanted to help us find the people responsible so he can both thank them and spit in their faces. As far as he's concerned, whoever murdered Lövgren did him a favour. And whoever murdered Maria ought to be beheaded in the public square."

Hansson got up. "I'll tell Martinsson. Anything else you need right now?"

Wallander looked at his watch.

"Let's have a meeting in my office in an hour. See if you can get hold of Rydberg. He was supposed to go to Malmö to find a man who makes sails."

Hansson gave him a questioning look.

"The noose. The knot. I'll fill you in later."

Hansson left, and Wallander was alone. A breakthrough, he thought. All successful criminal investigations reach a point where we break through the wall. We don't know what we're going to find. But there's always a solution somewhere.

He went over to the window and looked out into the twilight. A cold draught was seeping through the window frame, and he could see from the way a streetlight was swaying that the wind was blowing harder.

He thought about Nyström and his wife. For a lifetime they had lived in close contact with a man who had not been the man he pretended to be at all.

How would they react when the truth came out? With denial? Bitterness? Amazement?

He went back to the desk and sat down. The first feeling of relief that followed a breakthrough like this one often faded quite rapidly. Now there was a possible motive, the most common of all: money. But so far there was no invisible finger pointing in a specific direction. No murderer yet.

Wallander cast another glance at his watch. If he hurried, he could drive down to the hot dog stand at the railway station and get a bite to eat before the meeting. This day too was going to pass without a change in his eating habits.

He was just about to put on his jacket when the phone rang. At the same time there was a knock on the door. The jacket fell to the floor as he grabbed the phone and shouted, "Come in."

Rydberg stood in the doorway. He was holding a large plastic bag.

He heard Ebba's voice on the phone.

"The TV people insist on speaking to you," she said.

He quickly decided to talk to Rydberg before he had to deal with the media again.

"Tell them I'm in a meeting and won't be available for half an hour," he said.

"Are you sure?"

"Sure of what?"

"That you'll talk to them in half an hour? Swedish TV doesn't like to be kept waiting. They take it for granted that everyone will fall to their knees when they call."

"That I will not do. But I can talk to them in half an hour."

He hung up.

Rydberg had sat down on the chair by the window. He was busy drying off his hair with a paper napkin.

"I've got good news," said Wallander.

Rydberg went on drying his hair.

"I think we've got a motive. Money. And I think we should look for the killers among people who were close to the Lövgrens."

Rydberg tossed the wet napkin into the wastebasket.

"I've had a miserable day," he said. "Good news is welcome."

Wallander spent five minutes recounting the meeting with the farmer, Lars Herdin. Rydberg stared gloomily at the shards of glass on the floor.

"Strange story," said Rydberg when Wallander was finished. "It's strange enough to be true."

"I'll try to sum it up," Wallander went on. "Someone

knew that Johannes Lövgren from time to time kept large sums of money at home. This gives us robbery as a motive. And the robbery developed into a murder. If Herdin's description of Lövgren is right, that he was an unusually stingy man, he would naturally have refused to reveal where he had hidden the money. Maria Lövgren, who can't have understood much of what was happening on the last night of her life, was forced to accompany Johannes on his final journey. So the question is who besides Herdin knew about the irregular but substantial cash withdrawals. If we can answer that, we can probably answer everything."

Rydberg sat there thinking after Wallander fell silent.

"Did I leave anything out?" asked Wallander.

"I'm thinking about what she said before she died," said Rydberg. " 'Foreign.' And I'm thinking about what I've got in this plastic bag."

He stood up and dumped the contents of the bag onto the desk. A heap of pieces of rope. Each one artfully tied in a knot.

"I've been with an old sail maker in a flat that smells worse than anything you can imagine," said Rydberg with a grimace. "It turns out that this man is almost ninety, and practically senile. I wonder whether I shouldn't contact the social services. He was so confused he thought I was his son. Later one of the neighbours told me that his son has been dead for thirty years. But he certainly knows about knots. When I finally got out of there, it was four hours later. These pieces of rope were a present."

"Did you find out what you wanted to know?"

"The old man looked at the noose and said he thought the knot was ugly. Then it took me three hours to get him to tell me something about this ugly knot. In the meantime he managed to nod off for a while."

Rydberg gathered up the bits of rope in his plastic bag as he went on. "When he woke up he started talking about his days at sea. And then he said that he'd seen that knot in Argentina. Argentine sailors used that knot for making leads for their dogs."

Wallander nodded.

"So you were right. The knot was foreign. The question now is how this all fits in with Herdin's story."

They went out in the corridor, Rydberg went to his office, and Wallander went to see Martinsson and study the printouts. It turned out that there were exhaustive statistics on overseas-born citizens who had either committed or been suspected of committing crimes in Sweden. Martinsson had also managed to run a check on attacks involving old people. At least four different individuals or gangs were known to have assaulted old, isolated people in Skåne during the past twelve months. But Martinsson had also found out that every one of them was in prison. He was still waiting for word on whether any of them had been granted leave on the day in question.

They held the case meeting in Rydberg's office, since

one of the office clerks had offered to sweep up the glass from Wallander's floor. Wallander's phone rang almost nonstop, but the clerk didn't pick it up.

The meeting was long. Everyone agreed that Lars Herdin's testimony was a breakthrough. Now they had a direction to go in. At the same time they went over everything that had been gleaned from the interviews with the residents of Lunnarp, and the people who had telephoned the police or responded to the questionnaire they had sent out. A car that had driven through a village a few kilometres from Lunnarp at high speed late on Saturday night attracted special attention. A lorry driver who had set out on a journey to Göteborg at 3 a.m. had almost been hit going around a tight curve. When he heard about the double murder he called the police. He wasn't sure, but after going through pictures of various cars he decided it was probably a Nissan.

"Don't forget rental cars," said Wallander. "People on the move want to be comfortable these days. Robbers rent cars as often as they steal them."

It was already 6 p.m. by the time the meeting was over. Wallander realised that all his colleagues were now on the offensive. There was palpable optimism after Lars Herdin's visit.

He went to his office and typed up his notes of the interview with Herdin. He had Hansson's notes of the earlier interview so he could compare them. He realised at once that Lars Herdin had not been evasive. The information was the same in both.

Just after 7 p.m. he put the papers aside. He realised that the TV people hadn't called back. He asked the switchboard whether Ebba had left any message before she went home.

The girl who answered was a temp. "There's nothing here," she said.

He went to the canteen and switched on the TV, on a whim. The local news had just started. He leaned on a table and distractedly watched a report about how short of funds the city of Malmö was.

He thought about Sten Widén. And Johannes Lövgren, who had sold meat to the Nazis during the war. He thought about himself, and about his stomach, which was far too big.

He was just about to turn off the TV when the anchorwoman started talking about the murders in Lunnarp. In astonishment he heard that the police in Ystad were concentrating their search on as-yet-unidentified foreign citizens. The police were convinced that those responsible were foreigners. It could not be ruled out that they might be refugees seeking asylum.

Finally the reporter talked about Wallander himself. Despite repeated efforts, it had been impossible to get any of the detectives in charge to comment on the information, which had been obtained from anonymous but reliable sources.

The reporter was speaking in front of a shot of the Ystad police station. Then she moved straight on to the weather report. A storm was approaching from the west. The wind would increase, but there was no risk of snow. The temperature would continue to stay above freezing level.

Wallander turned off the TV. He couldn't make up his mind whether he was upset or merely tired. Or maybe he was just hungry.

Someone at the police station had leaked the information. Perhaps nowadays people got paid for passing on confidential information. Did the state-run television monopoly have slush funds too?

Who? he wondered. It could have been anyone except me. And why? Was there some other explanation besides money? Racial hatred? Fear of refugees? As he walked back to his room, he could hear the phone ringing all the way down the corridor.

It had been a long day. He would have liked to drive home and cook himself some dinner. With a sigh he sat down and pulled over the phone. I guess I'll have to get started, he thought. Start denying the information on the TV. And hope that nobody burns any wooden crosses in the days to come.

CHAPTER 6

Overnight a storm moved in across Skåne. Kurt Wallander was sitting in his untidy flat as the winter wind tore at the roof tiles, drinking whisky and listening to a German recording of *Aïda*, when everything went dark and silent. He went over to the window and looked out into the darkness. The wind was howling, and somewhere an advertising sign was banging against a wall.

The luminous hands on his wristwatch showed 2:50 a.m. Oddly enough, he no longer felt tired. It had been after midnight by the time he got away from the station. The last caller had been a man who refused to give his name. He had proposed that the police join forces with the domestic nationalist movements and chase the foreigners out of the country once and for all. For a moment Wallander had tried to listen to what the man was saying. Then he had slammed down the receiver, called the switchboard, and had all incoming calls held. He'd turned off the lights in his office, walked down the silent corridor, and driven straight home. By the time he unlocked his front door, he had decided to find out who had leaked the information. It wasn't really his business at all. If conflicts arose within the police force, it was the duty of the chief of police to intervene. In a few days Björk would be back from his winter holiday. Then he could deal with it. The truth would have to come out.

But as Wallander drank his first glass of whisky, it had occurred to him that Björk would do nothing. Even though each individual police officer was bound by an oath of silence, it could hardly be considered a criminal offence if an officer called up a contact at Swedish Television and told him what was discussed at a case meeting. Nor would it be easy to prove any irregularities if Swedish Television had paid its secret informant. Wallander wondered briefly how Swedish Television entered such an expense in their books. And in any case Björk wouldn't be disposed to question internal loyalty in the middle of a murder investigation.

By the second glass of whisky he was back to worrying who could have been the source of the leak. Apart from himself, he felt he could safely eliminate Rydberg. But then why was he so sure of Rydberg? Could he see more deeply into him than into any of the others?

The storm had obviously knocked out the power. He sat alone in the dark, thinking. His thoughts about the murdered couple, about Lars Herdin, about the strange knot on the noose were mixed with thoughts of Sten Widén and Mona, of Linda and his ageing father. Somewhere in the dark a vast meaninglessness was beckoning. A sneering face that laughed scornfully at every attempt he made to manage his life.

He woke up when the power came back on. He had slept for over an hour. The record was still spinning on the record player. He emptied his glass and went to lie down on his bed.

I've got to talk to Mona, he thought. I've got to talk to her after all that's happened. And I've got to talk to my daughter. I have to visit my father and see what I can do for him. On top of all that I really ought to catch the murderers...

He had dozed off again. He thought he was in his office when the telephone rang. Drowsily he snatched the phone. Who could be calling him at this hour? As he answered, he prayed that it was Mona.

At first he thought that the man on the line sounded like Sten Widén.

"Now you've got three days to make good," said the man.

"Who is this?" said Wallander.

"It doesn't matter who I am," replied the man. "I'm one of the Ten Thousand Redeemers."

"I refuse to talk to anyone if I don't know who it is," said Wallander, wide-awake now.

"Don't hang up," said the man. "You now have three days to make up for shielding foreign criminals. Three days, no more."

"I don't understand what you're talking about," said Wallander, feeling uneasy at the unknown voice.

"Three days to catch the killers and put them on display," said the man. "Or else we'll take over."

"Take over what? And who's 'we'?"

"Three days. No more. Then something's going to burn."

The connection was broken off.

Wallander went into the kitchen, turned on the light, and sat down at the table. He wrote down the conversation in an old notebook that Mona used to use for her shopping lists. At the top of the pad it said "bread." He couldn't read what she had written below that.

It wasn't the first time in his years as a policeman that Wallander had received an anonymous threat. Several years earlier, a man who considered himself unjustly convicted of assault and battery had harassed him with insinuating letters and nighttime phone calls. It was Mona who finally got fed up and demanded that he do something about it. Wallander had sent Svedberg to the man with a warning that he was risking a long jail sentence. Another time his tyres had been slashed.

But this man's message was different. "Something's going to burn," he had said. That meant anything from refugee camps to restaurants to houses owned by foreigners.

Three days—seventy-two hours. That meant Friday, or Saturday the thirteenth at the latest.

He went and lay down on the bed again and tried to sleep. The wind tore and ripped at the walls of the house. How could he sleep when he kept waiting for the man to call again?

At 6:30 a.m. he was back at the station. He exchanged a few words with the duty officer and learned that the stormy night had been peaceful at least. An articulated lorry had tipped over outside Ystad, and some scaffolding had blown down in Skårby. That was all.

He got himself some coffee and went to his office. With an old electric shaver that he kept in a desk drawer he got rid of the stubble on his cheeks. Then he went out for the morning papers. The more he looked through them, the more irritated he became. Despite the fact that he had been on the telephone talking to a number of reporters until late the night before, they had printed only vague and incomplete denials that the police were concentrating their investigation on foreign citizens. It was as though the papers had only reluctantly accepted the truth.

He decided to call another press conference for that afternoon and to present an account of the status of the investigation. He would also disclose the anonymous threat he had received during the night.

From a shelf behind his desk, he took down a folder in which he kept records on the various refugee centres in the region. Besides the big refugee camp in Ystad, several smaller ones were scattered throughout the district.

But what was there to prove that the threat actually had to do with a refugee camp in Ystad's police district?

Nothing. The threat might equally be directed at a restaurant or a house. For instance, how many pizzerias were there in the Ystad area? Twelve? More?

There was one thing he was quite sure of. The threat had to be taken seriously. In the past year there had been too many incidents that confirmed that these were well-organised factions that would not hesitate to resort to open violence against foreigners living in Sweden or refugees seeking asylum.

He looked at his watch. It was 7:45 a.m. He picked up the phone and dialled the number of Rydberg's house. After ten rings he hung up. Rydberg was on his way.

Martinsson stuck his head around the door.

"Hello," he said. "What time is the meeting today?"

"Ten o'clock," said Wallander.

"Awful weather, isn't it?"

"As long as we don't get snow. I can live with the wind."

While he waited for Rydberg, he looked for the note Sten Widén had given him. After Herdin's visit he realised that perhaps it wasn't so unusual for someone to have given the horse hay during the night. If the killers were among Johannes and Maria Lövgren's acquaintances, or even members of their family, they would naturally know about the horse. Maybe they also knew that Johannes Lövgren made a habit of going out to the stable in the night.

Wallander had only a vague idea of what Widén would be able to add. Maybe the real reason he had called him was to avoid losing touch with him. No one answered, even though he let the phone ring for over a minute. He hung up and decided to try again a little later.

He also had another phone call he wanted to make before Rydberg arrived. He dialled the number and waited.

"Public prosecutor's office," a cheerful female voice answered.

"This is Kurt Wallander. Is Åkeson there?"

"He's on leave of absence. Did you forget?"

He had forgotten. It had completely slipped his mind that public prosecutor Per Åkeson was taking some university courses. And they had had dinner together as recently as the end of November.

"I can connect you with his deputy, if you'd like," said the receptionist.

"Do that," said Wallander.

To his surprise a woman answered. "Anette Brolin."

"I'd like to talk with the prosecutor," said Wallander.

"Speaking," said the woman. "What is this about?"

Wallander realised that he hadn't introduced himself. He gave her his name and went on. "It's about this double murder. I think it's time we presented a report to the public prosecutor's office. I had forgotten that Per was on leave."

"If you hadn't called this morning, I would have called you," said the woman.

Wallander thought he detected a reproachful tone

in her voice. Bitch, he thought. Are you going to teach me how the police are supposed to cooperate with the prosecutor's office?

"We actually don't have much to tell you," he said, noticing that his voice sounded a little hostile.

"Is an arrest imminent?"

"No. I was thinking more of a short briefing."

"All right," said the woman. "Shall we say eleven o'clock at my office? I've got a warrant application hearing at quarter past ten. I'll be back by eleven."

"I might be a little late. We have a case meeting at ten. It might run on."

"Try to make it by eleven."

She hung up, and he sat there holding the receiver.

Cooperation between the police and the prosecutor's office wasn't always easy. But Wallander had established an informal and confidential relationship with Per Åkeson. They often called each other to ask advice. They seldom disagreed on when detention or release was justified.

"Damn," he said out loud. "Anette Brolin, who the hell is she?"

Just then he heard the unmistakable sound of Rydberg limping by in the corridor. He stuck his head out of the door and asked him to come in. Rydberg was dressed in an outmoded fur jacket and beret. When he sat down he grimaced.

"Bothering you again?" asked Wallander, pointing at his leg.

"Rain is OK," said Rydberg. "Or snow. Or cold. But this damned leg can't stand the wind. What do you want?"

Wallander told him about the call he had received during the night.

"What do you think?" he asked when he'd finished. "Serious or not?"

"Serious. At least we have to proceed as if it is."

"I'm thinking about a press conference this afternoon. We'll present the status of the investigation and concentrate on Lars Herdin's story. Without mentioning his name, of course. Then I'll speak about the threat. And say that all rumours about foreigners being involved are groundless."

"But that's actually not true," Rydberg mused.

"What do you mean?"

"The woman said what she said. And the knot may be Argentine."

"How do you intend to make that fit in with a robbery that was presumably committed by someone who knew Lövgren very well?"

"I don't know yet. I think it's too soon to draw conclusions. Don't you?"

"Provisional conclusions," said Wallander. "All police work deals with drawing conclusions, which you later discard or keep building on."

Rydberg shifted his sore leg.

"What are you thinking of doing about the leak?" he asked.

"I'm thinking of giving them hell at the meeting," said Wallander. "Then Björk can deal with it when he gets back."

"What do you think he'll do?"

"Nothing."

"Exactly."

Wallander threw his arms wide.

"We might as well admit it right now. Whoever leaked it to the TV people isn't going to get his nose twisted off. By the way, how much do you think Swedish Television pays policemen for leaks?"

"Probably far too much," said Rydberg. "That's why they don't have money for any good programmes."

He got up from his chair.

"Don't forget one thing," he said as he stood with his hand on the door frame. "A policeman who snitches can snitch again."

"What does that mean?"

"He can insist that one of our leads does point to foreigners. It's true, after all."

"It's not even a lead," said Wallander. "It's the last confused words of a dying woman."

Rydberg shrugged.

"Do as you like," he said. "See you in a while."

The case meeting went as badly as it could have. Wallander had decided to start with the leak and its possible consequences. He would describe the anonymous call he had received and then invite suggestions on a plan of action before the deadline. But when he announced angrily that there was someone at the meeting disloyal enough to betray confidential information, possibly for money, he was met by equally furious protests. Several officers said that the leak could have come from the hospital. Hadn't doctors and nurses been present when the old woman uttered those last words?

Wallander tried to refute their objections, but they kept protesting. By the time he finally managed to steer the discussion to the investigation itself, a sullen mood had settled over the meeting. Yesterday's optimism had been replaced by a slack, uninspired atmosphere. Wallander had got off on the wrong foot.

The effort to identify the car with which the lorry driver had almost collided had yielded no results. An additional man was assigned to concentrate on this.

The investigation of Lars Herdin's past was continuing. On the first check nothing remarkable had come to light. He had no police record and no conspicuous debts.

"We're going to run a vacuum cleaner over this man," said Wallander. "We have to know everything there is to know. I'm going to meet the prosecutor in a few minutes. I'll ask for authorisation to go into the bank."

Peters delivered the biggest news of the day.

"Lövgren had two safe-deposit boxes," he said. "One at the Union Bank and one at the Merchants' Bank. I went through the keys on his key ring."

"Good," said Wallander. "We'll check them out later today."

The charting of Lövgren's family, friends, and relatives would go on.

It was decided that Rydberg should take care of the daughter who lived in Canada, who would be arriving at the hovercraft terminal in Malmö just after 3 p.m.

"Where's the other one?" asked Wallander. "The handball player?"

"She's already arrived," said Svedberg. "She's staying with relatives."

"You go and talk to her," said Wallander. "Do we have any other tip-offs that might produce something? Ask the daughters if either of them was given a wall clock, by the way."

Martinsson had sifted through the tip-offs. Everything that the police learnt was fed into a computer. Then he did a rough sort. The most ridiculous ones never got beyond the printouts.

"Hulda Yngveson phoned from Vallby and said that it was the disapproving hand of God that dealt the blow," said Martinsson.

"She always calls," sighed Rydberg. "If a calf runs off, it's because God is displeased."

"I put her on the C.F. list," said Martinsson.

The sullen atmosphere was broken by a little amusement when Martinsson explained that C.F. stood for "crazy fools."

They had received no tip-offs of immediate interest.

But every one would be checked. Finally there was the question of Johannes Lövgren's secret relationship in Kristianstad and the child that they had together.

Wallander looked around the room. Thomas Näslund, a thirty-year veteran who seldom called attention to himself but who did solid, thorough work, was sitting in a corner, pulling on his lower lip as he listened.

"You can come with me," said Wallander. "See if you can do a little footwork first. Ring Herdin and pump him for everything you can about this woman in Kristianstad. And the child too, of course."

The press conference was fixed for 4 p.m. By then Wallander and Näslund hoped to be back from Kristianstad. Rydberg had agreed to preside if they were late.

"I'll write the press release," said Wallander. "If no one has anything more, we'll adjourn."

It was 11:25 a.m. when he knocked on Per Åkeson's door in another part of the police building. The woman who opened the door was very striking and very young. Wallander stared at her.

"Seen enough yet?" she said. "You're half an hour late, by the way."

"I told you the meeting might run over," he replied.

He hardly recognised the office. Per Åkeson's spartan, colourless space had been transformed into a room with pretty curtains and potted plants round the walls.

He followed her with his eyes as she sat down behind

her desk. She couldn't be more than thirty. She was wearing a rust-brown suit that he was sure was of good quality and no doubt quite expensive.

"Have a seat," she said. "Maybe we ought to shake hands, by the way. I'll be filling in for Åkeson all the time he's away. So we'll be working together for quite a while."

He put out his hand and noticed at the same time that she was wearing a wedding ring. To his surprise, he realised that he felt disappointed. She had dark brown hair, cut short and framing her face. A lock of bleached hair curled down beside one ear.

"I'd like to welcome you to Ystad," he said. "I have to admit that I quite forgot that Per was on leave."

"I assume we'll be using our first names. Mine is Anette."

"Kurt. How do you like Ystad?"

She shook off the question brusquely. "I don't really know yet. Stockholmers no doubt have a hard time getting used to the leisurely pace of Skåne."

"Leisurely?"

"You're half an hour late."

Wallander could feel himself getting angry. Was she provoking him? Didn't she understand that a case meeting might run over? Did she regard all Scanians as leisurely?

"I don't think Scanians are any lazier than anyone else," he said. "All Stockholmers aren't stuck-up, are they?"

"I beg your pardon?"

"Forget it."

She leaned back in her chair. He was having difficulty looking her in the eye.

"Perhaps you would give me a summary of the case," she said.

Wallander tried to make his report as concise as possible. He could tell that, without intending to, he had wound up in a defensive position. He avoided mentioning the leak in the police department. She asked a few brief questions, which he answered. He could see that despite her youth she did have professional experience.

"We have to take a look at Lövgren's bank statements," he said. "He also has two safe-deposit boxes we want to open."

She wrote out the documents he needed.

"Shouldn't a judge look at this?" asked Wallander as she pushed them over to him.

"We'll do that later," she said. "And I'd appreciate receiving copies of all the investigative material."

He nodded and got up to leave.

"This article in the papers," she inquired. "About foreigners who may have been involved?"

"Rumour," replied Wallander. "You know how it is."

"I do?" she asked.

When he left her office he noticed that he was sweating. What a babe, he thought. How the hell can someone like that become a prosecutor? Devote her life to catching small-time crooks and keeping the streets clean?

He stopped in the reception area of the station, unable to decide what to do next. Eat, he decided. If I don't get some food now, I never will. I can write the press release over lunch.

When he walked out of the police station he was almost blown over. The storm had not died down.

He ought to drive home and make himself a simple salad. Despite the fact that he had hardly had a thing all day, his stomach felt heavy and bloated. But instead he allowed himself to be tempted by the Hornpiper down by the square. He wasn't going to tackle his eating habits seriously today either.

At 12:45 he was back at the station. Since he had once again eaten too fast, he had an attack of diarrhea and made for the men's room. When his stomach had settled somewhat, he handed the press release to one of the office clerks and then headed for Näslund's room.

"I can't get hold of Herdin," said Näslund. "He's on some kind of winter hike with a conservation group in Fyledalen."

"Then I suppose we'll have to drive out there and look for him," said Wallander.

"I thought I might as well do that, then you can check the safe-deposit boxes. If everything was so secret with this woman and their child, maybe there's something locked up there. We'll save time that way, I mean."

Wallander nodded. Näslund was right. He was charging like a bull at a gate.

"OK, that's what we'll do," he said. "If we don't make it today we'll go up to Kristianstad tomorrow morning."

Before he got into his car to drive down to the bank, he tried once more to get hold of Sten Widén. There was no answer this time either.

He gave the number to Ebba at the reception desk.

"See if you can get an answer," he said. "Check whether this number is right. It's supposed to be in the name of Sten Widén. Or a racing stable with a name I don't know."

"Hansson probably knows," said Ebba.

"I said racehorses, not trotters."

"He bets on anything that moves," said Ebba with a laugh.

"I'll be at the Union Bank if there's anything urgent," said Wallander.

He parked across from the bookshop on the square. The powerful wind almost blew the parking ticket out of his hand after he put the money in the machine. The town seemed abandoned. The winds were keeping people indoors.

He stopped at the electrical shop by the square. He was considering buying a VCR in an attempt to conquer the loneliness of his evenings. He looked at the prices and tried to work out whether he could afford to buy one this month. Or should he invest in a new stereo instead? After all, it was music he turned to when he lay tossing and turning, unable to sleep.

He tore himself away from the window and turned down the pedestrian street by the Chinese restaurant. The Union Bank was right next door. He walked in through the glass doors, finding only one customer inside the small lobby. A farmer with a hearing aid, complaining about interest rates in a high, shrill voice. To the left, an office door stood open. Inside a man sat studying a computer screen. Wallander assumed this was where he was supposed to go. As he appeared in the doorway, the man looked up quickly, as though he might be a bank robber. He walked into the room and introduced himself.

"We're not happy about this at all," said the man. "In all the years I've been at this bank we've never had any trouble with the police."

Wallander was instantly annoyed by the man's attitude. Sweden had turned into a country where people seemed to be afraid of being bothered more than anything else. Nothing was more sacred than ingrained routine.

"It can't be helped," said Wallander, handing over the documents that Anette Brolin had drawn up. The man read them carefully.

"Is this really necessary?" he asked. "The whole point of a safe-deposit box is that it's protected from inspection."

"Yes, it is necessary," said Wallander. "And I haven't got all day."

With a sigh the man got up from his desk. Wallander could see that he had prepared himself for this visit. They passed through a barred doorway and entered the safe-deposit vault. Lövgren's box was at the bottom in one corner. Wallander unlocked it, pulled out the drawer, and put it on the table. He raised the lid and started going through the contents. There were some papers for burial arrangements and some title deeds to the farm in Lunnarp, some old photographs and a pale envelope with old stamps on it. That was all.

Nothing, he thought. Nothing that I had hoped for.

The man stood to one side; watching him. Wallander wrote down the number of the title deed and the names on the burial documents. Then he closed the box.

"Will that be all?"

"For the time being," said Wallander. "Now I'd like to take a look at the accounts that Lövgren had here at the bank."

On the way out of the vault something occurred to him. "Did anyone else besides Lövgren have access to his safe-deposit box?" he asked.

"No," replied the bank official.

"Do you know whether he opened the box recently?"

"I've checked the register," was the reply. "It has to be many years since he last opened the box."

The farmer was still complaining when they returned to the lobby. He had started on a tirade about the declining price of grain.

"I have all the information in my office," said the man.

Wallander sat down by his desk and went through two sheets of printouts. Johannes Lövgren had four different accounts. Maria Lövgren was a joint signatory on two of them. The total amount in these two accounts was 90,000 kronor. Neither of the accounts had been touched for a long time. In the past few days interest had been paid into the accounts. The third account was left over from Lövgren's days as a working farmer. The balance in that one was 132 kronor and 97 öre.

There was one more. Its balance was almost a million kronor. Maria Lövgren was not a signatory to it. On January 1, interest of more than 90,000 kronor had been paid into the account. On January 4, Johannes Lövgren had withdrawn 27,000 kronor. Wallander looked up at the man sitting on the other side of the desk.

"How far back can you trace records for this account?" he asked.

"Theoretically, for ten years. But it'll take some time, of course. We'll have to run a computer search."

"Start with last year. I'd like to see all activity in this account during 1989."

The official rose and left the room. Wallander started studying the other document. It showed that Johannes Lövgren had almost 700,000 kronor in various mutual funds that the bank administered.

So far Herdin's story seems to hold up, he thought.

He recalled the conversation with Nyström, who had sworn that his neighbour didn't have any money. That's how much he knew about his neighbours.

After about five minutes the man came back from the lobby. He handed Wallander another printout. On three occasions in 1989 Johannes Lövgren had taken out a total of 78,000 kronor. The withdrawals were made in January, July, and September.

"May I keep these papers?" he asked.

The man nodded.

"I'd very much like to speak with the clerk who paid out the money to Johannes Lövgren the last time," he said.

"Britta-Lena Bodén," said the man.

The woman who came into the office was quite young. Wallander thought she was hardly more than twenty.

"She knows what it's all about," said the man.

Wallander nodded and introduced himself. "Tell me what you know."

"It was quite a lot of money," said the young woman. "Otherwise I wouldn't have remembered it."

"Did he seem uneasy? Nervous?"

"Not that I recall."

"How did he want the money?"

"In thousand-krona notes."

"Only thousands?"

"He took a few five hundreds too."

"What did he put the money in?"

The young woman had a good memory.

"A brown briefcase. One of those old-fashioned ones with a strap around it."

"Would you recognise it if you saw it again?"

"Maybe. The handle was tatty."

"What do you mean by tatty?"

"The leather was cracked."

Wallander nodded. The woman's memory was excellent. "Do you remember anything else?"

"After he got the money, he left."

"And he was alone?"

"Yes."

"You didn't see whether anyone was waiting for him outside?"

"I wouldn't be able to see that from the counter."

"Do you remember what time it was?"

The woman thought before she replied. "I went to lunch straight afterwards. It was around midday."

"You've been a great help. If you remember anything else, please let me know."

Wallander got up and went into the lobby. He stopped for a moment and looked around. The young woman was right. From the counters it was impossible to see whether anyone was waiting on the street outside.

The farmer was gone, and new customers had arrived. Someone speaking a foreign language was changing money at one of the counters.

Wallander went outside. The Merchants' Bank was in Hamngatan close by.

A much friendlier bank officer accompanied him down to the vault. When Wallander opened the steel drawer, he was disappointed at once. The box was empty. No one but Johannes Lövgren had access to this safe-deposit box either. He had rented it in 1962.

"When was he here last?" asked Wallander. The answer gave him a start.

"On the fourth of January," the official replied after studying the register of visitors. "At 1:15 p.m., to be precise. He stayed for twenty minutes."

But when Wallander asked all the employees, no one remembered whether Lövgren had anything with him when he left the bank. No one remembered him having a briefcase. That young woman from the Union Bank, he thought. Every bank ought to have someone like her.

Wallander struggled down windblown backstreets to Fridolf's Café, where he had a cup of coffee and ate a cinnamon bun.

I would like to know what Lövgren did between midday and 1:15, he thought. What did he do between his first and second bank visits? And how did he get to Ystad? How did he get back? He didn't own a car.

He took out his notebook and brushed some crumbs off the table. After half an hour he had drawn up a summary of the questions that had to be answered as soon as possible.

On the way back to the car he went into a menswear shop and bought a pair of socks. He was shocked at the price but paid without protesting. Mona had always bought his clothes. He tried to remember the last time he had bought a pair of socks.

When he got back to his car, he found a parking ticket stuck under his windscreen wiper. If I don't pay it, they'll eventually start legal proceedings against me, he thought. Then acting public prosecutor Brolin will be forced to stand up in court and take me to task.

He tossed the ticket into the glove compartment, thinking again how good-looking she was. Good-looking and charming. Then he remembered the bun he'd just eaten.

It was 3 p.m. before Näslund rang. By then Wallander had decided to postpone the trip to Kristianstad.

"I'm soaked," Näslund said. "I've been tramping around in the mud after Herdin all over Fyledalen."

"Give him a thorough going over," said Wallander. "Put a little pressure on him. We want to know everything he knows."

"Should I bring him in?" asked Näslund.

"Go home with him. Maybe he'll talk more freely at home at his own kitchen table."

The press conference started at 4 p.m. Wallander looked for Rydberg, but nobody knew where he was.

The room was full. Wallander saw that the reporter from the local radio station was there, and he made up his mind to find out what she really knew about Linda.

He could feel his stomach churning. I'm repressing things, he thought. Along with everything else I don't have time for. I'm searching for the slayers of the dead and can't even manage to pay attention to the living. For a dizzying instant his entire consciousness was filled with only one urge. To take off. Flee. Disappear. Start a new life.

He stepped onto the little dais and welcomed his audience to the press conference.

After just under an hour it was over. Wallander thought that he probably came off pretty well by denying all rumours that the police were searching for foreign citizens in connection with the murders. He hadn't been asked any questions that gave him trouble. When he stepped down, he felt satisfied.

The young woman from the local radio station waited while he was interviewed for television. As always when a TV camera was pointed at his face, he got nervous and stumbled over his words. But the reporter was satisfied and didn't ask for another take.

"You'll have to get yourself some better informants," said Wallander when it was all over.

"I might have to at that," replied the reporter and laughed.

When the TV crew had left, Wallander suggested that the young woman from the local radio station accompany him to his office.

He was less nervous with a radio microphone than in front of the camera. When she was finished, she turned off the tape recorder. Wallander was just about to bring up Linda when Rydberg knocked on the door and came in.

"We've almost finished," said Wallander.

"We have finished" said the young woman, getting up.

Crestfallen, Wallander watched her go. He hadn't managed to get in one word about Linda.

"More trouble," said Rydberg. "They just called from the refugee processing unit here in Ystad. A car drove into the courtyard and someone threw a bag of rotten turnips at an old man from Lebanon, hitting him in the head."

"Damn," said Wallander. "What happened?"

"He's at the hospital getting bandaged up. But the director is nervous."

"Did they get the registration number?"

"It all happened too quickly."

Wallander thought for a moment.

"Let's not do anything conspicuous just now," he said. "In the morning there will be strong denials about the foreigners in all the papers. It'll be on TV tonight. Then we just have to hope that things calm down. We could ask the night patrols to check the camp."

"I'll tell them," said Rydberg.

"Come back afterwards and we'll do an update," said Wallander.

It was 8:30 p.m. when Wallander and Rydberg finished.

"What do you think?" asked Wallander as they gathered up their papers.

Rydberg scratched his forehead. "It's obvious that this Herdin lead is a good one. As long as we can get hold of that mystery woman and the child, the son. There's a lot to indicate that the solution might be close at hand. So close that we can't see it. But at the same time—" Rydberg broke off.

"At the same time?"

"I don't know," Rydberg went on. "There's something funny about all this. Especially that noose. I don't know what it is."

He shrugged and stood up. "We'll have to go on tomorrow," he said.

"Do you remember seeing a brown briefcase at Lövgren's house?" Wallander asked.

Rydberg shook his head.

"Not that I can recall," he said. "But a whole pile of old junk fell out of the wardrobes. I wonder why old people turn into such hoarders?"

"Send someone out there tomorrow morning to look for an old brown briefcase," said Wallander. "With a cracked handle."

Rydberg left. Wallander could see that his leg was bothering him a lot. He should find out whether Ebba had reached Sten Widén. But he didn't bother. Instead he looked up Anette Brolin's home address in a department directory. To his surprise he discovered that she was almost his neighbour.

I could ask her to dinner, he thought. Then he remembered that she wore a wedding ring.

He drove home through the storm and took a bath. Then he lay on his bed and flicked through a biography of Giuseppe Verdi.

He woke up with a start a few hours later because he was cold. His watch showed almost midnight. He felt dejected. Now he'd have another sleepless night. Driven by despondency, he got dressed. He might as well spend a few nighttime hours in his office.

Outside, he noticed that the wind had died down. It was getting cold again. Snow, he thought. It'll be here soon.

He turned onto Österleden. A lone taxi was heading in the opposite direction. He drove slowly through the empty streets. On an impulse, he decided to drive past the refugee camp on the west side of town.

The camp consisted of huts in long rows in an open field. Floodlights lit up the green-painted structures. He stopped in the car park and got out of the car. The waves were breaking on the beach not far away.

He looked at the camp. Put a fence around it and it'd be a concentration camp, he thought. He was just about to get back in his car when he heard a faint crash of glass breaking. In the next instant there was a dull boom.

Then tall flames were shooting out of one of the huts.

CHAPTER 7

He had no idea how long he stood there, stunned by the flames raging in the winter night. Perhaps it was minutes, perhaps only a few seconds. But when he managed to break out of his paralysis, he had enough presence of mind to grab the car phone and raise the alarm.

The static on the phone made it difficult to hear the man who answered.

"The refugee camp in Ystad is on fire!" shouted Wallander. "Get the fire department out here! The wind is blowing hard."

"Can I have your name?" asked the man at the emergency switchboard.

"This is Wallander of the Ystad police. I just happened to be driving past when the fire started."

"Can you identify yourself?" continued the voice on the phone, unmoved.

"Damn it! 4-7-1-1-2-1! And get a bloody move on!"

He hung up the phone to avoid answering any more questions. Besides, he knew that the emergency switchboard could identify all the police officers on duty in the district. He ran across the road towards the burning huts. The fire was blazing in the wind. He wondered fleetingly what would have happened if the fire had started the night before, during the heavy storm. Even now the flames were getting a firm grip on the hut next door.

Why didn't someone sound the alarm? he thought. But he didn't know whether there were refugees living in all the huts. The heat of the fire hit him in the face as he pounded on the door of the hut that had so far only been licked by the flames.

The hut where the fire had started was now completely engulfed. Wallander tried to approach the door, but was driven back. He ran around one side. There was only one window. He banged on the glass and tried to look inside, but the smoke was so thick that he found himself staring straight into a white haze. He looked around for something to break the glass with but found nothing. He tore off his jacket, wrapped it around his arm, and smashed his fist through the windowpane. He held his breath to keep from inhaling the smoke and groped for the latch. Twice he had to leap back to catch his breath before he managed to open the window.

"Get out!" he shouted into the fire. "Get out! Get out!"

Inside the hut were two bunk beds. He hauled himself up onto the window ledge and felt the splinters of glass cutting into his thigh. The upper bunks were empty. But someone was lying on one of the lower bunks.

Wallander yelled again but got no response. Then he heaved himself through the window, banging his head on the edge of a table as he fell to the floor. He was almost suffocating from the smoke as he fumbled his way towards the bed. At first he thought he was touching a lifeless body. Then he realised that what he had taken for a person was only a rolled-up mattress. At the same moment his jacket caught fire and he threw himself headfirst out of the window. He could hear sirens far off, and as he stumbled away from the fire he saw crowds of half-dressed people milling around outside the huts. Two more of the low buildings were now in flames. Wallander threw open doors and saw that people were living in these huts. But those who had been asleep inside had fled. His head was pounding and his thigh hurt, and he felt sick from the smoke he had inhaled. At that moment the first fire engine arrived, followed closely by an ambulance. He saw that the fire captain on duty was Peter Edler. He was in his midthirties and Wallander remembered that his hobby was flying kites. Wallander had heard only favourable things about him. He was a man who was never unsure of himself. As Wallander staggered over to Edler, he realised that he had burns on one arm.

"The huts that are burning are empty," he said. "I don't know about the other ones."

"You look terrible," said Edler. "I think we can handle this."

The firemen were already hosing down the huts. Wallander heard Edler order a tractor to drag away those that were already burning in order to isolate the fire.

The first police car came to a skidding stop, its blue light flashing and its siren wailing. Wallander saw that it was Peters and Norén. He hobbled over to their car.

"What's happening?" asked Norén.

"It'll be OK," said Wallander. "Start cordoning off the area and ask Edler if he needs any help."

Peters stared at him. "You look awful. How did you happen to be here?"

"I was just driving by," replied Wallander. "Now get moving."

For the next hour a peculiar mixture of chaos and efficient firefighting prevailed. The dazed director of the refugee camp was wandering around aimlessly, and Wallander had to exert real pressure to get him to try to find out how many refugees should be at the camp and then do a count. To his great surprise, it turned out that the Immigration Service's records were hopelessly confused. And the director couldn't help either. In the meantime a tractor dragged away the smouldering huts, and before long the firefighters had the blaze under control. The ambulance had taken only a few of the refugees to the hospital, most of them suffering from shock, although there was a little Lebanese boy who had fallen and hit his head on a rock.

Edler pulled Wallander aside. "Go and get yourself patched up."

Wallander nodded. His arm was stinging and burning, and he could feel that one leg was sticky with blood.

"I hate to think about what might have happened if you hadn't raised the alarm the moment the fire broke out," said Edler.

"Why the hell do they put the huts so close together?" asked Wallander.

Edler shook his head. "The boss here is starting to get tired. You're right of course—the buildings are too damn close."

Wallander went over to Norén, who had just finished cordoning off the area.

"I want that director in my office first thing tomorrow morning," he said.

Norén nodded.

"Did you see anything?" he asked.

"I heard a crash. Then the hut exploded. But no cars. No people. If it was set, then it was done with a delayed-action detonator."

"Shall I drive you home or to the hospital?"

"I can drive myself. But I'd better go now."

At the casualty ward, Wallander found that he had suffered more damage than he had supposed. On one forearm he had a large burn, his groin and one thigh had been cut by the glass, and above his right eye he had a big lump and several nasty abrasions. He had also bitten his tongue without being aware of it.

It was almost 4 a.m. by the time Wallander could leave the hospital. His bandages were too tight, and he still felt sick from the smoke.

As he left the hospital, a camera flashed in his face. He recognised the photographer from the biggest morning newspaper in Skåne. He waved his hand to dismiss a reporter who appeared out of the shadows, wanting an interview. Then he drove home.

To his own great amazement he was actually feeling sleepy. He undressed and crawled under the bed covers. His body ached, and flames were dancing in his head. And yet he fell asleep at once.

At 8 a.m. Wallander woke because somebody was pounding a sledgehammer inside his head. He had once again dreamed of the mysterious black woman. But when he stretched out his hand for her, Sten Widén was suddenly there with the whisky bottle, and the woman had turned her back on Wallander and gone off with Sten.

He lay still, taking stock of how he felt. His neck and arm were stinging. His head was pounding. For a moment he was tempted to turn to the wall and go back to sleep. To forget all about the investigation and the night's blaze.

He didn't get a chance to decide. He was interrupted by the ringing of the telephone. I don't feel like answering it, he thought.

It was Mona.

"Kurt," she said. "It's Mona."

He was filled with an overwhelming sense of joy.

Mona, he thought. Dear God! Mona! How I've missed you!

"I saw your picture in the paper," she said. "Are you all right?"

He remembered the photographer outside the hospital and the flash of a camera.

"Fine," he said. "A little sore."

"No worse than that?"

His joy was gone. Now the bad feelings came back, the sharp pain in his stomach.

"Do you really care how I am?"

"Why shouldn't I care?"

"Why should you?"

He heard her breathing in his ear.

"I think you're so brave," she said. "I'm proud of you. The papers say that you risked your life to save people."

"I didn't save anybody! What kind of rubbish is that?"

"I just wanted to be sure you weren't hurt."

"What would you have done if I was?"

"What would I have done?"

"If I was hurt. If I was dying. What would you have done then?"

"Why do you sound so angry?"

"I'm not angry. I'm just asking you. I want you to come home. Back here. To me."

"You know I can't do that. But I wish we could talk to each other."

"You never call! So how are we supposed to talk to each other?"

He heard her sigh. That made him furious. Or maybe scared.

"Of course we can meet," she said. "But not at my place. Or at yours."

He made up his mind swiftly. What he said was not entirely true. But it wasn't really a lie either.

"There are a lot of things we need to talk about," he told her. "Practical matters. I can drive over to Malmö if you like."

There was a pause before she answered.

"Not tonight," she said. "But I could tomorrow."

"Where? Shall we have dinner? The only places I know are the Savoy and the Central."

"The Savoy is expensive."

"Then how about the Central? What time?"

"Eight o'clock?"

"I'll be there."

The conversation was over. He looked at his pummelled face in the hall mirror. Was he looking forwards to the meeting? Or did he feel uneasy? He wasn't sure. He felt confused. Instead of picturing his meeting with Mona, he saw himself with Anette Brolin at the Savoy. And although she was still the acting public prosecutor in Ystad, she was transformed into a black woman.

Wallander dressed, skipped his morning coffee, and went out to his car. It had turned warmer again. The remnants of a damp fog were drifting from the sea over the town. There was no wind at all.

He was greeted with friendly nods and pats on the back when he entered the police station. Ebba gave him a hug and a jar of pear jam. He felt embarrassed, but also a little proud.

Björk should have been here, he thought. In Ystad instead of in Spain. This was the kind of thing Björk dreamed of. Heroes on the force.

By 9:30 a.m. everything was back to normal. By then he had already managed to give the director of the refugee camp a tough lecture on the sloppy supervision of the refugees. The director, who was short and plump and who radiated apathy and laziness, nevertheless defended himself vigorously, insisting that he had followed the rules and regulations of the Immigration Service to the letter.

"It's the police's job to ensure that the camp is safe," he said, trying to turn Wallander's lecture on its head.

"How are we supposed to guarantee anything at all when you have no idea how many people are living in those damned huts or who they are?"

The director was red-faced with fury when he left.

"I'm going to file a complaint," he said.

"Complain to the king," replied Wallander. "Complain to the prime minister. Complain to the European Court. Complain to whoever the hell you like.

But from now on you're going to have accurate lists of how many people there are at your camp, what their names are, and which huts they live in."

Just before the case meeting was due to start, Edler called.

"How do you feel?" he asked. "The hero of the day."

"Piss off," replied Wallander. "Have you found anything?"

"It wasn't hard," replied Edler. "A handy little detonator that ignited some rags soaked in petrol."

"Are you sure?"

"Damn right I'm sure! You'll have the report in a few hours."

"We'll have to try and run the arson investigation parallel with the murders. But if anything else happens, I'm going to need reinforcements from Simrishamn or Malmö."

"Are there any police left in Simrishamn? I thought the station there was closed down."

"It was the volunteer firefighters who were disbanded. In fact, I've heard rumours that we're going to have some new positions opening up down here."

Wallander started the meeting by reporting what Edler had told him. A brief discussion followed concerning possible motives for the attack. All were agreed that it was most likely a rather well-organised youthful prank, but no one denied the seriousness of what had happened.

"It's important for us to catch those responsible,"

said Hansson. "Just as important as catching the killers at Lunnarp."

"Maybe it was the same people who threw the turnips at the old man," said Svedberg.

Wallander noticed the contempt in his voice.

"Talk to him. Maybe he can give you a description."

"I don't speak Arabic," said Svedberg.

"We have interpreters, for God's sake! I want to know what he has to say by this afternoon."

The meeting was brief. This was one of those days when the police officers were busy trying to establish facts. Conclusions and results were sparse.

"We'll skip the afternoon meeting," Wallander decided, "provided nothing out of the ordinary happens. Martinsson will go out to the camp. Svedberg, maybe you could take over whatever Martinsson was doing that can't wait."

"I'm searching for the car that the lorry driver saw," said Martinsson. "I'll give you my paperwork."

When the meeting was over, Näslund and Rydberg stayed behind in Wallander's office.

"We're starting to go into overtime," said Wallander. "When is Björk due back?"

Neither man knew.

"Does he have any idea about what's happened?" Rydberg wondered.

"Does he care?" Wallander countered.

He called Ebba and got an answer at once. She even knew which airline he would be coming in on.

"Saturday night," he told the others. "But since I'm the acting chief, I'm going to authorise all the overtime we need."

Rydberg raised his visit to the Lövgren farm.

"I've been snooping about," he said. "In fact I've turned the whole place upside down. I've even dug around in the hay bales out in the stable. But there was no brown briefcase."

Wallander knew that that was that. Rydberg never gave up until he was 100 percent sure.

"So now we know this much," he said. "One brown briefcase containing 27,000 kronor is missing."

"People have been killed for much less," said Rydberg.

They sat in silence for a moment, pondering these words.

"I can't understand why it should be so hard to locate that car," said Wallander, touching the tender lump on his forehead. "I gave out its description at the press conference and asked the driver to contact us."

"Patience," said Rydberg.

"What came out of the interviews with the daughters? If there are any reports, I can read them in the car on the way to Kristianstad. By the way, do either of you think that the attack last night had anything to do with the threat I received?"

Both Rydberg and Näslund shook their heads.

"I don't either," said Wallander. "That means that we need to be prepared for something to happen on Friday or Saturday. I thought that you, Rydberg, could think this matter through and come up with some suggestions for action by this afternoon."

Rydberg made a face.

"I'm not good at things like that."

"You're a good policeman. You'll do just fine."

Rydberg gave him a skeptical look.

Then he stood up to go. He paused at the door.

"The daughter that I talked to, the one from Canada, had her husband with her. The Mountie. He wondered why we don't carry guns."

"In a few years we probably will," said Wallander.

Näslund was just about to brief him on his conversation with Lars Herdin when the phone rang. Ebba told him that the head of the Immigration Service was on the line.

Wallander was surprised to be speaking to a woman. He assumed that all senior government officials were still elderly gentlemen full of arrogant self-esteem.

The woman had a pleasant voice, but what she said annoyed him instantly.

"We are most displeased," the woman said. "The police have an obligation to guarantee the safety of our refugees."

Just like that damned director, thought Wallander.

"We do what we can," he said, trying to conceal his irritation. It occurred to him that it might be a breach of conduct for an acting police chief in a small town to contradict what the high priestess of a government civil service agency had to say.

"Obviously that is not sufficient."

"Our job would have been much easier if we had received up-to-date information about how many refugees were at each of the various camps."

"The service has complete data on the refugees."

"That's not my impression at all."

"The Minister of Immigration is very concerned."

Wallander brought to mind a red-haired woman who was regularly interviewed on TV.

"She's welcome to contact us," said Wallander, making a face at Näslund, who was leafing through some papers.

"It's clear that the police are not allocating enough resources to the protection of these refugees."

"Or maybe there are just too many to cope with. And you have no idea where they are lodged."

"What do you mean by that?" The polite voice was now cool.

Wallander felt his anger growing.

"Last night's fire highlighted the shocking disarray at the camp. That's what I mean. In general, it's difficult to get any clear directives from the Immigration Service. You often ask the police to instigate deportations, but we have no idea where to find the deportees. Sometimes we waste several weeks searching for the people we are supposed to deport."

What he said was true. He had heard of colleagues in Malmö being driven to despair at the inability of the Immigration Service to handle its job.

"That's simply not the case," said the woman, "and I'm not going to waste valuable time arguing with you."

The conversation was over.

"Bitch," said Wallander, slamming down the phone.

"Who was that?" asked Näslund.

"The head of the Immigration Service," replied Wallander, "who's living in cloud-cuckoo-land. Feel like getting some coffee?"

Rydberg turned in transcripts of the interviews that he and Svedberg had held with Lövgren's two daughters. Wallander described his phone conversation.

"The Minister of Immigration will be calling soon, and she'll be concerned," said Rydberg, with a wicked laugh.

"You can deal with her," said Wallander. "I'll try to be back from Kristianstad by four."

When Näslund reappeared with the two mugs of coffee, Wallander no longer wanted his. He had to get out of the building. His bandages were too tight, and his head ached. A drive would do him good.

"Tell me about it in the car," he said, pushing the coffee away.

Näslund looked doubtful.

"I don't really know where we should go. Herdin knew virtually nothing about the mystery woman, for all that he was well-informed about Lövgren's financial assets."

"He must have known something."

"I gave him a thorough grilling," said Näslund. "I actually think he was telling the truth. The only thing he knew for sure was that she existed."

"How did he know that?"

"He happened to be in Kristianstad once, and saw Lövgren and her in the street."

"When was that?"

Näslund flipped through his notes.

"Eleven years ago."

Wallander toyed with his coffee.

"It doesn't fit," he said. "He has to know a great deal more. How can he be so sure that there's a son? How does he know about the payments to the woman? Couldn't you force it out of him?"

"He claimed that somebody had written to him and told him."

"Who?"

"He wouldn't say."

Wallander thought about this for a moment.

"We'll go to Kristianstad anyway," he said. "Our colleagues up there will have to help us. Then I'm going to take on Herdin myself."

They took a squad car. Wallander clambered into the back seat and left the driving to Näslund. When they had left town, Wallander noticed that Näslund was driving much too fast.

"This isn't an emergency," he said. "Slow down. I have to read these papers and think."

Näslund drove more slowly.

The landscape was grey and foggy. Wallander stared out at the dreary desolation. Although he felt at home in the Scanian spring and summer, he felt alienated by the barren silence of autumn and winter.

He leaned back and closed his eyes. His body ached and the burn on his arm stung. And he was having palpitations. Divorced men have heart attacks, he thought. We put on weight from eating too much and feel tormented about being abandoned. Or else we throw ourselves into new relationships, and in the end our hearts just give out.

The thought of Mona made him both furious and sad. He opened his eyes and looked out again at the landscape of Skåne.

He read through the transcripts of the interviews with Lövgren's daughters. There was nothing there to give them a lead. No enemies, no simmering hostilities. And no money either. Johannes Lövgren had even kept his own daughters in the dark about his vast assets.

Wallander tried to imagine this man. How had he operated? What had driven him? What did he suppose would happen to the money after he was gone?

He was startled by his train of thought. Somewhere there should be a will. But if it wasn't in one of the safe-deposit boxes, then where was it? Did the murdered man have another safe-deposit box somewhere else?

"How many banks are there in Ystad?" he asked Näslund.

Näslund knew everything about the town. "Ten, I should say."

"Tomorrow I want you to investigate the ones we haven't visited so far. Did Lövgren have more safe-deposit boxes? I also want to know how he got back and forth from Lunnarp. Taxi, bus, whatever."

Näslund nodded. "He could have taken the school bus."

"Someone would have seen him."

They took the Tomelilla route, crossing the main road to Malmö and continuing north.

"What did the inside of Herdin's house look like?" Wallander asked.

"Old-fashioned. But clean, tidy. Strangely enough, he uses a microwave to do his cooking. He offered me homemade rolls. He has a big parrot in a cage. The farm is well cared for. The whole place looks neat. No broken-down fences."

"What make of car does he drive?"

"A red Mercedes."

"A Mercedes?"

"Yes, a Mercedes."

"I thought he told us it was hard making ends meet."

"Well, that Mercedes of his would have set him back 300,000 plus."

Wallander thought for a moment. "We need to know more about Lars Herdin. Even if he says he has no idea who killed them, he could easily know something without realising it himself."

"What's that got to do with the Mercedes?"

"Nothing. I've just got a hunch that Herdin is more important to us than he thinks he is. And we might wonder how a farmer today can afford to buy a car for 300,000 kronor. Maybe he has a receipt that says he bought a tractor."

They drove into Kristianstad and parked outside the police station just as sleet started to fall. Wallander registered the first vague prickles in his throat, warning him that a cold was coming on. Damn, he thought. I can't get sick now. I don't want to meet Mona with a fever and sniffles.

The Ystad police and the Kristianstad police had no special relationship with each other beyond cooperating whenever the occasion arose. But Wallander knew several of the officers rather well from various conferences at county level. He was hoping, above all, that Göran Boman would be on duty. He was the same age as Wallander, and they had met over a whisky at Tylösand. Together they had endured a tedious study day organised by the educational department of the national police. The purpose had been to inspire them to improve and make more effective the staff policies at their respective workplaces. In the evening they sat and shared half a bottle of whisky and soon discovered that they had a lot in common. In particular, both their fathers had been extremely reluctant at their decision to go into police work.

Wallander and Näslund stepped into the reception

area. The young woman at the switchboard, who oddly enough spoke with a lilting Norrland accent, told them that Göran Boman was indeed on duty.

"He's in an interview at present," said the woman. "But it probably won't last long."

Wallander went out to use the toilet. He gave a start when he caught sight of himself in the mirror. The bruises and abrasions were bright red. He splashed his face with cold water. At that moment he heard Boman's voice in the corridor.

The reunion was a hearty one. Wallander was delighted to see Boman again. They got some coffee and took it to his office. Wallander noted that they had exactly the same kind of desk, but otherwise Boman's office was better furnished. It made his office more pleasant, in the same way that Anette Brolin had transformed the sterile office she had taken over.

Boman knew, of course, about the murders in Lunnarp, as well as the attack on the refugee camp and Wallander's rescue attempt that had been so exaggerated in the papers. They talked for a while about refugees. Boman had the same impression as Wallander, that people seeking asylum were dealt with in a chaotic and disorganised fashion. The Kristianstad police also had numerous examples of deportation orders that could be executed only with great difficulty. As recently as a few weeks before Christmas they had been advised that several Bulgarian citizens were to be expelled. According to the Immigration Service, they were living at a camp in Kristianstad. Only after several days' work did the police find out that the Bulgarians were living at a camp in Arjeplog, more than one thousand kilometres to the north.

They switched to the reason for their visit. Wallander gave Boman a detailed rundown.

"And you want us to find her for you," said Boman when he was done.

"That wouldn't be a bad plan."

Näslund had been sitting in silence.

"I've got an idea," he said. "If Johannes Lövgren had a son by this woman, and we assume that he was born in this town, we should be able to look it up in the town's records. Lövgren must have been listed as the child's father, don't you think?"

Wallander nodded. "Besides, we know approximately when the child was born. We can concentrate on a ten-year period, from about 1947 to 1957, if Herdin's story is correct. And I think it is."

"How many children are born over a ten-year period in Kristianstad?" asked Boman. "It would have taken an awfully long time to check before we had computers."

"It's of course possible that the record will state 'father unknown,'" said Wallander. "But then we just have to go through all of those cases with extra care."

"Why don't you just put out a public appeal for the woman?" asked Boman. "And ask her to contact you."

"Because I'm quite sure that she wouldn't do that," said Wallander. "It's just a feeling I have. It may not be particularly professional. But I think I'd rather try this route instead."

"We'll find her," said Boman. "We live in a society and an age when it's almost impossible to disappear. Unless you commit suicide in such an ingenious fashion that your body is completely obliterated. We had a case like that last summer. At least that's what I assume happened. A man who was sick of it all. He was reported missing by his wife. His boat was gone. We never found him. And I don't think we're ever going to, either. I think he put out to sea, scuttled the boat, and drowned himself. But if this woman and her son exist, we'll find them. I'll put an officer on it right away."

Wallander's throat hurt. He had started to sweat. He would have liked most of all to stay sitting there, discussing the case with Boman. He had the feeling that Boman was a talented policeman. His opinion would be valuable. But Wallander was too tired. They tied up the loose ends and Boman accompanied them out to the car.

"We'll find her," he repeated.

"Let's get together some evening," said Wallander. "In peace and quiet. And have some whisky."

Boman nodded. "Maybe on another pointless study day," he said.

The sleet was still coming down. Wallander felt the dampness seeping into his shoes. He crawled again

into the back seat and huddled up in the corner. Soon
he fell asleep.

He didn't wake until Näslund pulled up in front of
the police station in Ystad. He was feverish and miserable. It continued to sleet. He managed to beg a couple
of aspirin from Ebba. He knew that he ought to go
home to bed, but he couldn't resist getting an update
on the day's developments. And he wanted to hear
what Rydberg had come up with regarding protection
for the refugees.

His desk was piled high with phone messages.
Anette Brolin was among the many people who had
called. And his father. But not Linda. Or Widén. He
shuffled through the messages and then put them
aside except for the ones from Anette Brolin and his
father. Then he called Martinsson.

"Bingo," said Martinsson. "I think we've found it.
A car that fits the description was rented last week by
an Avis office in Göteborg. It hasn't been returned.
There's just one thing that's strange."

"What's that?"

"The car was rented by a woman."

"What's strange about that?"

"I have a little trouble picturing a woman as the
killer."

"Now you're on the wrong track. We have to get hold
of that car. And the driver. Even if it is a woman. Then
we'll see if they were involved. Eliminating someone
from an investigation is just as important as getting a

positive lead. And give the registration number to the lorry driver in case he recognises it."

He hung up and went into Rydberg's office.

"How's it going?" he asked.

"This is certainly not much fun," replied Rydberg gloomily.

"Who said police work was supposed to be fun?"

But Rydberg had made a thorough job of it, just as Wallander had known he would. The various camps were pinpointed, and Rydberg had written a brief memo about each one. For the time being he suggested that the night patrols should make rounds of the camps according to a schedule he had devised.

"Good," said Wallander. "Just make sure the patrols understand that it's a serious matter."

He gave Rydberg a report of his visit to Kristian-stad. Then he stood up.

"I'm going home now," he said.

"You're looking a little bedraggled."

"I'm coming down with a cold. But everything seems to be moving along by itself right now."

He went straight home, made some tea, and crawled into bed. When he woke up several hours later, the tea-cup was still at his bedside untouched. He was feeling a little better. He threw out the cold tea and made coffee instead. Then he called his father.

Wallander realised he had heard nothing about the fire. "Weren't we going to play cards?" he snapped.

"I'm ill," said Wallander.

"But you're never ill."

"I've got a cold."

"I don't call that being ill."

"Not everybody is as healthy as you are."

"What does that mean?"

Wallander sighed. If he didn't come up with something, this conversation with his father was going to end badly.

"I'll come out and see you early tomorrow," he said. "Around eight o'clock. If you're up by then."

"I never sleep past four."

"No, but I do."

He said goodbye and hung up the phone. In the same instant he regretted the arrangement. Starting off the day by driving out to visit his father was equivalent to accepting a whole day filled with feelings of depression and guilt.

He looked around his flat. There were layers of dust everywhere. Even though he frequently aired the place out, it still smelled musty. Lonely and musty.

He thought about the black woman who visited him night after night. Where did she come from? Where had he seen her? Was she in a photograph in the newspaper, or had he seen her on TV?

He wondered why it was that in his dreams he had an erotic obsession that was so different from his experience with Mona. The thought excited him. Perhaps he should call Anette Brolin. But he couldn't bring himself to do that. Angrily he sat down on the floral-patterned sofa and switched on the TV. He found one of the Danish channels, where the news was just about to start.

The anchorman reviewed the top stories. Another catastrophic famine. Chaos spreading in Romania. A huge cache of drugs confiscated in Odense. Wallander reached for the remote control and turned off the TV. He couldn't take any more news.

He thought about Mona. But his thoughts took an unexpected turn. He was no longer sure that he really wanted her back. How could he be sure anything would be better? He couldn't. He was just fooling himself.

Restless, he went out to the kitchen and drank a glass of juice.

Then he sat down and wrote a detailed progress report on the investigation. When he had finished, he spread out all his notes on the table and looked at them as if they were pieces of a puzzle. He had a strong feeling that they might not be too far from finding a solution. Even though there were still a lot of loose ends, a number of details did fit together.

It wasn't possible to point to a particular person. There weren't even any actual suspects. But still he had the feeling that the police were close. This made him feel both gratified and uneasy. Too many times he had been in charge of a complicated criminal investigation that seemed promising at first but later petered out in a dead end, and in the worst instances they had had to drop the case altogether.

Patience, he thought. Patience.

Once more he thought of calling Anette Brolin. But he had no idea what he would say to her. And her husband might answer the phone.

He sat down and switched on the TV again. To his immense surprise he was confronted by his own face. He heard the droning voice of a woman reporter. The gist of it was that Wallander and the police in Ystad seemed to be showing no concern for the safety of the refugees in their various camps.

Wallander's face disappeared and was replaced by a woman being interviewed outside a large office block. When her name appeared on the screen, he realised that he should have recognised her. It was the head of the Immigration Service, whom he had talked to that very day.

"It cannot be ruled out that there may be an element of racism behind the lack of interest shown by the police," she stated.

Bitterness welled up inside him. You're a bitch, he thought. And what you're saying is a bloody lie. And why didn't those damned reporters contact me? I could have shown them Rydberg's protection plan. Racists? What was she talking about? His anger was mixed with the shame of being unjustly accused.

Then the phone rang. He considered not answering it. But then he went out to the hall and picked up the receiver.

It was the same voice. A little hoarse, muffled.

Wallander guessed that the man was holding a handkerchief over the mouthpiece.

"We're waiting for results," he said.

"Go to hell!" roared Wallander.

"By Saturday at the latest."

"Were you the bastards who started the fire last night?" he shouted into the phone.

"Saturday at the latest," repeated the man, unmoved.

Then the line went dead.

Wallander felt sick. He couldn't rid himself of a sense of foreboding. It was like an ache in his body, slowly spreading.

Now you're scared, he thought. Now Kurt Wallander is scared. He went back to the kitchen and stood at the window, looking out into the street. There was no wind. The streetlight was hanging motionless.

Something was going to happen. He was sure of it. But what? And where?

CHAPTER 8

In the morning he got out his best suit. He stared despondently at a spot on a lapel.

Ebba, he thought. This is a good project for her. When she hears that I'm going to meet Mona, she'll put her heart into getting rid of this spot. Ebba is a woman who thinks that the level of divorces is a considerably greater threat to the future of our society than the increase in crime and violence.

He laid the suit on the back seat and drove off. A thick cloud cover hung over the town. Is this snow? he wondered. Snow that I really don't want. He drove slowly eastwards, through Sandskogen, past the abandoned golf course, and turned off towards Kåseberga.

For the first time in days he felt that he had had enough sleep. Nine hours straight. The swelling on his forehead had started to go down, and the burn on his arm didn't sting any longer.

Methodically he rehearsed the summary he had written the night before. The vital thing was to find Lövgren's mystery woman. And their son. Somewhere,

in the circles surrounding these people, those responsible would be found. The murders had to be connected to the missing 27,000 kronor, maybe even to
Lövgren's other assets.

Someone who knew about the money, and who
had taken the time to feed the horse before making
off. People who were familiar with Johannes Lövgren's
routine.

The rental car from Göteborg didn't fit the puzzle.
Maybe it had nothing at all to do with the case. He
looked at his watch. 7:40 a.m. Thursday, January 11.

Instead of driving straight to his father's house, he
went a few kilometres past it and turned off on the
little gravel road that wound through rolling sand
dunes up towards Backåkra, Dag Hammarskjöld's
old estate, which the statesman had bequeathed to the
Swedish people. Wallander left his car in the car park
and walked up the hill. From there he could see the sea
stretching out along the strand below him.

There was a stone circle there. A stone circle of con-
templation, erected some years earlier. It was an invi-
tation to solitude and peace of mind. He sat down on a
stone and looked out to sea.

He had never been particularly inclined to philo-
sophical meditation, never felt a need to delve into
himself. Life for him was a matter of juggling practical
questions that needed resolution. Whatever lay ahead
was inescapable, something he could not change, no
matter how much he tried to give it meaning.

Having a few minutes of solitude was another thing altogether. Not having to think at all, just listen, observe, sit motionless, gave him great peace.

There was a boat on its way somewhere. A large sea bird glided soundlessly on the breeze. Everything was quiet. After ten minutes he stood up and went back to the car.

His father was in his studio painting when Wallander walked in. This time it was going to be a canvas with a grouse. His father looked at him crossly. Wallander could see that the old man was filthy. And he smelled terrible.

"Why are you here?" his father said.

"We made a date yesterday."

"Eight o'clock, you said."

"Good grief, I'm only eleven minutes late."

"How the hell can you be a policeman if you can't keep track of time?"

Wallander didn't answer. Instead he thought about his sister Kristina. Today he would have to make time to call her. Ask her whether she was aware of their father's rapid decline. He had always imagined that senility was a slow process. That wasn't the case at all, he realised now.

His father was searching for a colour with his brush on the palette. His hands were still steady. Then he confidently daubed a hint of pale red on the grouse's plumage.

Wallander sat down on the old toboggan to watch.

The stench of his father's body was acrid. Wallander was reminded of a foul-smelling man lying on a bench in the Paris Metro, when he and Mona were on their honeymoon.

I have to say something, he thought. Even if my father is on his way back to his childhood, I still have to speak to him as if he's an adult.

His father went on painting with great concentration. How many times has he painted that same motif? Wallander wondered. A quick and incomplete reckoning in his head came up with the figure of seven thousand. He'd painted seven thousand sunsets.

He got up and poured coffee from the kettle steaming on the kerosene stove.

"How are you feeling?" he asked.

"When you're as old as I am, how you're feeling is how you're feeling," his father replied brusquely.

"Have you thought about moving?"

"Where would I move to? And why should I move anyway?"

The answers were like the cracks of a whip.

"To a retirement home."

His father pointed his brush at him ferociously, as if it were a weapon.

"Do you want me to die?"

"Of course not! It would be for your own good."

"How do you think I'd survive with a bunch of old fogies? And they certainly wouldn't let me paint in my room."

"Nowadays you can have your own flat."

"I've already got my own house. Maybe you didn't notice that. Or maybe you're too ill to notice?"

"I just have a little cold."

At that moment he realised that the cold hadn't come to anything. He had been through this a few times before. When he had a lot to do, he refused to permit himself to get ill. But once the investigation was over, he would succumb almost at once.

"I'm going to see Mona tonight," he said.

Continuing to talk about an old people's home or a flat in sheltered accommodation was pointless. First he had to talk to his sister.

"If she left you, she left you. Forget her."

"I have absolutely no wish to forget her."

His father kept on painting. Now he was working on the pink clouds. The conversation had died.

"Is there anything you need?" asked Wallander.

His father replied without looking at him. "Are you leaving already?"

The reproach was unconcealed. Wallander knew it would do no good to try and stifle the guilt that flared up in him.

"I've got a job to do," he said. "I'm the acting chief. We're trying to solve a double murder. And track down some pyromaniacs."

His father snorted and scratched his crotch. "Chief of police. Is that supposed to impress me?"

Wallander got up.

"I'll be back, Dad," he said. "I'm going to help you clean up this mess."

The old man flung his brush to the floor and stood in front of his son shaking his fist. The outburst took Wallander completely by surprise.

"You think you can come here and tell me this place is a mess?" he shouted. "You think you can come here and meddle in my life? Let me tell you this: I have both a cleaning woman and a housekeeper here. And by the way, I'm taking a trip to Rimini for my winter holiday. I'm going to have a show there. I'm demanding 25,000 kronor per canvas. And you come here talking about old people's homes. But you're not going to kill me off, I can tell you that!"

He walked out of the studio, slamming the door behind him.

He's off his perch, thought Wallander. I've got to put a stop to this. Maybe he really imagines he has a cleaning woman and a housekeeper. That he's going to Italy to open a show. He wasn't sure if he should follow his father inside. He could hear him banging around in the kitchen. It sounded as if he was throwing pots and pans on the floor.

Wallander went out to his car. The best thing would be to call his sister. Now, right away. Together maybe they could persuade their father that he couldn't go on like this.

At 9 a.m. he walked into station and left his suit with

Ebba, who promised to have it cleaned and pressed by that afternoon.

At 10 a.m. he called a case meeting for all the team members who were still in the station. The ones who had seen the spot on the news the night before shared his indignation. After a brief discussion they agreed that Wallander should write a sharp rebuttal and distribute it on the wire service.

"Why doesn't the chief of the national police respond?" Martinsson wondered.

His question was met with disdainful laughter.

"That guy?" said Rydberg. "He only responds if he has something to gain from it. He doesn't give a damn about how the police in the provinces are doing."

Nothing new had happened that demanded the attention of the investigators. They were still laying the groundwork. Material was collected and gone over, various tip-offs were checked and entered in the daily log.

Everyone agreed that the mystery woman in Kristianstad and her son were the hottest lead. No one had any doubt either that the murder they were trying to solve had robbery as a motive. Wallander asked whether things had been quiet at the various refugee camps.

"I checked the nightly report," said Rydberg. "It was calm. The most dramatic thing to happen last night was an elk running about on the E65."

"Tomorrow is Friday," said Wallander. "Yesterday I

got another anonymous phone call. The same individual. He repeated the threat that something was going to happen tomorrow or Saturday at the latest."

Rydberg suggested that they contact the national police. Let them decide whether additional manpower should be provided.

"Let's do that," said Wallander. "We might as well be on the safe side. In our own district we'll send out an extra night patrol to concentrate on the refugee camps."

"Then you'll have to authorise overtime," said Hansson.

"I know," said Wallander. "I want Peters and Norén on this special night detail. And I want someone to call and talk to the directors at all of the camps. Don't scare them. Just ask them to be a little more vigilant."

After about an hour the meeting was finished. Wallander was left alone in his office, getting ready to write the response to Swedish Television.

The telephone rang. It was Göran Boman in Kristianstad.

"I saw you on the news last night," he said, laughing.

"Wasn't that a bugger?"

"You're right. You ought to protest."

"I'm writing a letter as we speak."

"What the hell are those reporters thinking of?"

"Not about the truth, that's for sure, but how big a headline they can get."

"I've got good news for you."

Wallander felt himself go tense.

"Did you find her?"

"Maybe. I'm faxing you some papers now. We've found nine possibilities. The register of citizens isn't such a silly thing to have. I thought you ought to take a look at what we came up with. Call me and tell me which ones you want us to check first."

"Great, Göran," said Wallander. "I'll call you."

The fax machine was in the reception area. A young female temp he had never seen before was just taking a fax sheet out of the tray.

"Which one is Kurt Wallander?" she asked.

"That's me," he said. "Where's Ebba?"

"She had to go to the dry cleaners," said the woman.

Wallander felt ashamed. He was making Ebba run his personal errands.

Boman had sent four pages in all. Wallander went back to his room and spread them on the desk. He studied one woman after another, their birth dates, when their babies with "fathers unknown" had been born. It didn't take him long to eliminate four. That left five who had given birth to sons during the 1950s.

Two were still living in Kristianstad, one in Gladsax outside Simrishamn. Of the other two, one lived in Strömsund and one had emigrated to Australia. He smiled at the idea that the investigation might require someone to be sent to the other side of the world.

He called Göran Boman.

"This looks promising," he said. "If we're on the right track, we've got five to choose from."

"Should I start bringing them in for a talk?"

"No, I'll take care of it myself. Or rather, I thought we might do it together. If you have time, I mean."

"I'll make time. Are we starting today?"

Wallander looked at his watch.

"Let's wait till tomorrow," he said. "I'll try to get up there by nine. If there's no trouble tonight, that is."

He quickly told Göran about the anonymous threats.

"Did you catch the arsonist from the other night?"

"Not yet."

"I'll set things up for tomorrow, and I'll make sure none of them has moved."

"Maybe I should meet you in Gladsax," Wallander suggested. "It's about halfway."

"Nine o'clock at the Hotel Svea in Simrishamn," said Boman. "A cup of coffee to start the day with."

"Sounds good. See you there. And thanks for your help."

Now, you bastards, thought Wallander after he hung up. I'm going to let you have it. He wrote the letter to Swedish Television. He did not mince words, and he decided to send copies to the Immigration Service, the Immigration Ministry, the county chief of police, and the chief of the national police.

In the corridor, Rydberg read through what he had written.

"Good," he said. "But don't think they'll do anything about it. Reporters in this country, especially on
television, can do no wrong."

He dropped the letter off to be typed and went into
the canteen to get himself some coffee. He hadn't had
time to think about eating yet. It was almost 1 p.m.,
and he decided to go through all his phone messages
before he went out to eat.

The night before, he had felt sick to his stomach
when he took the anonymous phone call. Now he had
cast off all sense of foreboding. If anything happened,
the police were ready.

He punched in the number for Sten Widén. But
before the phone started to ring, he put the receiver
down. Widén could wait. There would be time enough
later to amuse themselves by measuring how long it
took a horse to finish off a ration of hay.

Instead he tried the number of the public prosecutor's office. The woman at the switchboard told him
that Anette Brolin was in. He hung up and walked to
the other wing of the building. Just as he raised his
hand to knock, the door opened.

She had her coat on. "I'm just on my way to lunch."

"May I join you?"

She seemed to think about it for a moment. Then
she gave him a quick smile. "Why not?"

Wallander suggested the Continental. They got a
window table, and both ordered salted salmon.

"I saw you on the news yesterday," said Anette

Brolin. "How can they broadcast such inaccurate and biased reports?"

Wallander, who had braced himself for criticism, relaxed.

"Reporters regard the police as fair game," he said. "Whether we do too much or too little, we get criticised for it. And they don't understand that sometimes we have to hold back certain information for investigative reasons."

He told her about the leak. How furious he had been when information from the case meeting had gone straight to a TV broadcast. He noticed that she was listening, and felt that he had discovered someone human behind the prosecutor's role and the expensive clothes.

After lunch they ordered coffee.

"Did your family move here too?" he asked.

"My husband is still in Stockholm," she said. "And the children aren't going to change schools for a year."

Wallander's disappointment was palpable. Somehow he had hoped that the wedding ring meant nothing.

The waiter came with the bill, and he reached out to pay.

"We'll split it," she said.

They ordered more coffee.

"Tell me about this town," she said. "I've looked through a number of criminal cases from the last few years. It's a lot different from Stockholm."

"That's changing fast," he said. "Soon the entire Swedish countryside will be nothing but suburbs of the big cities. There were no narcotics here twenty years ago. Ten years ago drugs had come to towns like Ystad and Simrishamn, but we still had some control over what was happening. Today drugs are everywhere. When I drive by one of the beautiful old Scanian farms, I sometimes think: there might be a huge amphetamine factory hidden in there."

"There are fewer violent crimes," she said. "And they're not quite as brutal."

"It's coming," he said. "Unfortunately, I guess I'm supposed to say. But the differences between the big cities and the countryside have been almost erased. Organised crime is widespread in Malmö. The open borders and all the ferries coming in are like candy for the underworld."

"Still, there's a sense of calm here," she said pensively. "Something that's been totally lost in Stockholm."

They left the Continental. Wallander had parked his car in Stickgatan nearby.

"Are you really allowed to park here?" she asked.

"No," he replied. "But when I get a ticket I pay it. Although it might be an interesting experience to say to hell with it and get taken to court."

They drove back to the police station.

"I was thinking of asking you to dinner some evening," he said. "I could show you round the area."

"I'd like that," she said.

"How often do you go home?" he asked.

"Every other week."

"And your husband? The children?"

"He comes down when he can. And the children when they feel like it."

I love you, thought Wallander. I'm going to see Mona tonight and I'm going to tell her that I love another woman.

They said goodbye in reception.

"You'll get a briefing on Monday," said Wallander. "We're starting to get a few leads."

"Any closer to an arrest?"

"No. But the searches at the banks produced good results."

She nodded.

"Preferably before ten on Monday," she said. "The rest of the day I have detention hearings and negotiations in the district court."

They settled on 9 a.m. Wallander watched her as she disappeared down the corridor. He felt strangely exhilarated when he got back to his office. Anette Brolin, he thought. In a world where everything is said to be possible, anything could happen.

He devoted the rest of the day to reading the notes from various interviews that he had only skimmed before. The definitive autopsy report had also arrived. Once again he was shocked at the degree of violence the old couple had been subjected to. He read the reports of the interviews with the two daughters and the door-to-door canvassing in Lunnarp. All the information matched and added up.

No one had any idea that Johannes Lövgren was a significantly more complex person than he had appeared. The simple farmer had been hiding a split personality. Once during the war, in the autumn of 1943, he had been taken to court in a case of assault and battery. But he had been acquitted. Someone had dug up a copy of the report, and Wallander read through it carefully. But he could not see a reasonable motive for revenge. It seemed to have been an ordinary quarrel that led to blows at the community centre at Erikslund.

Ebba brought in his suit.

"You're an angel," he said.

"Hope you have a wonderful time tonight," she said with a smile.

Wallander felt a lump in his throat. She really meant what she said.

He spent the time until 5 p.m. filling in a football lottery form, making an appointment to have his car serviced, and thinking through the important interviews he had the following day. He also wrote a reminder to himself that he had to prepare a memo for Björk for his return.

Just after 5 p.m., Thomas Näslund stuck his head round the door.

"Are you still here?" he said. "I thought you'd gone home."

"Why would I have done that?"

"That's what Ebba said."

Ebba keeps watch over me, he thought with a smile. Tomorrow I'll bring her some flowers before I leave for Simrishamn.

Näslund came into the room.

"Do you have time right now?" he asked.

"Not much."

"I'll make it quick. It's about Klas Månson."

Wallander had to think for a moment before he remembered who that was.

"The one who robbed that shop?"

"That's the one. We have witnesses who can identify him, even though he had a stocking over his head. A tattoo on his wrist. There's no doubt that he's the one. But this new prosecutor doesn't agree with us."

Wallander raised his eyebrows. "What do you mean?"

"She thinks the investigation was sloppy."

"Was it?"

Näslund looked at him in amazement.

"It was no sloppier than any other investigation. It's a cut-and-dried case."

"So what did she say?"

"If we can't come up with more convincing proof she's considering opposing the detention order. It's bullshit that a Stockholm bitch like that can come here and pretend she's somebody!"

Wallander could feel himself getting angry, but he was careful not to betray his feelings.

"Per wouldn't have given us a problem," Näslund went on. "It's bloody obvious that this bastard is the one who robbed the shop."

"Have you got the report?" asked Wallander.

"I asked Svedberg to read it through."

"Leave it here for me so I can look at it tomorrow."

Näslund stood up.

"Somebody ought to tell that bitch," he said.

Wallander nodded and smiled. "We can't have a prosecutor coming down from Stockholm and interfering with the way we do things."

"I thought you'd say that," said Näslund and left.

An excellent excuse to have dinner, thought Wallander. He put on his jacket, hung his clean suit over his arm, and turned off the light.

After a quick shower he made it to Malmö just before 7 p.m. He found a car park near Stortorget and went down the steps to Kock's Tavern. He would knock back a couple of drinks before meeting Mona at the restaurant.

Even though the price was outrageous, he ordered a large whisky. He would have preferred a malt, but an ordinary blend would have to do.

At the first gulp he spilled some on himself. Now he'd have a new spot on his lapel. Almost in the same place as the old one. I'm going home, he thought, full of self-reproach. I'll go home and go to bed. I can't even hold a glass without spilling it all over myself. At the same time he knew this feeling was pure vanity.

Vanity and nervousness at seeing Mona. It might be their most important meeting since the occasion on which he had proposed to her. Now he was trying to prevent a divorce that was already set in motion.

But what did he really want? He wiped off his lapel with a paper napkin, drained the glass, and ordered another. He would have to go in ten minutes. By then he would have to make up his mind. What was he going to say to Mona? And what would her answer be?

His drink came and he tossed it back. The liquor burned in his temples, and he could feel himself starting to sweat. Deep inside he hoped that Mona would say the words he was waiting to hear.

She had been the one who wanted the divorce, so she was also the one who should take the initiative and put a stop to it.

He paid his bill and left. He walked slowly so as not to arrive too early.

He decided two things while he waited for the light to turn green on the corner of Vallgatan. He was going to have a serious talk with Mona about Linda. And he would ask her advice about his father. Mona knew the old man well. Even though they hadn't really got along, she understood his changeable moods.

I should have called Kristina, he thought as he crossed the street. I probably forgot about it on purpose. He walked across the canal bridge and was passed by a carload of youths. A boy, obviously drunk, was leaning right out of the open window and bellowing something.

Wallander remembered how he used to walk across this bridge more than twenty years before. In these neighbourhoods the city still looked the same. He had walked the beat here as a young policeman, usually with an older partner, and they would go into the railway station to check up on things. Occasionally they had to throw out someone who was drunk and didn't have a ticket, but there was seldom any violence.

That world doesn't exist anymore, he thought. It's gone, and we'll never get it back. He went into the station. It had changed a lot, but the stone floor was the same. And the sound of the screeching carriage wheels and braking engines.

Suddenly he caught sight of his daughter. At first he thought he must be imagining it. It could just as easily have been the girl tossing hay at Sten Widén's farm. But then he was sure. It was Linda. She was standing with a coal-black man, trying to get a ticket from the automatic machine. He was almost a foot-and-a-half taller than she was. He had frizzy black hair and was dressed in purple overalls.

As if he were on surveillance, Wallander swiftly drew back behind a pillar. The man said something and Linda laughed. He realised it had been years since he had seen his daughter laugh.

What he saw saddened him. He sensed that he couldn't reach her. She was beyond his grasp, even though she was so close.

My family, he thought. I'm in a railway station

spying on my daughter. And her mother, my wife, has probably already arrived at the restaurant so that we can meet and have dinner and maybe manage to talk without starting to shout and scream at each other.

He realised that he was having a hard time seeing. His eyes were misted over with tears. He hadn't had tears in his eyes for a long time. It was as distant a memory as the last time he had seen Linda laugh.

The black man and Linda were walking towards the platform. He wanted to rush after her, pull her to him. Then they were gone from his field of vision, and he continued his surveillance. He slunk along in the shadows of the platform where the icy wind from the sound blew. He watched them walk hand in hand, laughing. The last thing he saw was the blue doors hissing shut and the train leaving towards Landskrona or Lund.

He tried to focus on the fact that she had looked happy. Just as carefree as when she was a young girl. But all he seemed to feel was his own misery. Pathetic Inspector Wallander and his pitiful family life.

Now he was late. By now Mona would have turned on her heel and left. She was always punctual and hated having to wait. Especially for him.

He started along the platform at a run. A bright-red engine screeched alongside him like an angry beast. He was in such a hurry that he stumbled on the stairs leading to the restaurant. The shaven-headed doorman gave him a sour look.

"Where do you think you're going?" he asked.

Wallander was paralysed by the question. Its implication was immediately clear to him. The doorman thought he was drunk. He wasn't going to let him in.

"I'm going to have dinner with my wife," he said.

"No, I don't think you are," said the doorman. "I think you'd better go on home."

Wallander felt his blood boil.

"I'm a police officer!" he shouted. "And I'm not drunk, if that's what you think. Now let me in before I really get angry."

"Piss off!" said the doorman. "Before I call the police."

For a moment he felt like punching the doorman in the nose. Then he regained composure and calmed down. He took his identity card out of his inside pocket.

"I really am a police officer," he said. "And I'm not drunk. I stumbled. And my wife is here waiting for me."

The doorman gave the card a skeptical scrutiny. Then his face lit up.

"Hey, I recognise you," he said. "You were on TV the other night."

Finally, some benefit from the TV, he thought.

"I'm with you," said the doorman. "All the way."

"With me about what?"

"Keeping those damned niggers on a short leash. What kind of shit are we letting into this country, going around killing old people? I'm with you, we should kick 'em all out. Chase 'em out with a stick."

Wallander could see that there was no point to getting into a discussion with the man. Instead, he attempted a smile.

"Well, I guess I'll go and have dinner. I'm starving," he said.

The doorman held open the door for him.

"You understand we have got to be careful?"

"No problem," replied Wallander and went into the warmth of the restaurant.

He hung up his coat and looked around. Mona was sitting at a window table with a view over the canal. He wondered whether she had been watching him arrive. He sucked in his stomach as best he could, ran his hand over his hair, and walked over to her.

Everything went wrong right from the start. He saw that she noticed the spot on his lapel, and this made him furious. And he didn't know if he entirely succeeded in hiding his fury.

"Hello," he said, sitting down across from her.

"Late as usual," she said. "And you've really put on weight!"

She had to start off with an insult. Not even a friendly word, no affection.

"But you look just the same. You've got a lovely tan."

"We spent a week in Madeira."

Madeira. First Paris, then Madeira. Their honeymoon. The hotel perched way out on the cliffs, the little fish restaurant down by the beach. And now she had been there again. With someone else.

"I see," he said. "I thought Madeira was our island."

"Don't be childish!"

"I mean it!"

"Then you are being childish."

"Of course I'm childish! What's wrong with that?"

The conversation was spinning out of control. When a friendly waitress came to their table it was like being rescued from a deep hole in the ice.

The wine arrived and the mood improved. Wallander sat looking at the woman who had been his wife and thought that she was extremely beautiful. He tried to avoid thoughts that gave him a sharp stab of jealousy.

He did his best to give the impression of being very calm, which he definitely was not. They said *skål* and raised their glasses.

"Come back," he begged. "Let's start again."

"No," she said. "You have to understand that it's finished. All over."

"I went to the station while I was waiting for you," he said. "I saw Linda there."

"Linda?"

"You seem surprised."

"I thought she was in Stockholm."

"What would she be doing in Stockholm?"

"She was supposed to visit a college to see if it might be the right place for her."

"I'm not blind. It was her."

"Did you talk to her?"

Wallander shook his head. "She was just getting onto a train. I didn't have time."

"Which train?"

"Lund or Landskrona. She was with an African."

"That's good, at least."

"What do you mean by that?"

"I mean that Herman is the best thing that's happened to Linda in a long time."

"Herman?"

"Herman Mboya. He's from Kenya."

"He was wearing purple overalls!"

"He does have an amusing way of dressing sometimes."

"What's he doing in Sweden?"

"He's in medical school. He'll be a doctor soon."

Wallander listened in amazement. Was she pulling his leg?

"A doctor?"

"Yes! A doctor! A physician, or whatever you call it. He's warm, thoughtful, and has a good sense of humour."

"Do they live together?"

"He has a student flat in Lund."

"I asked you if they were living together!"

"I think Linda has finally decided."

"Decided what?"

"To move in with him."

"Then how can she go to the college in Stockholm?"

"It was Herman who suggested that."

The waitress refilled their glasses. Wallander could feel himself starting to get drunk.

"She called me one day," he said. "She was in Ystad. But she never came to say hello. If you see her, you can tell her that I miss her."

"She does what she wants."

"All I'm asking is for you to tell her!"

"I will! Don't shout!"

"I'm not shouting!"

Just then the roast beef arrived. They ate in silence. Wallander couldn't taste a thing. He ordered another bottle of wine and wondered how he was going to get home.

"You seem to be well," he said.

She nodded, firmly and maybe defiantly too.

"And you?"

"I'm having a hell of a time. Otherwise, everything's fine."

"What was it you wanted to talk to me about?"

He had forgotten that he had been supposed to think of an excuse for their meeting. Now he had no idea what to say. The truth, he thought wryly. Why not try the truth?

"I just wanted to see you," he said. "The other stuff was all lies."

She smiled.

"I'm glad that we could see each other," she said.

Suddenly he burst into tears.

"I miss you terribly," he mumbled.

She reached out her hand and put it on his. But she said nothing. And it was in that instant that Wallander knew that it was over. The divorce wouldn't change anything. Maybe they'd have dinner once in a while. But their lives were irreversibly going in different directions. Her silence told him that.

He started thinking about Anette Brolin. And the black woman who visited him in his dreams. He had been unprepared for loneliness. Now he would be forced to accept it and maybe gradually build a new life.

"Tell me one thing," he said. "Why did you leave me?"

"If I hadn't left you, I would have died," she said. "I wish you could understand that it wasn't your fault. I was the one who felt the separation was necessary, I was the one who decided. One day you'll understand what I mean."

"I want to understand now."

When they were about to leave she wanted to pay her share. But he insisted he'd pay and she gave in.

"How are you getting home?" she asked.

"There's a night bus," he replied. "How are you getting home?"

"I'm walking," she said.

"I'll walk with you part of the way."

She shook her head.

"We'll say goodbye here," she said. "That would be best. But call me again sometime. I want to stay in touch."

She kissed him quickly on the cheek. He watched her walk across the canal bridge with a vigorous stride. When she disappeared between the Savoy and the tourist bureau, he followed her. Earlier that evening he had shadowed his daughter. Now he was tailing his wife.

Near the television shop at the corner of Stortorget a car was waiting. She got into the front seat. Wallander ducked into a stairwell as the car drove past. He had a quick glimpse of the man behind the wheel.

He walked to his car. There was no night bus to Ystad. He stopped at a phone box and called Anette Brolin at home. When she answered he hung up at once. He got back into his car and pushed in the Maria Callas cassette and closed his eyes.

He woke up with a start because he was cold. He had slept for almost two hours. Even though he wasn't sober, he decided to drive home. He would take the back roads through Svedala and Svaneholm. That way he wouldn't risk running into any police patrols.

But he did. He had completely forgotten that the night patrols from Ystad were watching the refugee camps. And he was the one who had given the order.

Peters and Norén came upon an erratic driver between Svaneholm and Slimminge, after they had checked that everything was quiet at Hageholm. Normally either of them would have recognised Wallander's car, but it didn't occur to them that he might be out driving around at this time of night. Besides, the licence plate was so covered with mud that it was unreadable. Not until they had stopped the car and knocked on the windscreen, and Wallander had rolled down the window did they recognise their acting chief.

None of them said a word. Norén's torch shone into Wallander's bloodshot eyes.

"Everything quiet?" Wallander asked finally.

Norén and Peters looked at each other.

"Yes," said Peters. "Everything seems quiet."

"That's good," said Wallander, about to roll up the window.

Then Norén stepped forward.

"You'd better get out of the car," he said. "Now, right away."

Wallander looked questioningly at the face he could hardly recognise in the sharp glare from the torch. Then he did as he was told. He got out of the car. The night was cold. He was freezing.

Something had come to an end.

CHAPTER 9

The last thing Wallander felt like was a laughing policeman as he stepped into the Svea Hotel in Simrishamn
at 7 a.m. on Friday morning. Almost impenetrable
sleet was falling over Skåne, and water had seeped into
his shoes on his way from the car to the hotel.

Also he had a headache. He asked the waitress for a
couple of aspirin. She came back with a glass of water
fizzing with white powder. As he drank his coffee, he
noticed that his hand was shaking.

He reckoned it was as much from fear as from relief. A few hours earlier, when Norén had ordered him
out of his car on the highway road between Svaneholm
and Slimminge, he had thought that it was all over.
He wouldn't be a policeman anymore. The charge of
driving under the influence would mean immediate
suspension. And even if someday he were allowed to
return to active duty on the force, having served a jail
sentence, he would never be able to look his former
colleagues in the eye.

He had explored the possibility that he might become

head of security for some company. Or he might slip through the background check of some less choosy guard service. But his twenty-year career with the police would be over. And he was a policeman to the core.

He didn't even consider trying to bribe Peters and Norén. He knew that was impossible. The only thing he could do was plead. Appeal to their team spirit, to their camaraderie, to a friendship which didn't really exist.

But he didn't have to do that.

"Go with Peters, and I'll drive your car home," Norén had said.

Wallander recalled his feeling of relief, but also the unmistakable hint of contempt in Norén's voice. Without a word he got into the back seat of the patrol car. Peters said not a word the whole way to Mariagatan in Ystad.

Norén had followed close behind; he parked the car and handed the keys to Wallander.

"Did anyone see you?" asked Norén.

"Nobody but you."

"You were damned lucky."

Peters nodded. And then Wallander realised that nothing was going to happen. Norén and Peters were committing a serious breach of duty for his sake. He had no idea why.

"Thank you," he said.

"That's all right," Norén replied. And then they had driven off.

Wallander went into his flat and polished off the dregs of a bottle of whisky. Then he fell asleep for several hours, lying on top of his bed. Without thinking, without dreaming. At 6:15 a.m. he got into his car again, after giving himself a cursory shave.

He knew, of course, that he was still intoxicated. But now there was no danger of running into Peters and Norén. They went off duty at 6 a.m.

He tried to concentrate on what was in store for him. He was going to meet Göran Boman, and together they would go seek a missing link to the investigation of the murders at Lunnarp.

Wallander pushed all other thoughts aside. He would let them come back when he had the energy to deal with them. When he no longer had a hangover, when he had managed to put everything in perspective.

He was the only person in the hotel dining room. He gazed out at the grey sea, barely visible through the sleet. A fishing boat was on its way out of the harbour, and he tried to read the number painted in black on the hull.

A beer, he thought. A good old Pilsner is what I need right now.

It was a strong temptation. He also thought that it would be as well to drop in at the state liquor outlet, so he would have something to drink in the evening. He realised that he wasn't ready to sober up too quickly.

A rotten policeman, that's what I am, he thought. A dubious cop.

The waitress refilled his coffee cup. He imagined himself going into a hotel room with her. Behind drawn curtains he would forget that he existed, forget everything around him, and sink into a world free from reality.

He drank the coffee and picked up his briefcase. He still had a little time to read through the investigation reports. Restless, he went out to reception and called the police station in Ystad. Ebba answered.

"Did you have a nice evening?" she asked.

"Couldn't have been better," he replied. "And thanks again for your help with my suit."

"Anytime."

"I'm calling from the Svea Hotel in Simrishamn, if you need to get hold of me. Later I'll be on the move with Boman from the Kristianstad police. But I'll call in."

"Everything's quiet. No trouble at the refugee camps."

He hung up and went into the men's room to wash his face. He avoided looking at himself in the mirror. With his fingertips he gingerly felt the bump on his forehead. It hurt. When he stretched he felt a twinge shoot through his thigh.

When he returned to the dining room, he ordered breakfast. He leafed through all his papers as he ate.

Boman was punctual. On the stroke of 9 a.m. he walked into the dining room.

"What awful weather!" he said.

"It's better than a snowstorm," said Wallander.

While Boman drank his coffee they worked out what had to be done in the course of the day.

"It seems we're in luck," said Boman. "It's going to be possible to get hold of the woman in Gladsax and the two in Kristianstad without much trouble."

They started with the woman in Gladsax.

"Her name is Anita Hessler," said Boman, "and she's fifty-eight. She married a couple of years ago; her husband is an estate agent."

"Is Hessler her maiden name?" Wallander wondered.

"Her name is Johanson now. Her husband is Klas Johanson. They live in a suburb not far outside the town. We've done a little snooping. As far as we know, she's a housewife."

He checked his papers.

"On March 9, 1951, she gave birth to a son at Kristianstad's maternity ward. At 4:13 a.m., to be exact. As far as we know, he's her only child. But Klas Johanson has four children from a previous marriage. He's also six years younger than she is."

"So her son is thirty-nine," said Wallander.

"He was christened Stefan," said Boman. "He lives in Åhus and works as a tax-assessment supervisor in Kristianstad. His finances are in order. He has a terrace house, a wife and two children."

"Do tax-assessment supervisors usually commit murder?" asked Wallander.

"Not very often," replied Boman.

They drove out to Gladsax. The sleet had changed to a steady rain. Just before entering the town, Boman turned left.

The two-storey houses in the residential neighbourhood were in sharp contrast to the low white buildings of the town itself. Wallander thought that it could just as well have been an affluent suburb outside any large city.

The house was at the end of a terrace. A huge satellite dish stood on a slab of cement next to the house. The yard was well kept. They sat in the car for a few minutes and stared at the red-brick building. A white Nissan was parked in the drive in front of the garage.

"The husband probably isn't home," said Boman. "His office is in Simrishamn. Apparently he specialises in selling property to well-heeled Germans."

"Is that legal?" asked Wallander, in surprise.

Boman shrugged.

"They use dummy owners," he said. "The Germans pay well and the deeds are placed in Swedish hands. There are people in Skåne who make a good living by assuming the illegal ownership of residential property."

All of a sudden they caught a glimpse of movement behind the curtains. It was so fast that only the practised eye of the police would have noticed.

"Somebody's home," said Wallander. "Shall we go and say hello?"

The woman who opened the door was astoundingly

attractive. Her radiance was unmistakable, even though she was wearing a baggy tracksuit. It occurred to Wallander fleetingly that she didn't look Swedish.

He also thought that their initial introduction might be just as important as all their questions put together. How would she react when they told her that they were policemen?

The only thing he noticed was that she slightly raised one eyebrow. Then she smiled, revealing even rows of white teeth. Wallander wondered whether Boman was right. Was she really fifty-eight? If he hadn't known better, he would have guessed forty-five.

"This is unexpected," she said. "Come in."

They followed her into a tastefully furnished living room. The walls were covered with crowded bookshelves. A top-of-the-line Bang & Olufsen TV stood in the corner. Tiger-striped fish swam in an aquarium. Wallander had trouble associating this room with Johannes Lövgren. There was nothing to suggest a connection.

"Can I offer you gentlemen anything?" asked the woman.

They declined and sat down.

"We've come to ask you some questions," said Wallander. "My name is Kurt Wallander, and this is Göran Boman from the Kristianstad police."

"How exciting to have a visit from the police," said the woman, still smiling. "Nothing unusual ever happens here in Gladsax."

"We just wanted to ask you whether you know a man named Johannes Lövgren," said Wallander.

She gave him a look of surprise.

"Johannes Lövgren? No. Who's he?"

"Are you sure?"

"Of course I'm sure!"

"He was murdered a few days ago along with his wife, in a village called Lunnarp. Maybe you read about it in the newspapers."

Her surprise looked genuine.

"I don't understand," she said. "I remember seeing something about it in the paper. But what does this have to do with me?"

Nothing, thought Wallander and glanced at Boman, who seemed to share his opinion. What could this woman have to do with Johannes Lövgren?

"In 1951 you had a son in Kristianstad," said Boman. "On all the documents in various records you listed the father as unknown. Is it possible that a man by the name of Johannes Lövgren might have been this unknown father?"

She gazed at them for a long time before she answered.

"I don't understand why you're asking these questions," she said. "And I understand even less what this has to do with that murdered farmer. But if it's any help, I can tell you that Stefan's father was named Rune Stierna. He was married to someone else. I knew what I was getting into, and I chose to thank him for the child by keeping his identity secret. He died twelve years ago. And Stefan got along well with his father throughout his childhood."

"I know that these questions must seem strange," said Wallander. "But sometimes we have to ask odd questions."

They asked a few more questions and took some notes. Then it was over.

"I hope you will excuse us for disturbing you," said Wallander as he got to his feet.

"Do you think I'm telling the truth?" she asked.

"Yes," said Wallander. "We think you're telling the truth. But if you're not, we'll find out. Sooner or later."

She burst out laughing. "I'm telling the truth," she said. "I'm not a very good liar. But feel free to come back if you have more strange questions."

They left the house and went back to the car.

"Well, that's that," said Boman.

"She's not the one," said Wallander.

"Do we need to talk to the son in Åhus?"

"I think we can skip him. For the time being, at any rate."

They got into Wallander's car and drove straight back to Kristianstad. The rain had stopped falling and the sky had begun to clear by the time they reached the hills around Brösarp. Outside the police station in Kristianstad they switched to a police car and continued.

"Margareta Velander," said Boman, "is forty-nine, and owns a beauty shop called 'The Wave' on Krokarps-gatan. Three children, divorced, remarried, divorced again. Lives in a terrace house out towards Blekinge. Gave birth to a son in December 1958. The son's name is Nils. Evidently quite an entrepreneur. Used to go around to markets and sell imported knick-knacks. Also listed as the owner of a company dealing in women's novelty underwear. Lives in Sölvesborg, of all places. Who the hell would buy women's novelty underwear sold by a mail order company from a town like that?"

"Plenty of people," said Wallander.

"Once did time for assault and battery," Boman continued. "I haven't seen the report. But he got one year. That means the assault must have been pretty serious."

"I want to see that report," said Wallander. "Where did it happen?"

"He was sentenced by the Kalmar district court. They're looking for the paperwork on the case."

"When did it happen?"

"In 1981, I think."

Wallander sat and thought while Boman drove through the town.

"So she was only seventeen when the boy was born. And if we're taking Lövgren to be the father, there was a big age difference."

"I've thought of that. But that could mean a lot of things."

The beauty salon was in the basement of a block of flats on the outskirts of Kristianstad.

"Maybe I should come here," said Boman. "Who cuts your hair, by the way?"

Wallander was just about to say that Mona took care of that.

"It varies," he replied evasively.

There were three chairs in the salon. Each was occupied. Two women were sitting under hair dryers while a third was having her hair washed. The woman who was washing the customer's hair looked up at them in surprise.

"I only work by appointment," she said. "I'm booked up today. And tomorrow too, if you want to make an appointment for your wives."

"Margareta Velander?" asked Göran Boman.

He showed her his identity card.

"We'd like to talk to you," he said.

Wallander could see that she was frightened.

"I can't leave right now," she said.

"We'd be happy to wait," said Boman.

"You can wait in the back room," said Margareta Velander. "I won't be long."

It was a very small room. A table covered with oil-cloth and a couple of chairs took up practically all the space. Between some coffee cups and a grimy coffee maker on a shelf there was a stack of tabloid newspapers. Wallander studied a black-and-white photograph pinned to the wall. It was a blurred and faded image of a young man in a sailor's uniform. Wallander could read the word *Halland* on the band around the cap.

"*Halland*," he said. "Was that a cruiser or a destroyer?"

"A destroyer. Scrapped ages ago."

Margareta Velander came into the room. She was drying her hands on a towel.

"I've got a few minutes now," she said. "What's it about?"

"We wonder whether you know a man named Johannes Lövgren," began Wallander.

"Is that so?" she said. "Would you like some coffee?"

They both declined, and Wallander was annoyed that she had turned her back to him when he asked the question.

"Johannes Lövgren," he repeated. "A farmer from a village outside of Ystad. Did you know him?"

"The man who was murdered?" she asked, looking him straight in the eye.

"Yes," he said. "The man who was murdered. That's the one."

"No," she replied, pouring coffee into a plastic cup. "Why should I know him?"

The police officers exchanged glances. There was something about her voice that suggested she felt pressured.

"In December 1958 you gave birth to a son who was christened Nils," said Wallander. "You listed the father as unknown."

The instant he mentioned the name of her son, she started to cry. The coffee cup tipped over and fell to the floor.

"What has he done?" she asked. "What has he done now?"

They waited until she had calmed down.

"We're not here to bring you bad news," Wallander assured her. "But we'd like to know whether Johannes Lövgren was Nils's father."

"No."

Her answer was not convincing.

"Then we'd like you to tell us the name of his father."

"Why do you want to know?"

"It's important for our investigation."

"I've told you that I don't know anybody named Johannes Lövgren."

"What's the name of Nils's father?"

"I can't tell you."

"It won't go any further than this room."

She paused a little too long before she answered. "I don't know who Nils's father was."

"Women usually know."

"I was sleeping with more than one man at the time. I don't know who it was. That's why I listed the father as unknown."

She stood up quickly.

"I've got to get back to work," she said. "The old ladies are going to be boiled alive under those dryers."

"We can wait."

"But I don't have anything else to tell you!" She seemed more and more upset.

"We have some more questions."

Ten minutes later she was back. She was holding some notes that she stuffed into her purse, which was hanging on the back of a chair. She now seemed composed and ready for an argument.

"I don't know anyone called Lövgren," she said.

"And you insist that you don't know who was the father of your son, born in 1958?"

"That's correct."

"Do you realise that you may have to answer these questions under oath?"

"I'm telling the truth."

"Where can we find Nils?"

"He travels a lot."

"According to our records, his place of residence is in Sölvesborg."

"So go out there then!"

"That's what we plan to do."

"I have nothing more to say."

Wallander hesitated for a moment. Then he pointed at the photograph pinned on the wall.

"Is that Nils's father?" he asked.

She had just lit a cigarette. When she exhaled, it sounded like a hiss.

"I don't know any Lövgren. I don't know what you're talking about."

"All right then," said Boman. "We'll be off now. But you may be hearing from us again."

"I have nothing more to say. Why can't you leave me alone?"

"Nobody gets left alone when the police are looking for a murderer," said Boman. "That's the way it goes."

When they came outdoors, the sun was shining. They stood next to the car for a moment.

"What do you think?" asked Boman.

"I don't know. But there's something there."

"Shall we try to find the son before we move on to the third woman?"

"I think so."

They drove over to Sölvesborg and with great difficulty located what appeared to be the right address: a dilapidated wooden house outside the centre of the town, surrounded by wrecked cars and pieces of machinery. A ferocious German shepherd was barking and pulling on its iron chain. The house looked deserted. Boman leaned forwards and looked at a sign with sloppy lettering that was nailed to the door.

"Nils Velander," he said. "This is the place."

He knocked several times, but no one answered. They walked all the way around the house.

"What a bloody rat hole," said Boman.

When they got back to the door, Wallander tried the handle. The house wasn't locked. Wallander looked at Boman, who shrugged.

"If it's open, it's open," he said. "Let's go in."

They stepped into a musty hallway and listened. Silence. They both jumped when a hissing cat leaped out of a dark corner and vanished up the stairs to the first floor. The room on the left seemed to be some sort of office. There were two battered filing cabinets and an exceedingly messy desk with a phone and an answering machine. Wallander lifted the top of a box sitting on the desk. Inside was a set of black leather underwear and a mailing label.

"Fredrik Åberg of Dragongatan in Alingsås ordered this stuff," he said with a grimace. "Plain brown wrapper, no doubt."

They moved on to the next room, which was a storeroom for Nils Velander's novelty underwear. There were also a number of whips and dog collars. Everything was jumbled up, with no appearance of organisation.

The next room was the kitchen, with dirty dishes stacked by the sink. A half-eaten chicken lay on the floor. The room stank of cat piss. Wallander threw open the door to the pantry. Inside was a home distillery and two large vats. Boman sniggered and shook his head.

They went upstairs and peeked into the bedroom. The sheets were dirty and clothes lay in heaps on the floor. The curtains were drawn, and together they counted seven cats scurrying off.

"What a pigsty," repeated Boman. "How can anybody live like this?"

The house looked as if it had been abandoned in a hurry.

"Maybe we'd better leave," said Wallander. "We'll need a search warrant before we can give the place a thorough going-over."

They went back downstairs. Boman stepped into the office and punched the button on the answering machine. A man they assumed was Nils Velander stated that no one was in the Raff-Sets office at the moment, but you were welcome to leave your order on the answering machine.

The German shepherd jerked on its chain as they came out into the courtyard. At the corner, on the left-hand side of the house, Wallander discovered a basement door almost hidden behind the remains of an old mangle.

He opened the unlocked door and stepped into the darkness. He fumbled his way over to a fuse box. An old oil furnace stood in the corner. The rest of the basement room was filled with empty birdcages. He called to Boman, who joined him.

"Leather underpants and empty birdcages," said Wallander. "What exactly is this guy up to?"

"I think we'd better find out," replied Boman.

As they were about to leave, Wallander noticed a small steel cabinet behind the furnace. He bent down and pressed on the handle. It was unlocked, like everything else in the house. He put his hand in and grabbed hold of a plastic bag. He pulled it out and opened it.

"Look at this," he said to Boman.

The plastic bag contained a bundle of 1,000-krona notes. Wallander counted twenty-three.

"I think we're going to have to have a talk with this chap," said Boman.

They stuffed the money back and went outside. The German shepherd was still barking.

"We'll have to talk to our colleagues here in Sölvesborg," said Boman. "They can check him out for us."

At the Sölvesborg police station they found an officer who was quite familiar with Velander.

"He's probably mixed up in all kinds of illegal activities," said the policeman. "But the only thing we have on him is suspicion of illegally importing caged birds from Thailand. And operating a distillery."

"He was once sentenced for assault and battery," said Boman.

"He doesn't usually get into fights," replied the officer. "But I'll try to check up on him for you. Do you really think he's graduated to murdering people?"

"We don't know," said Wallander. "But we need to find him."

They set off for Kristianstad. It was raining again. They had formed a good impression of the police officer in Sölvesborg and were counting on him to find Velander for them. But Wallander had doubts.

"We don't know anything," he said. "Thousand-krona notes in a plastic bag aren't proof of anything."

"But something is going on there," said Boman.

Wallander agreed. There was something about the owner of the beauty salon and her son.

They stopped for lunch at a hotel restaurant. Wallander thought he ought to check in with the station in Ystad, but the pay phone he tried was broken.

It was 1:30 p.m. by the time they got back to Kristianstad. Before they went to find the third woman on their list, Boman wanted to check in at his office. The young woman at the reception desk flagged them down.

"There was a call from Ystad," she said. "They want Inspector Wallander to call back."

"Let's go to my office," said Boman.

Full of foreboding, Wallander dialled the number while Boman went to get some coffee. Without a word Ebba connected him to Rydberg.

"You'd better come back," said Rydberg. "Some idiot has shot a Somali refugee at Hageholm."

"What the hell do you mean by that?"

"Exactly what I said. This Somali was out taking a stroll. Someone blasted him with a shotgun. I've had a hell of a time tracking you down. Where have you been?"

"Is he dead?"

"His head was blown off."

Wallander felt sick to his stomach. "I'm on my way," he said.

He hung up the phone just as Boman came in, balancing two mugs of coffee. Wallander gave him a rundown of what had happened.

"I'll get you emergency transport," said Boman. "I'll send your car over later with one of the boys."

Everything happened fast. In a few minutes Wallander was on his way to Ystad in a car with sirens wailing. Rydberg met him at the station and they drove at once to Hageholm.

"Do we have any leads?" asked Wallander.

"None. But the newsroom at *Sydsvenskan* got a call only a few minutes after the murder. A man said that it was revenge for the murder of Johannes Lövgren. And that next time they would take a woman for Maria Lövgren."

"This is insane," said Wallander. "We don't have foreign suspects anymore, do we?"

"Somebody seems to have a different opinion. Thinks that we're shielding some foreigners."

"But I've already denied that."

"Whoever did this doesn't give a shit about your denials. They see a perfect case for pulling out a gun and shooting foreigners."

"This is crazy!"

"You're damn right it's crazy. But it's true!"

"Did the newspaper tape the phone conversation?"

"Yes."

"I want to hear it. To see if it's the same person who's been calling me."

The car raced through the landscape of Skåne.

"What are we going to do now?" asked Wallander.

"We've got to catch the Lunnarp killers," said Rydberg. "And damned fast."

At Hageholm everything was in chaos. Distressed and weeping refugees had gathered in the dining hall, reporters were interviewing people, and phones were ringing. Wallander stepped out of the car onto a muddy dirt road several hundred metres from the residential buildings. The wind was blowing again, and he turned up the collar of his jacket. An area near the road had been cordoned off. The dead man was lying face down in the mud.

Wallander cautiously lifted the sheet covering the body.

Rydberg hadn't been exaggerating. There was almost nothing left of the head.

"Shot at close range," said Hansson, who was standing nearby. "Whoever did this must have jumped out of hiding and fired the shots from a few metres away."

"Shots?" said Wallander.

"The camp director says that she heard two shots, one after the other."

Wallander looked around.

"Car tracks?" he asked. "Where does this road go?"

"Two kilometres further along you come out on the E65.

"And no one saw anything?"

"It's hard to question refugees who speak fifteen different languages. But we're working on it."

"Do we know who the dead man is?"

"He had a wife and nine children."

Wallander stared at Hansson in disbelief. "Nine children?"

"Just imagine the headlines tomorrow morning," said Hansson. "Innocent refugee murdered taking a walk. Nine children left without a father."

Svedberg came running from one of the police cars.

"The police chief is on the phone," he said.

Wallander looked surprised.

"I thought he wasn't due back from Spain until tomorrow."

"Not him. The chief of the national police."

Wallander got into the car and picked up the phone. The chief's voice was emphatic, and Wallander was immediately annoyed by what he said.

"This looks very bad," said the chief. "We don't need racist murders in this country."

"No," said Wallander.

"This investigation must be given top priority."

"Yes. But we already have the murders in Lunnarp on our hands."

"Are you making any progress there?"

"I think so. But it takes time."

"I want you to report to me personally. I'm going to take part in a discussion programme on TV tonight, and I need all the information I can get."

"I'll see to it."

He hung up.

Wallander remained sitting in the car. Näslund will have to handle this, he thought. He'll have to feed the paperwork to Stockholm. He felt depressed. His hangover was gone, and he remembered what had happened the night before, as he saw Peters approaching from a police car that had just arrived.

He thought about Mona and the man who had picked her up. And Linda laughing, the black man at her side. His father, painting his everlasting landscape. He thought about himself too.

A time to live, and a time to die.

Wallander forced himself out of the car to take charge of the criminal investigation. Nothing else had better happen, he thought. We can't handle anything else.

It was still raining.

CHAPTER 10

Wallander stood in the driving rain, freezing. It was late afternoon, and the police had rigged floodlights around the murder scene. He watched two ambulance attendants squishing through the mud with a stretcher. They were taking away the dead Somali. When he looked at the sea of mud he wondered whether even as skilful a detective as Rydberg would be able to find any tracks.

Still, he felt slightly relieved. Until ten minutes ago the officers had been surrounded by a hysterical woman and nine howling children. The wife of the dead man had thrown herself down in the mud, and her wails were so piercing that several of the policemen couldn't tolerate the sound and had moved away. To his surprise, Wallander saw that the only one who was able to handle the grieving woman and the anguished children was Martinsson. The youngest policeman on the force, who so far in his career had never even been forced to notify someone of a relative's death. He had held the woman, kneeling in the mud, and in some way the two were able to understand each other across the language barrier. A priest who had been called out was unable to do anything, of course. But gradually Martinsson succeeded in getting the woman and the children back to the main building, where a doctor was ready to take care of them.

Rydberg came tramping through the mud. His trousers were splattered all the way up his thighs.

"What a hell of a mess," he said. "But Hansson and Svedberg have done a fantastic job. They managed to find two refugees and an interpreter who actually think they saw something."

"What did they see?"

"How should I know? I don't speak either Arabic or Swahili. But they're on their way to Ystad right now. The Immigration Service has promised us some interpreters. I thought it would be best if you handled the interviews."

Wallander nodded. "Have we got anything to go on?"

Rydberg took out his grimy notebook.

"He was killed at 1 p.m. precisely," he said. "The director was listening to the news on the radio when she heard the noise. There were two shots. But you know that already. He was dead before he hit the ground. It seems to have been regular buckshot. Gyttorp brand, I think. Nytrox 36, probably. That's about all."

"That's not much."

"It's absolutely nothing. But maybe the eyewitnesses will have something to tell us."

"I've authorised overtime for everyone," said

Wallander. "Now we'll have to bust our guts night and day if necessary."

Back at the station, the first interview almost drove him to despair. The interpreter, who was supposed to know Swahili, could barely understand the dialect spoken by the witness, a young man from Malawi. It took him almost twenty minutes to discover that the man for some strange reason knew Luvale, a language spoken in parts of Zaire and Zambia. One of the Immigration Service people knew a former missionary who spoke fluent Luvale. She was close to ninety and lived in sheltered accommodation in Trelleborg. After calling his colleagues there, he was promised that the missionary would be given police transport to Ystad. Wallander suspected that a ninety-year-old missionary might not be very sharp, but he was wrong. A little white-haired lady with lively eyes appeared at the door of his office, and before he knew it she was involved in an intense conversation with the young man.

But, it turned out that the man hadn't seen a thing. "Ask him why he volunteered as a witness," Wallander said wearily.

The missionary and the young man went off into a lengthy exchange.

"He just thought it was rather exciting," she said at last. "And that's understandable."

"It is?" Wallander wondered.

"You must have been young once yourself," said the woman.

The young man from Malawi was sent back to Hage-holm, and the missionary returned to Trelleborg. The next witness actually had something to tell them. He was an Iranian who worked as an interpreter and who spoke fluent Swedish. Like the murdered Somali, he had been walking close to Hageholm when the shots were fired.

Wallander picked out a section of the map that showed the area around Hageholm. He put an X at the scene of the murder, and the Iranian was able to point at once to where he had been when he heard the shots. Wallander calculated the distance as about three hundred metres.

"After the shots I heard a car," said the man.

"But you didn't see it?"

"No. I was in the woods. I couldn't see the road."

The Iranian pointed again. To the south.

Then he really surprised Wallander.

"It was a Citroën," he said.

"A Citroën?"

"The kind you call a turtle here in Sweden."

"How can you be sure of that?"

"I grew up in Tehran. When we were boys we learned to recognise the makes of cars by the sound of the en-gine. Citroëns are easy. Most of all the turtle."

Wallander had a hard time believing what he heard. "Come out to the car park with me, and when you get outside, turn your back and shut your eyes."

Outside in the rain he started his Peugeot and drove

around the car park. He watched the Iranian carefully the whole time.

"All right," he said when he returned. "What was that?"

"A Peugeot," replied the Iranian with the utmost confidence.

"Good," said Wallander. "Damned amazing."

He sent the man home and gave the instruction that an APB be issued on a Citroën that might have been seen between Hageholm and the E65 to the west. The wire service was also advised that the police were looking for a Citroën that was believed to be linked to the murder.

The third witness was a young woman from Romania. She sat in Wallander's office nursing her baby during the interview. Her interpreter spoke poor Swedish, but Wallander still had a good idea of what the woman was saying.

She had walked the same way as the Somali, and she had passed him on her way back to the camp.

"How long?" asked Wallander. "How long was it from when you passed him to when you heard the shots?"

"Maybe three minutes."

"Did you see anyone else?"

The woman nodded, and Wallander leaned over the desk in suspense.

"Where?" he asked. "Show me on the map!"

The interpreter held the baby while the woman searched on the map.

"There," she said, pressing the pen to the map.

Wallander saw that the spot was very near the scene of the murder.

"Tell me about it," he said. "There's no hurry. Think carefully."

The woman thought for a while.

"A man in blue overalls," she said. "He was standing out in the field."

"What did he look like?"

"He didn't have much hair."

"How tall was he?"

"Normal height."

"Am I a man of normal height?" Wallander stood up straight.

"He was taller."

"How old was he?"

"He wasn't young. Not old either. Maybe forty-five."

"Did he see you?"

"I don't think so."

"What was he doing out in the field?"

"He was eating."

"Eating?"

"He was eating an apple."

Wallander thought for a moment. "A man in blue overalls standing in a field near the road and eating an apple. Did I understand you correctly?"

"Yes."

"Was he alone?"

"I didn't see anyone else. But I don't think he was alone."

"Why not?"

"He seemed to be waiting for someone."

"Did this man have a weapon of any kind?"

The woman thought again. "There might have been a brown package at his feet. Maybe it was just mud."

"What happened after you saw the man?"

"I hurried home as fast as I could."

"Why in a hurry?"

"It's not a good idea to run into strange men in the woods."

Wallander nodded. "Did you see a car?" he asked.

"No. No car."

"Can you describe the man in more detail?"

She thought for a long time before she replied.

"He looked strong," she said. "I think he had big hands."

"What colour was his hair? What little he had."

"Swedish colour."

"Blond hair?"

"Yes. And he was bald like this."

She drew a half moon in the air.

Then she was allowed to go back to the camp. Wallander went to get a cup of coffee. Svedberg asked if he wanted pizza. He nodded.

At 9 p.m. the team met in the canteen. Wallander thought that everyone apart from Näslund still looked surprisingly alert. Näslund had a cold and a fever but stubbornly refused to go home.

As they divided up pizzas and sandwiches, Wallander

tried to sum up. At one end of the room he had taken down a picture and projected a slide that showed a map of the murder scene. He had put an X on the site of the crime and drawn in the location and movements of both witnesses.

"So we aren't totally out in the cold here," he began. "We've got the time, and we have two reliable witnesses. A few minutes before the first shot, the female witness sees a man in blue overalls standing in a field very close to the road. This fits exactly with the time it should have taken the dead man to reach that point. And we know that the killer took off in a Citroën and headed southwest."

Wallander's summary was interrupted when Rydberg came into the canteen. All the team members began to laugh. Rydberg was covered in mud all the way up to his chin. He kicked off his wet and filthy shoes and took a sandwich that someone handed him. Wallander repeated his summary of the interviews for Rydberg.

"You're just in time," said Wallander. "What have you found?"

"I've been slogging around in that field for hours," Rydberg replied. "The Romanian woman pointed out pretty well where the man was most likely standing. We took casts of some footprints there. From rubber boots. She said that's what the man was wearing. Ordinary green rubber boots. And I found an apple core."

Rydberg took a plastic bag out of his pocket.

"With a little luck we might get some prints from it," he said.

"Can you take fingerprints from an apple core?" Wallander wondered.

"You can take prints from anything," said Rydberg. "There might be a strand of hair, a little saliva, skin fragments."

He set the plastic bag on the table, carefully, as if it were made of porcelain.

"Then I followed the footprints," he went on. "And if the Apple Man is the killer, then this is how I think it happened."

Rydberg took his pen out of the notebook and went over to the map projected onto the wall.

"He saw the Somali coming up the road. He threw away the apple core and walked straight onto the road in front of him. I could see his tracks. There he fired off his two shots at a distance of about four metres. Then he turned around and ran about fifty metres down the road from the murder scene. The road widens a little, making it possible for a car to turn around. Sure enough, there were tyre tracks. And I also found two cigarette butts."

He took the next plastic bag from his pocket.

"The man hopped in the car and drove south. That's how I think it happened. By the way, I think I'll send my cleaning bill to the police department."

"I'll sign for it," promised Wallander. "But now we have to think."

Rydberg raised his hand, as if he were in school.

"I've got a couple of ideas," he said. "First of all, I'm sure there were two of them. One the driver and one the shooter."

"Why do you think that?" asked Wallander.

"People who choose to eat an apple in a tense situation are probably not smokers. I think there was one person waiting by the car. A smoker. And a killer who ate an apple."

"That sounds reasonable."

"Also, I've got a feeling that the whole thing was well planned. It doesn't take much to figure out that the refugees at Hageholm use this road to take walks. Most often they probably go in groups. But now and then someone will be walking alone. If you then dress like a farmer, no one would think it looked suspicious. And the spot was well chosen, because the car could wait right nearby without being seen. So I think that this was a cold-blooded execution. The only thing the killers didn't know was who would come walking up that road alone. And they didn't care."

Silence fell over the canteen. Rydberg's analysis had been so clear that no one had anything to say. The ruthlessness of the murder was now obvious.

It was Svedberg who finally broke the silence. "A messenger brought over a cassette tape from *Sydsvenskan*," he said.

Someone found a tape recorder. Wallander recognised the voice. It was the same man who had called him twice and threatened him.

"We'll send this tape up to Stockholm," he said. "Maybe they can figure out something by analysing it."

"I also think we should find out what kind of apple he was eating," said Rydberg. "With a little luck we might track down the shop where he bought it."

They moved on to the motive.

"Racial hatred," said Wallander. "It can be so many things. But I assume we have to start poking around in these Swedish Neo-Nazi groups. Obviously we've entered a new and more serious phase. They're not just painting slogans anymore. They're throwing fire bombs and killing people. But I don't think the same people did this as set fire to the huts in Ystad. I still think that was more of a prank or the act of a drunk who got worked up about refugees. This murder is different. It's individuals either acting on their own or in some way involved in one of these movements. We'll have to give them a good shake-up. We also need to go out and appeal to the public for tip-offs. I'm thinking of asking Stockholm for help in charting these Swedish Neo-Nazi movements. This murder is of national concern. That means we can have all the resources we need. And, someone must have seen that Citroën."

"There's a club for Citroën owners," said Näslund in a hoarse voice. "We could match their list against the list of registered vehicles. The people in the club probably know just about every Citroën on the road in the whole country."

The assignments were given out. It was almost 10:30 p.m. before the meeting was over. No one had even thought of going home.

Wallander arranged an impromptu press conference in the reception area of the police station. Again he urged anyone who had seen a Citroën on the E65 to get in touch with the police. He also gave a preliminary description of the murderer. When he was finished, the questions rained down.

"Not now," he said. "I've said all I'm going to say."

When Wallander was on the way back to his office, Hansson came and asked if he wanted to see a video tape of the discussion programme on which the chief of the national police had been a guest.

"I'd rather not," he replied. "Not right now, at least."

He cleared his desk. He stuck the note reminding him to call his sister on his telephone receiver. Then he called Göran Boman at home.

Boman answered. "How's it going?" he asked.

"We've got a good deal to go on," said Wallander. "We'll have to work hard."

"I've got good news for you too."

"I was hoping you would."

"Our colleagues in Sölvesborg found Nils Velander. Apparently he has a boat at a shipyard that he goes and works on once in a while. The transcript of the interview is coming tomorrow, but they told me the key things. He claims that he earned the money in the plastic bag from his underwear business. And he agreed to exchange the notes for new ones, so we can check for fingerprints."

"I'll have to visit the Union Bank here in Ystad," said Wallander. "We need to find out whether the serial numbers can be traced."

"The money is arriving tomorrow. But honestly, I don't think he's the one."

"Why not?"

"I don't know."

"I thought you said you had good news?"

"I do. Now I'm getting to the third woman. I didn't think you'd mind if I looked her up by myself."

"Of course not."

"As you recall, her name is Ellen Magnusson. She's sixty and she works at one of the chemists here in Kristianstad. I had in fact met her once before. Several years ago she ran over and killed a road worker. That was outside the airport at Everöd. She said that she had been blinded by the sun, which was no doubt true. In 1955 she had a son and listed the father as unknown. The son's name is Erik, and he lives in Malmö. He's a civil servant at the county council. I drove out to her house. She seemed frightened and upset, as if she'd been waiting for the police to turn up. She denied that Johannes Lövgren was the father of her boy. But I had a strong feeling that she was lying. If you trust my judgement, I'd like to focus on her. But of course I won't exclude the bird dealer and his mother."

"For the next twenty-four hours I doubt I'll be able

to do much beyond what I'm working on right now," said Wallander. "I'm grateful for all the time you're devoting to this."

"I'll send over the papers," said Boman. "And the money. I assume you'll have to give us a receipt for them."

"When all this is over we'll sit down and have that whisky," said Wallander.

"There's going to be a conference at Snogeholm Castle in March on the new narcotics routes in Eastern Europe," said Boman. "How would that be?"

"That sounds fine," said Wallander.

They hung up, and he went over to Martinsson's room to hear whether any information had come in on the Citroën.

Martinsson shook his head. Nothing yet.

Wallander went back to his office and put his feet up on his desk. It was 11:30 p.m. Slowly he let his thoughts take shape. First he methodically played out in his mind the murder outside the refugee camp. Had he forgotten anything? Was there any gap in Rydberg's account of what had happened, or something else that they ought to be working on right away?

He concluded that the investigation was rolling along as efficiently as could be expected. All they had to do now was wait for the various technical analyses and hope that the car could be traced. He shifted in his chair, loosened his tie, and thought about what Boman had told him. He had full confidence in his judgement.

If Boman felt the woman was lying, then that was undoubtedly the case. But why was he going so easy on Nils Velander?

He took his feet down from the desk and pulled over a blank sheet of paper. He made a list of everything he had to do in the next few days. He decided to try to get the Union Bank to open its doors for him tomorrow, even though it was Saturday.

When he finished his list, he stood up and stretched. It was just after midnight. Out in the corridor he could hear Hansson talking with Martinsson, but he couldn't hear what they were saying.

Outside the window a streetlight was swaying in the wind. He felt sweaty and dirty and considered taking a shower downstairs in the changing room. He opened the window and breathed in the cold air.

He felt restless. How would they be able to stop the murderer from striking again?

The next one was to be a woman, in retribution for Maria Lövgren's death. He sat down at his desk and pulled over the folder with the data on the refugee camps in Skåne.

It was improbable that the murderer would return to Hageholm. But there were any number of alternatives. And if the murderer was going to select his victim as randomly as he had at Hageholm, they had even less to go on. Besides, it was impossible to require the refugees to stay indoors.

He shoved the folder aside and rolled a sheet of

paper into his typewriter. He thought he might as well write his memo to Björk. Just then the door opened and Svedberg came in.

"News?" asked Wallander.

"You might call it that," said Svedberg, looking unhappy.

"What is it?"

"I don't quite know how to tell you. But we just got a call from a farmer out by Löderup."

"Did he see the Citroën?"

"No. But he claimed that your father was walking around out in the fields in his pyjamas. With a suitcase in his hand."

Wallander was stunned. "What the hell are you talking about?"

"The farmer sounds lucid enough. It was you he actually wanted to talk to. But the switchboard put it through to me by mistake. I thought you ought to decide what to do."

Wallander sat quite still, his expression blank.

Then he stood up. "Where?" he asked.

"It sounded like your father was walking down by the main highway."

"I'll handle this myself. I'll be back as soon as I can. Call me if anything happens."

"Do you want me or somebody else to go along?"

Wallander shook his head.

"My father is senile," he said. "I have to see about getting him into a home somewhere."

Just as Wallander was going out the main doors, he noticed a man standing in the shadows outside. He recognised him as a reporter from one of the afternoon papers.

"I don't want him following me," he told Svedberg.

Svedberg nodded. "Wait till you see me back out and stall in front of his car. Then you can get away."

Wallander waited. He saw the reporter making rapidly for his car. Seconds later, Svedberg drove up and turned off his ignition, blocking the reporter's way. Wallander drove away.

He drove fast. Much too fast. He ignored the speed limit through Sandskogen. He was alone. Hares fled terrified across the rain-slicked road.

When he reached the village where his father lived, he didn't even have to look for him. He caught the old man in his headlights, in his blue-trimmed pyjamas, squishing barefoot through a field. He was wearing his old hat and carrying a big suitcase. When the headlights blinded him, his father held his hand in front of his eyes in annoyance. Then he kept on walking. Energetically, as if on his way to some specific destination.

Wallander turned off his engine but left the headlights on and walked out into the field.

"Dad!" he yelled. "What the hell are you doing?"

His father didn't answer but kept going. Wallander followed him. He tripped and fell and got wet up to his waist.

"Dad!" he shouted again. "Stop! Where are you going?"

No answer. His father seemed to pick up speed. Soon they would be down by the main highway. Wallander ran and stumbled to catch up with him, grabbing him by the arm. But his father pulled away and kept going.

Wallander got angry. "Police," he yelled. "If you don't stop, we'll fire a warning shot."

His father stopped and turned around. Wallander saw him blinking in the glare of the headlights.

"What did I tell you?" the old man screamed. "You want to kill me!"

Then he flung his suitcase at Wallander. The lid flew open and revealed the contents: dirty underwear, tubes of paint, and brushes. Wallander felt a huge sadness well up inside him. His father had tramped out into the night with the bewildered notion that he was on his way to Italy.

"Calm down, Dad," he said. "I just thought I'd drive you down to the railway station. Then you won't have to walk."

His father gave him a skeptical look. "I don't believe you," he said.

"Of course I'd drive my own father to the station if he's going on a journey."

Wallander picked up the suitcase, closed the lid, and started for the car. He put the bag in the boot and stood waiting. His father looked like a wild beast caught in the headlights. An animal chased to exhaustion, waiting for the fatal shot.

He started to walk towards the car. Wallander couldn't decide whether what he saw was an expression of dignity or humiliation. He opened the rear door and his father crawled in. Wallander had taken a blanket from the boot, and now he wrapped it around his father's shoulders.

He gave a start when a man stepped out of the shadows. An old man, dressed in dirty overalls.

"I'm the one who telephoned," said the man. "How's it going?"

"Everything's fine," replied Wallander. "And thanks for the call."

"It was pure chance that I saw him."

"I understand. Thanks again."

He got behind the wheel. When he turned his head he could see that his father was so cold he was shaking beneath the blanket.

"Now I'll drive you to the station, Dad," he said. "It won't take long."

He drove straight to the emergency entrance of the hospital. He was lucky enough to run into the young doctor he had met at Maria Lövgren's deathbed. He explained what had happened.

"We'll admit him overnight for observation," said the doctor. "He may be suffering from exposure. Tomorrow the social worker will try to find a place for him."

"Thank you," said Wallander. I'll stay with him awhile."

His father had been dried off and was lying on a stretcher.

"Sleeping car to Italy," he said. "I'm finally on my way."

Wallander sat on a chair next to the stretcher.

"That's right," he said. "Now you'll get to Italy."

It was past 2 a.m. when he left the hospital. He drove the short distance to the station. Everyone except Hansson had gone home. Hansson was watching the taped discussion programme with the chief of the national police.

"Anything going on?" asked Wallander.

"Not a thing," said Hansson. "A few tip-offs, of course. But nothing earthshaking. I took the liberty of sending people home to get a few hours' sleep."

"That's good. Funny that nobody has called about the car."

"I was just thinking that. Maybe he just drove out on the E65 a little way and then took off on one of the back roads. I've looked at the maps. There's a whole maze of little roads in that area. Plus a big nature reserve, where no one goes in the winter. The patrols that check the camps are running a fine-tooth comb over those roads tonight."

Wallander nodded.

"We'll send in a helicopter when it gets light," he said. "The car might be hidden somewhere in that nature reserve."

He poured a cup of coffee.

"Svedberg told me about your father," said Hansson. "How did it go?"

"It went all right. The old boy is going senile. He's at the hospital. But it was OK."

"Go home and sleep for a few hours. You look exhausted."

"I've got some things to write up."

Hansson turned off the video.

"I'll stretch out on the sofa for a while," he said.

Wallander went into his office and sat down at the typewriter. His eyes stung with fatigue. And yet the weariness brought with it an unexpected clarity. A double murder is committed, he thought. And the manhunt triggers another murder. Which we have to solve fast, so as to prevent more murders. All this has happened in less than a week.

He wrote his memo to Björk, deciding to make sure that it was delivered to him by hand at the airport. He yawned. It was 3:45 a.m. He was too tired to think about his father. He was only afraid that the social worker at the hospital wouldn't be able to come up with a good solution.

The note with his sister's name on it was still sticking to the telephone. In a few hours, when it was morning, he would have to call her.

He yawned again and sniffed his armpits. He stank. Just then Hansson appeared in the half-open door. Wallander saw at once that something had happened.

"We've got something," said Hansson.

"What?"

"A guy from Malmö just called and said his car has been stolen."

"A Citroën?"

Hansson nodded.

"How come he discovers it at four o'clock in the morning?"

"He said he was leaving to go to a trade fair in Göteborg."

"Did he report this to our colleagues in Malmö?"

Hansson nodded. Wallander grabbed the phone.

"Then let's get moving," he said.

The police in Malmö promised to speed up their interrogation of the man. The registration number of the stolen car, the model, year, and colour were already being sent all over the country.

"BBM 160," said Hansson. "A dove-blue turtle with a white roof. How many of those can there be in this country? A hundred?"

"If the car isn't buried, we'll find it," said Wallander. "What time is sunrise?"

"Around eight or nine o'clock," replied Hansson.

"As soon as it gets light we need a helicopter over the reserve. You take care of that."

Hansson nodded. He was just leaving the room when he stopped.

"Damn it! There was one more thing."

"Yes?"

"The man who called and said that his car was stolen. He was a policeman."

Wallander gave Hansson a puzzled look.

"A policeman? What do you mean?"

"I mean that he was a policeman. Like you and me."

CHAPTER 11

Wallander went into one of the holding cells in the station and lay down for a nap. After a great deal of effort, he managed to set the alarm function on his watch. He was going to allow himself to sleep for two hours. When the beeping sound on his wrist woke him up, he had a slight headache. The first thing he thought about was his father. He took a few aspirin out of the first aid kit he found in a cupboard and washed them down with a cup of lukewarm coffee. Then he hesitated, trying to decide whether he should take a shower first or call his sister in Stockholm.

Finally he went down to the changing room and got into the shower. Slowly his headache evaporated. But he felt weighed down with weariness as he sank into the chair behind his desk. It was 7:15 a.m. His sister was always up early. She picked up the phone almost as soon as it started ringing. As gently as possible he told her what had happened.

"Why didn't you call me before?" she asked indignantly. "You must have noticed what was going on."

"I guess I noticed too late," he replied warily.

They agreed that she would wait until after he had spoken to the social worker before she decided when to come to Skåne.

"How are Mona and Linda?" she asked as the conversation was drawing to a close.

It dawned on him that she didn't know about the separation.

"Fine," he said. "I'll call you later."

He drove to the hospital. The temperature had fallen below freezing again. An icy wind was blowing through the town from the southwest.

A nurse, who had just received a report from the night staff, told Wallander that his father had slept fitfully. But he had not suffered from his nighttime promenade through the fields. Wallander decided to see the social worker first.

Wallander distrusted social workers. All too often in his career he had encountered welfare people, called in when the police had caught juvenile offenders, with misguided views on what action should be taken. Social workers were often too soft and yielding when they ought in his opinion to be making tough decisions. More than once he had raged at the welfare authorities because he felt that their pussyfooting encouraged young criminals to continue their activities.

Maybe this one is different, he thought. After a short wait he was greeted by a woman in her fifties.

Wallander described his father's sudden decline. How unexpected it was, how helpless he felt.

"It might be temporary," said the social worker. "Sometimes elderly people suffer from periods of confusion. If it passes, it might be enough to see that he gets regular home care. If it turns out that he really is senile, then we'll have to come up with some other solution."

They decided that his father should stay in over the weekend. Then she would discuss with the doctors what to do next. Wallander stood up. This woman seemed to know what she was talking about.

"It's hard to be sure what to do," he said.

She nodded. "Nothing is as troublesome as when we're forced to become parents to our own parents," she said. "I know. My mother finally became so difficult that I couldn't keep her at home."

Wallander went to see his father, who was in a room with four beds. All were occupied. One man was in a cast, another was curled up as if he had severe stomach pains. Wallander's father was lying staring at the ceiling.

"How are you, Dad?" he asked.

It was a moment before his father answered. "Leave me alone."

He spoke in a low voice. There was no hint of petulance. Wallander had the impression that his father's voice was full of sorrow. He sat on the edge of the bed for a while. Then he left.

"I'll be back, Dad. And Kristina says hello."

Wallander hurried out of the hospital, filled with a sense of helplessness. The icy wind whipped his face. He didn't feel like going back to the station, so he called Hansson on the scratchy car phone.

"I'm driving over to Malmö," he said. "Have we got a helicopter in the air?"

"It's been up for half an hour," replied Hansson. "Nothing yet. We have two dog patrols out too. If that damned car is anywhere in the reserve, we'll find it."

Wallander drove to Malmö. The morning traffic was fierce and intense. He was frequently forced over towards the shoulder by drivers passing without enough room. I should have taken a squad car, he thought. But maybe that doesn't make any difference these days.

Wallander arrived at the Malmö police station where the man who had had his car stolen was waiting for him. Before Wallander went in to see him, he talked to the officer who had taken the report of the theft.

"Is it true that he's a policeman?" Wallander asked.

"He was," the officer replied. "But he took early retirement."

"Why was that?"

The officer shrugged. "Problems with his nerves. I honestly don't know."

"Do you know him?"

"He mostly kept to himself. Even though we worked

together for ten years, I can't say that I really knew him."

"But surely someone does?"

The police officer shrugged again. "I'll find out," he said. "But remember, anybody can have his car stolen."

Wallander went into the room and said hello to the man, whose name was Rune Bergman. He was fifty-three and had been retired for four years. He was thin, with nervous, flitting eyes. Along one side of his nose he had a scar from what looked like a knife wound.

Wallander immediately sensed that the man sitting in front of him was on guard. He couldn't say why. But the feeling was palpable, and it grew stronger as the conversation progressed.

"Tell me what happened," he said. "At four o'clock in the morning you discovered your car was missing."

"I was going to drive to Göteborg. I like to get started before dawn when I'm going on a long drive. When I went outside, the car was gone."

"From the garage or from a parking place?"

"From the street outside my house. I have a garage. But there's so much junk in it that there's no room for the car."

"Where do you live?"

"In a suburb near Jägersrö."

"Do you think any of your neighbours saw anything?"

"I asked them. But no one heard or saw anything."

"When did you last see your car?"

"I was inside all day. But the car was there the night before."

"Locked?"

"Of course it was locked."

"Did it have a lock on the steering wheel?"

"Unfortunately, no. It was broken."

His answers came easily. But Wallander couldn't rid himself of the feeling that the man was on guard.

"What kind of trade show were you going to?" he asked.

The man sitting across from him looked surprised. "What does that have to do with this?"

"Nothing. I just wondered."

"An air show, if you must know."

"An air show?"

"I'm interested in old planes. I build model planes myself."

"Is it true that you took early retirement?"

"What the hell does that have to do with my stolen car?"

"Nothing."

"Why don't you start looking for my car instead of poking around in my personal life?"

"We're already onto it. As you know, we think that the person who stole your car may have committed a murder. Or maybe I should say an execution."

The man looked him straight in the eye. The nervous flitting had stopped.

"That's what I heard," he said.

Wallander had no more questions. "I thought we'd go over to your place. So I can see where the car was parked."

"I can't invite you in for coffee. The place is a mess."

"Are you married?"

"I'm divorced."

They went out to Wallander's car. The neighbourhood was an old one, situated just beyond the trotting track at Jägersrö. They stopped outside a yellow brick house with a small front lawn.

"This is where the car was, right where you're parked," said the man. "Right here."

Wallander backed up a few metres and they got out. Wallander noticed that the car must have been parked between two streetlights.

"Are there a lot of cars parked on this street at night?" he asked.

"Usually one in front of every house. A lot of people who live here have two cars. Their garages only hold one."

Wallander pointed at the streetlights. "Do they work?" he asked.

"Yes. I always notice if any of them are broken."

Wallander looked around, thinking. He had no further questions.

"I assume that we'll be talking to you again," he said.

"I want my car back," replied the man.

Wallander realised that he did have one more question.

"Do you have a licence to carry a gun?" he asked. "Do you own any guns?"

The man stiffened. At that moment a crazy idea flashed through Wallander's mind. The car theft was pure fiction. The man standing beside him was one of the two men who had shot the Somali the day before.

"What the hell do you mean?" said the man. "A gun licence? Don't tell me you're so fucking stupid that you think I had anything to do with that?"

"You were a policeman, so you should know that we have to ask these questions," said Wallander. "Do you have any guns in your house?"

"I have guns and a licence."

"What kind of guns?"

"I like to shoot once in a while. I have a Mauser for hunting moose."

"Anything else?"

"A shotgun. A Lanber Baron. It's a Spanish gun. For shooting rabbits."

"I'll send someone over to pick them up."

"Why is that?"

"Because the man who was killed yesterday was shot at close range with a shotgun."

The man gave him a disdainful look. "You're crazy," he said. "You're out of your fucking mind."

Wallander left. He drove straight back to the Malmö police station. He called Ystad. The car hadn't been found. Then he asked to speak to the officer in charge of the department for homicide and violent crimes in Malmö. Wallander had met him once before and found him to be overbearing and self-important. It had been on the same occasion that he met Göran Boman.

Wallander explained the case he was working on.

"I want his weapons checked," he said. "I want his house searched. I want to know whether he has any connections with racist organisations."

The police officer gave him a long look. "Do you have any reason whatsoever to believe that he made up the story about a stolen car? That he might be involved in the murder?"

"He owns guns. And we have to investigate everything."

"There are hundreds of thousands of shotguns in this country. And what makes you think I can get authorisation to search his house when the case is about a stolen car?"

"This case has top priority," said Wallander, starting to get annoyed. "I'll call the county police chief. The national police chief, if necessary."

"I'll do what I can," said the officer. "But no one likes it when you dig around in the private life of a colleague. And what do you think would happen if this got out to the press?"

"I don't give a shit," said Wallander. "I've got three murders on my hands. And somebody who's promised me a fourth. Which I intend to prevent."

On his way to Ystad, Wallander stopped at Hageholm. The technicians were just wrapping up their investigation. At the scene he went over Rydberg's theory about how the murder occurred, and he decided he was right. The car had probably been parked at the spot Rydberg had pinpointed. He realised that he hadn't asked the policeman whether he smoked. Or whether he ate apples.

He continued on to Ystad. On his way in he ran into a temp who was on her way out to lunch. He asked her to pick up a pizza for him.

He looked into Hansson's office: still no car.

"Case meeting in my office in fifteen minutes," said Wallander. "Try to round everybody up. Anyone who isn't here should be reached by phone."

Without taking off his overcoat, Wallander sat down and called his sister again. They agreed that he would pick her up at Sturup airport at 10 a.m. the following morning.

He felt the lump on his forehead, which was now changing colour, shifting to yellow and black and red. Within twenty minutes, everyone except Martinsson and Svedberg was there.

"Svedberg is out digging around in a gravel pit," said Rydberg. "Somebody called and said they saw a mysterious car out there. Martinsson is trying to track down a man in the Citroën club who apparently knows about all the Citroëns on the road in Skåne. A dermatologist from Lund."

"A dermatologist from Lund?" Wallander asked in surprise.

"There are hookers who collect stamps," said Rydberg. "Why shouldn't a dermatologist be into Citroëns?"

Wallander reported on his meeting with the ex-policeman in Malmö. He could hear how hollow it sounded when he said that he had ordered a thorough investigation of the man.

"That doesn't sound very likely," said Hansson. "A policeman who wants to commit a murder wouldn't be dumb enough to report his own car stolen, would he?"

"Maybe not," said Wallander. "But we can't afford to ignore a single lead, no matter how unlikely it seems."

The discussion turned to the missing car.

"We aren't getting tip-offs from the public," said Hansson. "Which reinforces my belief that the car never left the area."

Wallander unfolded a detailed map, and they leaned over it as if preparing for battle.

"The lakes," said Rydberg. "Krageholm Lake, Svaneholm Lake. Let's assume that they drove out there and ditched the car. There are minor roads all over the place."

"It still sounds risky," objected Wallander. "Somebody could easily have seen them."

They decided at any rate to drag the lakes. And to send some men out to search through abandoned barns. A dog patrol from Malmö had been out searching without finding a single trace. The helicopter search had produced no results either.

"Could your Iranian have been mistaken?" wondered Hansson.

Wallander thought about this for a moment.

"We'll bring him in again," he said. "We'll test him on six different kinds of cars. Including a Citroën."

Hansson was detailed to take care of the witness. They moved on to a summary of the search for the killers in Lunnarp. Here, too, the car that the early-morning lorry driver had seen still eluded them.

Wallander could see that his colleagues were tired. It was Saturday, and many of them had been working nonstop for a long time.

"We'll put Lunnarp on hold until Monday morning," he said. "Right now we're going to concentrate on Hageholm. Whoever isn't needed at the moment should go home and get some rest. It looks like next week is going to be just as busy as this one."

Then he remembered that Björk would be back at work on Monday.

"Björk will be taking over," he said. "So I want to take this opportunity to thank everyone for their efforts so far."

"Did we pass?" asked Hansson sarcastically.

"You get the highest marks," replied Wallander.

After the meeting he asked Rydberg to stay behind for a moment. He needed to talk through the situation with somebody in peace and quiet. And Rydberg was, as usual, the one whose opinion he respected most. He told him about Boman's efforts in Kristianstad. Rydberg nodded thoughtfully. Wallander saw that he was hesitant.

"It might be a dud," said Rydberg. "This double murder is puzzling me more and more, the longer I think about it."

"In what way?" asked Wallander.

"I can't get away from what the woman said before she died. I have a feeling that deep inside her tormented and wounded consciousness, she must have realised that her husband was dead. And that she was going to die too. I think it's human instinct to offer a solution to a mystery if there's nothing else left. And she said only one word: 'foreign.' She repeated it. Four or five times. It has to mean something. And that noose. The knot. You said it yourself. That murder smells of revenge and hatred. But still we're looking in a completely different direction."

"Svedberg has made a chart of all of Lövgren's relatives," said Wallander. "There are no foreign connections. Only Swedish farmers and one or two craftsmen."

"Don't forget his double life," said Rydberg. "Nyström described the neighbour he had known for forty years as an ordinary man. With few assets. After two days we discovered that none of this was true. So what's to prevent us from finding other false bottoms to this story?"

"So what do you think we should do?"

"Exactly what we are doing. But be open to the possibility that we might be on the wrong track."

They turned to the murdered Somali. Ever since he left Malmö, Wallander had been toying with an idea.

"Can you stay a little longer?" he asked.

"Sure," replied Rydberg, surprised. "Of course I can."

"There was something about that police officer," said Wallander. "I know it's mostly a hunch. An extremely unreliable trait in a policeman. But I thought we ought to keep an eye on that gentleman, you and I. Through the weekend, in any case. Then we can see whether we should continue and bring in more manpower. But if I'm right, that he might be involved, that his car wasn't stolen, then he should be feeling a little uneasy right now."

"I agree with Hansson that no policeman would be dim enough to pretend his car had been stolen if he were planning to commit a murder," Rydberg objected.

"I think you're both wrong," Wallander replied. "The same way that he was wrong in thinking that just because he had once been a policeman, that alone would steer all suspicion away from him."

Rydberg rubbed his aching knee.

"We'll do as you say, then," he said. "What I believe or don't believe is neither here or there if you think it's important."

"I want him under surveillance," said Wallander.

"We'll split up the shifts until Monday morning. It'll be rough, but we can do it. I can take the night shifts, if you like."

Rydberg said that he might as well handle the watch until midnight. Wallander gave him the address. The temp came into the office with the pizza he had ordered.

"Have you eaten?" Wallander asked.

"Yes," replied Rydberg hesitantly.

"No you haven't. Take this one and I'll get another."

Rydberg ate the pizza at Wallander's desk. He wiped his mouth and stood up.

"Maybe you're right," he said.

"Maybe," replied Wallander.

Nothing happened the rest of the day. The car continued to elude them. The fire department dragged the lakes, finding only parts of an old combine. Few tip-offs came in from the public.

Reporters from the newspapers, radio, and TV called constantly, wanting updates. Wallander repeated his appeal for information on a missing pale blue Citroën with a white roof. Directors of the various refugee camps called in, anxious and demanding increased police protection. Wallander answered as patiently as he could.

An old woman was hit and killed by a car in Bjäresjö. Svedberg, back from the gravel pit, took on that case, even though Wallander had promised him the afternoon off.

Näslund called at 5 p.m., and Wallander could tell that he was tipsy. He wanted to know whether anything was happening, or whether he could go to a party in Skillinge. Wallander told him to go ahead.

He called the hospital twice to ask about his father. Each time they told him that he was tired and uncommunicative. He also called Sten Widén. A familiar voice answered the phone.

"I was the one who helped you with the ladder up to the loft," Wallander said. "The man you guessed was a policeman. I'd like to talk to Sten, if he's there."

"He's in Denmark buying horses," replied Louise.

"When is he back?"

"Maybe tomorrow."

"Would you ask him to call me?"

"I'll do that."

He hung up. Wallander had the distinct impression that Sten Widén was not in Denmark at all. Maybe he was even standing right next to the young woman, listening. Maybe they were together in the unmade bed when he called.

Wallander gave his memo to one of the patrol officers, who promised to hand it to Björk the minute he stepped off the plane at Sturup airport that evening.

He decided to go through his bills, which he had forgotten to pay on the first of the month. He filled out a bunch of giro slips and enclosed a cheque in the manila envelope. He wasn't going to be able to afford either a VCR or a stereo this month.

Next he answered an inquiry about a trip to the Royal Opera in Copenhagen at the end of February. He said yes. *Woyzeck* was an opera he hadn't seen staged.

It was 8 p.m. He read through Svedberg's report on the fatal accident in Bjäresjö. He could see at once that there was no question of criminal proceedings. The woman had stepped out into the road slap in front of a car travelling within the speed limit. The farmer who was driving the car was not at fault, all the eyewitness accounts agreed on that. He made a note to see to it that Anette Brolin read through the report after the autopsy was done.

At 8:30 p.m. two men started slugging each other in a block of flats on the outskirts of Ystad. Peters and Norén swiftly separated the combatants. They were two brothers, well known to the police. They got into a fight about three times a year.

A greyhound was reported lost in Marsvinsholm. The dog had been seen heading west, so the report was passed to the station in Skurup.

At 10 p.m. Wallander left the police station. It was cold and the wind was blowing in gusts. The sky was clear and filled with stars. Still no snow. He went home and put on heavy-duty long underwear and a woollen cap. Absentmindedly he watered the drooping plants in the kitchen window. Then he drove to Malmö.

Norén was duty officer that night. Wallander had promised to call in regularly. But presumably Norén would have his hands full with Björk, who would be coming home to discover that his holiday was definitely over.

Wallander stopped at a hotel restaurant in Svedala. He hesitated before deciding on only a salad. He doubted that this was a wise moment to change his eating habits, but he knew that he might fall asleep if he ate too much before an all-night shift.

He drank several cups of strong coffee after his meal. An elderly woman came over to his table and tried to sell him *The Watch Tower*. He bought a copy, thinking that it would be sufficiently dull to last all night.

Wallander pulled out onto the E65 again and drove the last stretch to Malmö. He began to doubt the value of this assignment. Was he justified in trusting his intuition? Shouldn't Hansson's and Rydberg's objections have been enough for him to drop the idea of this surveillance? He felt unsure of himself. Irresolute. And the salad had not been enough.

It was 11:35 p.m. when he turned onto a street near the yellow house where Bergman lived. He pulled his cap over his ears as he stepped out into the freezing night. All around him were darkened houses. In the distance he heard the screech of car tyres. He kept to the shadows as far as possible and turned down the street called Rosenallé.

Almost at once he caught sight of Rydberg, who was standing under a tall chestnut tree. The trunk was so thick that it nearly hid him entirely.

Wallander slipped into the shadow of the huge tree trunk. Rydberg was freezing. He was rubbing his hands together and stamping his feet.

"Anything going on?" asked Wallander.

"Not much in twelve hours," replied Rydberg. "At four, he went to buy groceries. Two hours later he came out to close the gate, which had blown open. But he's definitely on his guard. I think you may be right after all."

Rydberg pointed at the house next door.

"That one's empty," he said. "From the yard you can see both the street and his back door. He might take it into his head to slip out that way. There's a bench where you can sit. If your clothes are warm enough."

Wallander had noticed a phone box on his way over to Bergman's house. He asked Rydberg to go over and call Norén. If nothing urgent was happening, Rydberg could get in his car and drive home.

"I'll be back around seven," said Rydberg. "Don't freeze to death."

He vanished without a sound. Wallander stood still for a moment, looking at the yellow house. Lights were on in two of the windows, one on the lower floor and one upstairs. The curtains were drawn. He looked at his watch. Just after midnight. Rydberg had not returned. So everything must be quiet at the station in Ystad.

He hurried across the street and opened the gate to the yard of the empty house. He fumbled his way in the dark and found the bench that Rydberg had mentioned. From there he had a good view. To keep warm, he started pacing, five steps forwards and five steps back.

The next time he looked at his watch, it was only 12:50. It was going to be a long night. He was already feeling cold. He tried to make the time pass by studying the starry sky. When his neck started to hurt, he resumed his pacing.

At 1:30 a.m. the light on the ground floor went out. Wallander thought he could hear a radio on the second floor. Mr. Bergman keeps late hours, he thought. Maybe that's what happens if you take early retirement. At 1:55 a.m. a car drove past, immediately followed by another one. Then all was quiet again. The light was still on upstairs. Wallander was freezing.

At 2:55 a.m. the light went out. Wallander listened for the radio. But everything was quiet. He flapped his arms to keep warm. In his head he hummed the melody of a Strauss waltz.

The sound was so slight that he almost missed it.

The click of a door latch. That was all. Wallander stood stock-still and listened. Then he noticed the shadow.

The man must have been moving very quietly. Even so, Wallander caught a glimpse of Rune Bergman as he slipped through the back yard of his house. Wallander waited a few seconds. Then cautiously he climbed over the fence. It was hard to get his bearings in the dark, but he could just make out a narrow passage between a shed and the yard opposite Bergman's house. He moved fast. Too fast, considering how little he could see.

He emerged onto the street parallel to Rosenallé. One second later and he would not have seen Bergman vanish down a cross-street to the right.

For a moment Wallander hesitated. His car was only fifty metres away. If he didn't get it now, and Bergman had another car parked somewhere nearby, he would have no chance of following him.

He ran like a madman. His frozen joints creaked and he was soon out of breath. He fumbled with his keys, and yanked open the door, deciding to try to intercept Bergman.

He turned into the street that he thought was the right one. Too late he saw that it was a dead end. He swore and backed up. Bergman probably had any number of streets to choose from. There was also a park nearby.

Make up your mind, he thought furiously. Make up your mind, damn it.

He drove towards the big car park between the Jägersrö track and some large department stores. He was just about to give up when he caught sight of Bergman. He was in a phone box over by a new hotel next to the stables.

Wallander pulled over and turned off his engine and headlights. The man in the phone box hadn't noticed him.

A few minutes later a taxi pulled up and Bergman got into the back. Wallander started the car. The taxi took the motorway heading towards Göteborg. Wallander had to let a lorry go by before he took up the chase. He glanced at the petrol gauge. He wasn't going to be able to follow the taxi further than Halmstad. Suddenly it indicated a right turn. He was going to take the exit for Lund. Wallander followed.

The taxi stopped at the railway station. As Wallander drove past, Bergman was paying the driver. He turned off the main road and parked hurriedly. Bergman was walking fast. Wallander followed him, hugging the shadows.

Rydberg had been right. The man was on his guard. Without warning he stopped short and looked around. Wallander threw himself headlong into a doorway. He struck his forehead on the edge of a step and could feel the lump above his eye split open. Blood ran down his face. He wiped it off with his glove, counted slowly to ten, and took up his pursuit. The blood over his eye was sticky.

Bergman stopped outside a building covered with scaffolding and protective sacking. Again he looked around, and Wallander crouched down behind a parked car.

Then he was gone. Wallander waited until he heard a door shut. Soon afterwards the lights went on in rooms on the third floor.

He ran across the street and pushed his way behind

the sacking. Without hesitating, he climbed up onto the scaffolding. It creaked and groaned under him. He had to keep wiping away the blood trickling into his eye. He heaved himself up onto the second level. The lit windows were barely a metre above his head. He took out his handkerchief and tied it around his head to stem the blood.

Cautiously he hauled himself up onto the next platform. The effort so exhausted him that he had to remain lying down for over a minute before he could go on. He crept forwards along the freezing planks, which were covered with scraped-off stucco. He dared not think how far above the ground he was, or he would get vertigo at once.

He peered over the window ledge into the first lit room. Through the net curtains he could see a woman sleeping in a double bed. The covers next to her had been thrown back as if someone had got out in a hurry.

He crawled further along. When he looked over the next window ledge, he saw Bergman talking to a man wearing a dark-brown dressing gown. Wallander felt as if he had actually seen him before. That was how well the Romanian woman had described the man standing in the field eating an apple.

He felt his heart pounding. So he had been right after all. It had to be the same man. They were talking in low voices. Too low to hear what they were saying. The man in the dressing gown disappeared through a door and at the same moment Bergman looked straight at Wallander.

Caught, he thought, as he pulled back his head. Those bastards won't hesitate to shoot me. He was paralysed with fear. I'm going to die, he thought desperately. They're going to blow my head off. But nothing happened.

Finally he got up the nerve to peer inside again. The man in the dressing gown was standing there, eating an apple. Bergman was holding two shotguns. He laid one of them on a table. The other one he stuffed under his coat. Wallander realised he had seen more than enough. He turned and crept back the way he had come.

How it happened, he would never know.

He lost his footing in the dark. When he reached for the scaffolding, his hand grabbed at empty space. He fell. He had no time to think that he was going to die. One of his legs caught between two planks. He jerked to a halt, the pain excruciating. He was hanging upside down with his head a metre above the ground.

He tried to wriggle loose. But his foot was wedged tight. He was hanging in midair, unable to do anything. The blood was pounding in his temples. The pain was so bad that he had tears in his eyes. At that moment he heard the outside door open.

Bergman had left the flat. Wallander bit his knuckles to keep from screaming. Through the sacking he saw the man stop suddenly. Right in front of him. He saw a flash. The shot, thought Wallander. Now I'm going to die.

He realised that Bergman had lit a cigarette. The footsteps moved away. Wallander was about to pass out. An image of Linda flickered before him.

With enormous effort he swung his body and with one hand managed to grab hold of one of the uprights on the scaffolding. He pulled himself up far enough to get a grip on the planks where his foot was wedged tight. He gathered all his remaining strength. Then he tugged hard. His foot broke loose, and he lost his grip. He landed on his back in a mound of gravel. He lay perfectly still, trying to feel if anything was broken.

When he stood up, he was so dizzy that he had to hold on to the wall so he wouldn't fall. It took him almost twenty minutes to make his way back to the car. He saw the hands of the station clock pointing to 4:30 a.m.

Wallander sank into the driver's seat and closed his eyes. Then he drove back to Ystad. I have to get some sleep, he thought. Tomorrow is another day. Then I'll do what has to be done.

He groaned when he saw his face in the bathroom mirror. He rinsed his wounds with warm water.

It was almost 6 a.m. by the time he crawled between the sheets. He set the alarm clock for 6:45. He didn't dare sleep any later than that.

He tried to find the position that hurt the least. Just as he was falling asleep, he was jerked awake by a bang on the front door. The morning paper. Then he stretched out again. In his dreams Anette Brolin was coming towards him. Somewhere a horse neighed.

It was Sunday, January 14. The day dawned with increased wind from the northeast.

Kurt Wallander slept.

CHAPTER 12

He thought he had slept for a long time, but when he woke up and looked at the clock, he realised that he had been asleep only briefly. The telephone had woken him. Rydberg was calling from a phone box in Malmö.

"Come on back," said Wallander. "You don't have to stand there freezing. Come here, to my place."

"What happened?"

"It's him."

"Are you sure?"

"Absolutely positive."

"I'm on my way."

Wallander climbed painfully out of bed. His body ached and his temples were throbbing. While the coffee was brewing, he sat at the kitchen table with a pocket mirror and a piece of cotton wool. With great difficulty he succeeded in fastening a gauze pad over the wound on his forehead. His whole face was a palette of shades of blue and purple.

Rydberg appeared in the doorway less than an hour

later. While they drank coffee, Wallander told him his story.

"Good," Rydberg said afterwards. "Excellent work. Now we'll bring in those bastards. What was the name of the guy in Lund?"

"I forgot to look at the name in the doorway. And we're not the ones who'll bring them in. That's Björk's job."

"Is he back?"

"He was supposed to get in last night."

"Then let's haul him out of his bed."

"The prosecutor too. And we'll have to coordinate with Malmö and Lund, right?"

While Wallander was dressing, Rydberg was on the phone. Wallander was gratified to hear that he wasn't taking no for an answer. He wondered whether Anette Brolin's husband was visiting this weekend.

Rydberg stood in the bedroom doorway and watched him knot his tie.

"You look like a boxer," he said, laughing. "A punch-drunk boxer."

"Did you get Björk?"

"He seems to have spent the evening catching up with everything that's happened. He was relieved to hear that we had solved one of the murders, at least."

"The prosecutor?"

"She'll come right away."

"Was she the one who answered the phone?"

Rydberg looked at him in surprise. "Who else would have answered?"

"Her husband, for instance."

"What difference would that have made?"

Wallander didn't feel like answering. "God, I feel like shit," he said instead. "Let's go."

They went out into the early dawn. A gusty wind was still blowing and the sky was overcast with dark clouds.

"You think it's going to snow?" asked Wallander.

"Not before February," said Rydberg. "I can feel it. But then it'll be a hard winter."

A Sunday calm prevailed at the station. Norén had been relieved by Svedberg. Rydberg gave him a swift rundown of what had happened during the night.

"Well, I'll be damned," said Svedberg. "A police-man?"

"An ex-policeman."

"Where did he hide the car?"

"We don't know yet."

"Is the case airtight?"

"I think so."

Björk and Anette Brolin arrived at the station at the same moment. Björk, who was fifty-four and originally from Västmanland, had a nice tan. Wallander had always imagined him to be the ideal chief for a medium-sized police district. He was friendly, not too intelligent, and at the same time extremely concerned with the good name and reputation of the police.

He gave Wallander a dismayed look. "You look really terrible."

"They beat me up," said Wallander.

"Beat you up? Who?"

"The other officers. That's what happens when you're acting chief. They let you have it."

Björk laughed.

Anette Brolin looked at him with what seemed to be genuine sympathy.

"That must hurt," she said.

"I'll be all right," replied Wallander.

He turned his face away when he answered, remembering that he had forgotten to brush his teeth. They all went into Björk's office. Since there was no written report, Wallander gave a summary of the case. Björk and Anette Brolin both asked a lot of questions.

"If it had been anyone but you who dragged me out of bed on Sunday morning with this kind of cops-and-robbers story, I wouldn't have believed it," said Björk.

Then he turned to Anette Brolin. "Do we have enough to detain them? Or should we just bring them in for questioning?"

"I'll get the detention order on them based on the interrogation results," said Anette Brolin. "Then, of course, it would be good if that Romanian woman could identify the man in Lund in a lineup."

"We'll need a court order for that," said Björk.

"Yes," said Anette Brolin. "But we could do a provisional identification."

Wallander and Rydberg looked at her with interest.

"We could bring in the woman," she went on. "Then they could pass each other in the corridor by chance."

Wallander nodded in approval. Anette Brolin was a prosecutor who was Per Åkeson's equal when it came to taking a flexible view of the rules.

"Right," said Björk. "I'll get in touch with our colleagues in Malmö and Lund. Then we'll pick up the suspects in two hours. At ten o'clock."

"What about the woman in the bed?" asked Wallander. "The one in Lund?"

"We'll bring her in too," said Björk. "How should we divide up the interrogations?"

"I want Bergman," said Wallander. "Rydberg can talk to the man who munches on apples."

"At 3 p.m. we'll decide about the detention order," said Anette Brolin. "I'll be at home until then."

Wallander accompanied her out to reception. "I was thinking about asking you to dinner last night," he said. "But something came up."

"There'll be plenty more evenings," she said. "I think you've done a good job on this case. How did you work out that he was the one?"

"I didn't. It was just a hunch."

He watched her as she headed towards town. It came to him that he hadn't thought of Mona at all since the evening they had had dinner together.

Everything started to move very fast. Hansson was wrenched out of his Sunday peace and told to collect the Romanian woman and an interpreter.

"Our colleagues don't sound happy," Björk said with concern. "It's never anyone's idea of fun to bring in someone from your own force. It's going to be a wretched winter because of this."

"What do you mean by wretched?" asked Wallander.

"Fresh attacks on the police force."

"He'd retired early, hadn't he?"

"Even so. The papers will be screaming about the fact that the murderer was a policeman. There will be new persecution of the force."

Shortly before 10 a.m. Wallander arrived at the building that was covered in scaffolding and sacking. He had four plainclothes policemen from Lund with him.

"He has guns," said Wallander while they were still sitting in the car. "And he has committed a cold-blooded execution. Still, I think we can take it easy. He's certainly not anticipating us. Two guns drawn should be enough."

Wallander had brought along his revolver. On the way to Lund he tried to remember when he had last taken it out. He'd realised that it was more than three years earlier, in the course of the capture of an escaped convict from Kumla prison who had barricaded himself in a summerhouse near Mossby beach.

Now they were sitting in a car outside the building in Lund. Wallander realised that he had climbed much higher than he had thought. If he had fallen all the way to the ground, he would have crushed his spine.

That morning the police in Lund had sent out an inspector pretending to do the paper round to case the flat.

"Let's review the situation," said Wallander. "No back stairs?"

The officer sitting next to him shook his head.

"No scaffolding on the rear side?"

"Nothing."

According to the officer, the flat was occupied by a man named Valfrid Ström. He wasn't listed in any police files. Nor did anyone know how he made his living.

At 10 a.m. on the dot they got out of the car and crossed the street. One officer stayed at the main door of the building. There was an intercom system, but it wasn't working. Wallander jimmied the door open with a screwdriver.

"One man should stay in the stairwell," he said. "You and I will go upstairs. What's your name?"

"Enberg."

"You've got a first name, haven't you?"

"Kalle."

"OK, Kalle, let's go."

They listened in the dark outside the door. Wallander drew his revolver and nodded to Enberg to do the same. Then he rang the doorbell.

The door was opened by a woman wearing a dressing gown. Wallander recognised her. It was the same woman who had been asleep in the double bed. He hid his revolver behind his back.

"We're with the police," he said. "We're looking for your husband, Valfrid Ström."

The woman, who was in her forties and had a harried expression, looked scared. She stepped aside and let the policemen in.

Suddenly Valfrid Ström was standing in front of them. He was dressed in a green tracksuit.

"Police," said Wallander. "We need to ask you to come with us."

The man with the half-moon-shaped bald patch looked at him tensely. "Why?"

"For questioning."

"About what?"

"You'll find out at the station."

Wallander turned to the woman. "You'd better come along too. Put on some clothes."

The man seemed completely calm. "I'm not going anywhere if you don't tell me why," he said. "Perhaps you could start by showing me some identification."

When Wallander put his right hand in his inside pocket, he couldn't hide the fact that he was carrying a gun. He switched it over to his left hand and fumbled for his wallet, where he kept his identity card.

In the same instant Ström leapt straight at him. He butted Wallander right in the forehead, smack in the middle of his wound. Wallander went sailing backwards, and the revolver flew out of his hand. Enberg didn't have time to react before the man in the green tracksuit had disappeared out the door. The woman shrieked, and Wallander fumbled for his revolver. He dashed down the stairs after the man, yelling a warning to the two officers posted below.

Ström was fast. He gave the policeman standing inside the door an elbow to the chin. The man outside was rammed by the front door when Ström flung himself out into the street. Wallander, who could hardly see for the blood streaming into his eyes, stumbled over the unconscious policeman in the stairwell. He pulled at the safety catch on his revolver, which was stuck.

Then he was out on the street.

"Which way did he go? he called to the bewildered policeman who was entangled in the sacking.

"Left."

Wallander ran. He caught sight of Ström's tracksuit just as he disappeared into an underpass. He tore off his cap and wiped his face. Several elderly women, who looked as though they were on their way to church, jumped aside in fright. He ran into the underpass just as a train rumbled overhead.

When he reached street level again, he just had time to see Ström stop a car, drag the driver out, and drive off.

The only vehicle nearby was a large horsebox. The driver was pulling a pack of condoms from a vending machine on a shop wall. When Wallander came racing up, his gun drawn and blood streaming down his face, the man dropped the condoms and ran for his life.

Wallander climbed into the driver's seat. He heard

a horse whinny behind him. The engine was still running, and he threw it into first gear.

He thought he had lost sight of Ström, but then he saw the car again. It drove through a red light and continued down a narrow street straight towards the cathedral. Wallander was changing gears fast, trying not to lose sight of the car. Horses were whinnying behind him, and he smelled the odour of warm manure.

In a tight curve he almost lost control. He bounced off two parked cars, but finally managed to straighten up.

The chase proceeded towards the hospital and then through an industrial area. Wallander saw that the horsebox was equipped with a phone. He tried dialling the emergency number with one hand while struggling to keep the heavy vehicle on the road.

Just as the emergency operator answered, he had to negotiate a curve. The phone fell from his grasp, and he realised that he wouldn't be able to recover it without stopping.

This is crazy, he thought in desperation. Stark raving mad. And then he remembered his sister. He was supposed to be meeting her at Sturup airport right now.

In the roundabout by the entrance to Staffanstorp the chase ended.

Ström was forced to brake hard to avoid a bus that was heading across his path. He lost control, and the car ran straight into a concrete pillar. Wallander, about a hundred metres behind him, saw flames shooting out of the car. He braked so hard that the horsebox slid into the ditch and toppled over. The back doors flew open and two horses disentangled themselves and galloped away across the fields.

Ström had been flung out of the car on impact. One foot was sliced off. His face had been gashed by shards of glass. Even before he reached him Wallander could tell that he was dead.

People came running from the nearby houses. Cars pulled over to the side of the road. Too late he realised that he had his gun in his hand. A few minutes later the first squad car arrived. Then an ambulance. Wallander showed his identity card and made a call from the squad car. He asked to be put through to Björk.

"Did it go all right?" asked Björk. "Bergman has been picked up and is on the way here. Everything went without a hitch. And the Yugoslav woman is waiting here with her interpreter."

"Send them over to the morgue at Lund General Hospital," said Wallander. "She'll have to identify a corpse. By the way, she's Romanian."

"What the hell do you mean by that?" said Björk.

"Just what I said," replied Wallander and hung up.

At that moment he saw one of the horses come galloping back across the field. It was a beautiful white stallion. He didn't think he'd ever seen such a beautiful horse.

When he got back to Ystad the news of Ström's death had already made the rounds. The woman who was his wife had collapsed, and a doctor refused to let the police interrogate her.

Rydberg told Wallander that Bergman denied everything. He hadn't stolen his own car and then ditched it. He hadn't been at Hageholm. He hadn't visited Ström the night before. He demanded to be taken back to Malmö at once.

"What a damned weasel," said Wallander. "I'll crack him."

"Nobody is doing any cracking here," said Björk. "That ludicrous high-speed chase through Lund has caused enough trouble already. I don't understand why five full-grown policemen can't manage to bring in one unarmed man for questioning. By the way, do you know that one of those horses was run over? Its name was Super Nova, and its owner put a value of a hundred thousand kronor on it."

Wallander felt anger welling up inside him. Why couldn't Björk grasp that it was support he needed? Not this officious whining.

"Now we're going to wait for the Romanian woman's identification," said Björk. "Nobody talks to the press or the media except me."

"Thank heavens for that," said Wallander.

He went back to his office with Rydberg and closed the door.

"Do you have any idea how you look?" Rydberg asked.

"Don't tell me, please."

"Your sister called. I asked Martinsson to drive out and collect her from the airport. I assumed that you had forgotten. He said he'd take care of her until you were free."

Wallander nodded gratefully. A few minutes later, Björk barrelled in.

"The identification is positive," he said. "We've got the murderer we were looking for."

"She recognised him?"

"Not a shadow of a doubt. It was the man who was eating the apple out in the field."

"Who was he?" asked Rydberg.

"Ström called himself a businessman," replied Björk. "He was forty-seven. But the Security Police in Stockholm didn't take long to answer our inquiry. He has been engaged in nationalist movements since the 1960s. First in something called the Democratic Alliance, later in much more militant factions. But how he ended up a cold-blooded murderer is something Bergman may be able to tell us. Or his wife."

Wallander stood up. "Now we'll tackle Bergman," he said.

All three of them went into the room where Bergman sat smoking. Wallander led the interrogation. He went on the offensive at once.

"Do you know what I was doing last night?" he asked.

Bergman gave him a look of contempt. "How would I know that?"

"I tailed you to Lund."

Wallander thought he caught a fleeting shift in the man's face.

"I followed you to Lund," repeated Wallander. "And I climbed up on the scaffolding outside the building where Ström lived. I saw you exchange your shotgun for another one. Now Ström is dead. But a witness has identified him as the murderer at Hageholm. What do you have to say to all that?"

Bergman didn't say anything. He lit another cigarette and stared into space.

"OK, we'll take it from the top," said Wallander. "We know how everything happened. There are only two things we don't know yet. First, what did you do with your car? Second, why did you shoot the Somali?"

Bergman wasn't talking. Just after 3 p.m. he was formally put under arrest and assigned a legal aid lawyer. The charge was murder or accessory to murder.

At 4 p.m. Wallander briefly questioned Valfrid Ström's wife. She was still in shock, but she answered his questions. He learned that Ström imported exclusive cars. She told him that Ström was violently opposed to Sweden's policy on refugees. She had been married to him for just a little over a year. Wallander formed the conviction that she would get over her loss rather quickly.

After the interrogation he talked with Rydberg and Björk. Then they released the woman with a warning not to leave Lund and she was taken home.

Wallander and Rydberg made another attempt to

get Bergman to talk. The legal aid lawyer was young and ambitious, and he claimed that there were no grounds for submission of evidence, and that in his opinion the arrest was equivalent to a preliminary miscarriage of justice.

They talked some more, and Rydberg had an idea.

"Where was Ström trying to escape to?" he asked Wallander.

He pointed at a map.

"The chase ended at Staffanstorp. Maybe he had a warehouse there or somewhere in the vicinity. It's not far from Hageholm, if you know the back roads."

A call to Ström's wife confirmed that Rydberg was on the right track. He did indeed have a warehouse between Staffanstorp and Veberöd. It was where he kept his imported cars. Rydberg drove there in a squad car. Very soon he called Wallander.

"Bingo," he said. "There's a pale-blue Citroën here."

"Maybe we ought to teach our children to identify cars by their sound," said Wallander.

He tackled Bergman again. But the man said nothing.

Rydberg returned to Ystad after a preliminary examination of the Citroën. In the glove compartment he found a box of shotgun shells. In the meantime the police in Malmö and Lund searched Bergman's and Ström's apartments.

"It seems as though these two gentlemen were members of some sort of Swedish Ku Klux Klan movement," said Björk. "I'm afraid this is going to be difficult to untangle. There might be more people involved."

And Bergman still wasn't talking.

Wallander was greatly relieved that Björk was back and could deal with the media. His face stung and burned, and he was very tired. By 6 p.m. he finally had time to call Martinsson and talk to his sister. Then he drove over and picked her up. She was startled when she saw his battered face.

"It might be best if Dad didn't see me," said Wallander. "I'll wait for you in the car."

His sister said she had already visited their father. The old man was still tired, but he brightened up a little when he saw his daughter.

"I don't think he remembers much about that night," she said as they drove up to the hospital.

"Maybe that's just as well."

Wallander sat in the car and waited while she visited their father again. He closed his eyes and listened to a Rossini opera. When she opened the car door, he jumped. He had fallen asleep. Together they drove to the house in Löderup.

Wallander could see that his sister was shocked at their father's decline. Together they cleaned out the stinking rubbish and filthy clothes.

"How could this happen?" she asked, and Wallander felt that she was blaming him.

Maybe she was right. Maybe he could have done

more. At least recognised his father's decline earlier. They stopped and bought groceries and then returned to Mariagatan. Over dinner they talked about what would happen to their father.

"He'll die if we put him in a retirement home," she said.

"What's the alternative?" asked Wallander. "He can't live here. He can't live with you. The house in Löderup won't work either. What's left?"

They agreed that it would be best, all the same, if their father could keep on living in his own house, with regular home visits.

"He has never liked me," said Wallander as they were drinking coffee.

"Of course he does."

"Not since I decided to be a policeman."

"You think maybe he had something else in mind for you?"

"Yes, but what? He's never said."

Wallander made up the sofa for his sister. When they had no more to say about their father, Wallander told her everything that had happened. And in the telling he realised that the old sense of intimacy, which had always bound them before, was gone. We haven't seen each other often enough, he thought. She doesn't even dare ask me why Mona and I went our separate ways.

He brought out a half-empty bottle of cognac. She shook her head, so he poured one for himself.

The late news was dominated by the story of Ström.

Bergman's identity was not revealed. Wallander knew that it was because of his having been a policeman. He assumed that the chief of the national police was hard at work setting out the necessary smoke screens so they could keep Bergman's identity secret for as long as possible. Sooner or later, of course, the truth would have to come out.

When the news was finished, the telephone rang.

Wallander asked his sister to answer it. "Find out who it is and say you'll check to see if I'm home," he told her.

"It's someone called Brolin," she said when she came back from the corridor.

Painfully, he got up from his chair and took the telephone.

"I hope I didn't wake you," said Anette Brolin.

"Not at all. My sister is visiting."

"I just thought I'd call and say that I think all of you did an extraordinary job."

"Mostly we were lucky."

Why is she calling? he wondered. He made a quick decision.

"How about a drink?" he suggested.

"Great. Where?" He could hear that she was surprised.

"My sister is just going to bed. How about your place?"

"That's fine."

He hung up and went back into the living room.

"I wasn't planning to go to bed at all," said his sister.

"I have to go out for a while. Don't wait up for me. I don't know how long I'll be."

The cool evening made it easy to breathe. He turned down Regementsgatan and felt a sudden sense of relief. They had solved the murder in Hageholm within forty-eight hours. Now they had to turn their attention back to the murders in Lunnarp.

He knew that he'd done a good job. He had trusted his intuition, acted without hesitation, and it had produced results. The thought of the crazy chase with the horsebox gave him the shakes. But the relief was still there.

Anette Brolin lived on the third floor of a turn-of-the-century building. He called her on the intercom and she answered. The flat was large but sparsely furnished. Against one wall were several paintings still waiting to be hung up.

"Gin and tonic?" she asked. "I'm afraid I don't have much of a selection."

"Please," he said. "Right now anything is fine. Just so as long as it's strong."

She sat down across from him on a sofa and pulled her legs up under her. He thought she was extremely beautiful.

"Do you have any idea how you look?" she asked with a laugh.

"A lot of people ask me that," he replied.

Then he remembered Klas Månson. The man who robbed the shop, whom Anette Brolin had refused to detain. He really didn't think he should talk about work, but he couldn't help it.

"Klas Månson," he said. "Do you remember that name?"

She nodded.

"Hansson told me that you thought our investigation was poor. That you didn't intend to apply for Månson's remand in custody to be extended unless it was done more carefully."

"The investigation was poor, sloppily written. Insufficient evidence. Vague testimony. I'd be in dereliction of my duty if I sought further detention based on material like that."

"The investigation was no worse than most. Besides, you forgot one important fact."

"What was that?"

"That Klas Månson is a guilty man. He's robbed shops before."

"Then you'll have to come up with better investigative work."

"I don't think there's anything wrong with the report. If we let the man loose, he'll just commit more crimes."

"You can't just put people in jail willy-nilly."

Wallander shrugged. "Will you hold off releasing him if I rustle up some more exhaustive testimony?" he asked.

"That depends on what the witness says."

"Why are you so stubborn? Månson is guilty. If we just hold him for a while, he'll confess. But if he has the slightest inkling that he can get out, he'll clam up."

"Prosecutors have to be stubborn. Otherwise what do you think would happen to law and order in this country?"

Wallander could feel that the gin had made him reckless.

"That question can also be asked by an insignificant, provincial police detective," he said. "Once I believed that being on the force meant that you were involved in protecting the property and safety of ordinary people. Probably I still believe it. But I've seen law and order being eroded away. I've seen young people who commit crimes being almost encouraged to continue. No one intervenes. No one cares about the increasing number of victims. It just gets worse and worse."

"Now you sound like my father," she said. "He's a retired judge. A true old-fashioned, reactionary civil servant."

"Could be. Maybe I am conservative. But I mean what I say. I actually understand why people sometimes take matters into their own hands."

"So you probably also understand how some misguided individuals can fatally shoot an innocent asylum seeker?"

"Yes and no. The insecurity in this country is enormous. People are afraid. Especially in farming communities like this one. You'll soon find out that there's a big hero right now at this end of the country. A man who is applauded behind drawn curtains. The man who saw to it that there was a municipal vote that said no to accepting refugees."

"So what happens if we put ourselves above the decisions of parliament? We have a policy for refugees in this country and it must be adhered to."

"Wrong. It's precisely the absence of a clear policy on refugees that creates chaos. Right now we're living in a country where anyone for any reason can come across the border in any manner. Control has been eliminated. The customs service is paralysed. There are plenty of unsupervised airfields where the dope and the illegal immigrants are unloaded every night."

He was aware that he was losing his cool. The murder of the Somali was a crime with many layers.

"Bergman, of course, must be locked up with the most severe punishment," he went on. "But the Immigration Service and the government have to take their share of the blame."

"That's nonsense."

"Is it? People who belonged to the fascist secret police in Romania are starting to show up here in Sweden. Seeking asylum. Should it be granted to them?"

"The principle has to apply equally."

"Does it really? Always? Even when it's wrong?"

She got up from the sofa and refilled their glasses. Wallander was starting to feel depressed. We're too different, he thought. We talk for ten minutes and a chasm opens.

He felt aggressive. And he looked at her and could feel himself getting aroused. How long was it since the last time he and Mona had made love? A year ago almost. A whole year with no sex.

He groaned at the thought.

"Are you in pain?" she asked.

He nodded. He wasn't, but he yielded to his desire for sympathy.

"Maybe it would be best if you went home," she said.

That was the last thing he wanted to do. He didn't feel that he even had a home since Mona moved out. He finished his drink and held out his glass for a refill. Now he was so intoxicated that he was starting to shed his inhibitions.

"One more," he said. "I've earned it."

"Then you have to go," she said.

Her voice had suddenly turned cool. But he didn't let it bother him. When she brought his glass, he grabbed her and pulled her down in the chair.

"Sit here by me," he said, laying his hand on her thigh.

She pulled herself free and slapped him. She hit him with the hand with the wedding ring, and he could feel it tear his cheek.

"Go home now," she said.

He put his glass down on the table. "Or you'll do what?" he asked. "Call the police?"

She didn't answer, but he could see that she was furious. He stumbled when he stood up. Suddenly he realised what he had tried to do.

"Forgive me," he said. "I'm exhausted."

"We'll forget all about this," she replied. "But now you have to go home."

"I don't know what came over me," he said, putting out his hand.

She took it.

"We'll just forget it," she said. "Good night."

He tried to think of something more to say. Somewhere in his muddled consciousness the thought gnawed at him that he had done something both unforgivable and dangerous. Just as he had driven his car home from the meeting with Mona when he was drunk. He left, and heard the door close behind him.

I have to stop drinking, he thought angrily. I can't handle it. Down on the street he sucked the cool air deep into his lungs.

How the hell could anyone be so stupid? he thought. No better than a drunken boy who doesn't know a thing about himself, women, or the world.

He went home to Mariagatan. The next day he would have to get back onto the hunt for the Lunnarp killers.

CHAPTER 13

Early on Monday morning, January 15, Wallander drove out to the shopping centre on the Malmö road and bought two bouquets of flowers. Just over a week earlier he had driven the same road, towards Lunnarp and the scene of the crime that was still demanding all of his attention. The past week had been the most intense of his career. When he looked at his face in the rearview mirror, he thought that every scratch, every lump, every discolouration from purple to black, was a memento of the week's events.

It was −6° C. There was no wind. The white ferry from Poland was making its way into the harbour.

When Wallander arrived at the police station a little after 8 a.m., he gave one of the bouquets to Ebba. At first she refused to take it, but he could see that she was pleased. He took the other bouquet with him to his office. He took a card from his desk drawer and pondered a long time what to write to Anette Brolin. Too long. By the time he managed a few lines, he had abandoned all attempts to find the perfect words. He simply apologised for his rash behaviour the night before. He blamed his rashness on fatigue.

"I'm actually quite shy by nature," he wrote. Which was not entirely true. But he thought this might give Anette Brolin the opportunity to turn the other cheek.

He was on the point of going over to the prosecutor's office when Björk came in. As usual, he had knocked so softly that Wallander hadn't heard him.

"Somebody sent you flowers?" said Björk. "You deserve them, as a matter of fact. I'm impressed how quickly you solved the murder of the Negro."

Wallander disliked Björk referring to the Somali as the Negro. A person lying under that tarpaulin was what there had been. But he had no intention of getting into an argument about it.

Björk was wearing a flowery shirt that he had bought in Spain. He sat down on the rickety wooden chair near the window.

"I thought we ought to go over the murders at Lunnarp," he said. "I've looked through the investigation reports. There seem to be a lot of gaps. I've been thinking that Rydberg should take over the primary responsibility for the investigation while you concentrate on getting Bergman to talk. What do you think about that?"

Wallander countered with a question. "What does Rydberg say?"

"I haven't talked to him yet."

"I think we should do it the other way around. Rydberg has a bad leg, and there's still a lot of footwork to be done in that investigation."

What Wallander said was true enough, but it wasn't concern for Rydberg's rheumatism that made him suggest reversing the responsibilities. He didn't want to give up the hunt for the Lunnarp killers. Police work was a team effort, but he thought of the murderers as belonging to him.

"There's a third option," said Björk. "We could let Svedberg and Hansson handle Bergman."

Wallander nodded. He'd go along with that.

Björk got up from the rickety chair.

"We need some new furniture," he said.

"We need more manpower," replied Wallander.

After Björk had left, Wallander sat down at his typewriter and typed up a comprehensive report on the arrest of Rune Bergman and the death of Valfrid Ström. He made a particular effort to compile something that Anette Brolin would not object to. It took him over two hours. Finally, he pulled the last page out of the typewriter, signed it, and took it to Rydberg.

Rydberg was sitting at his desk. He looked tired. When Wallander came into his office, he was just putting the telephone down.

"I hear that Björk wants to split us up," he said. "I'm glad to be spared dealing with Bergman."

Wallander put his report on the desk. "Read through

it," he said. "If you have no quarrel with it, give it to Hansson."

"Svedberg had a go at Bergman this morning," said Rydberg. "But he still refuses to talk. Even though the cigarettes match. The same brand that was lying in the mud next to where the car must have been."

"I wonder what's going to turn up," said Wallander. "What's behind this whole thing? Neo-Nazis? Racists with connections all over Europe? Why would someone commit a crime like this anyway? Jump out into the road and shoot a complete stranger? Just because he happened to be black?"

"No way of knowing," said Rydberg. "But it's something we're going to have to learn to live with."

They agreed to meet again in half an hour, after Rydberg had been through the report. Then they would start on the Lunnarp investigation in earnest.

Wallander went over to the prosecutor's office. Anette Brolin was in district court. He left the flowers with the young woman at reception.

"Is it her birthday?" she asked.

"Sort of," said Wallander.

When he got back to his office, Kristina was waiting for him. She had already left the flat by the time he woke up that morning. She told him that she had talked to both a doctor and the social worker.

"Dad seems better," she said. "They don't think he's slipping into chronic senility. Maybe it was just a temporary period of confusion. We agreed to try regular home care. I was thinking about asking you to drive us out there around midday today. If you can't do it, maybe I could borrow your car."

"Of course I can drive you. Who's going to do the home care?"

"I'm supposed to have a meeting with a woman who doesn't live far from Dad."

Wallander nodded. "I'm glad you're here. I couldn't have handled this alone."

They agreed that he would come to the hospital right after midday. After his sister left, Wallander straightened up his desk and placed the thick folder of material on the Lövgren case in front of him. It was time to get started.

Björk had told him that for the time being, there would be four people on the investigative team. Since Näslund was laid up with the flu, only three of them were at the case meeting in Rydberg's office. Martinsson had nothing to say and seemed to have a hangover. But Wallander remembered the decisive manner with which he had taken care of the hysterical widow at Hageholm.

They began with a thorough review of all the material. Martinsson was able to add information produced by his work with the central criminal records. Wallander felt a great sense of security in this methodical and meticulous scrutiny of details. To an outside observer such work would probably seem unbearably tedious. But that was not the case for the three police officers. The solution and the truth might be found through the combination of the most inconsequential information.

They isolated the loose ends that had to be dealt with first.

"You take Lövgren's trip to Ystad," Wallander said to Martinsson. "We need to know how he got to town and how he got home. Are there other safe-deposit boxes? What did he do during the hour between his appearances at the two banks? Did he go into a shop and buy something? Who saw him?"

"I think Näslund has already started calling around the banks," said Martinsson.

"Call him at home and find out," said Wallander. "This can't wait until he's feeling better."

Rydberg was to pay a visit to Lars Herdin and Wallander to drive over to Malmö again to talk to the man called Erik Magnusson, the one Göran Boman thought might be Lövgren's secret son.

"All the other items will have to wait," said Wallander. "We'll start with these and meet again at five o'clock."

Before he left for the hospital, Wallander called Boman in Kristianstad.

"Erik Magnusson works for the county council," said Boman. "Unfortunately, I haven't discovered exactly what he does. We've had an unusually rowdy weekend up here with a lot of fights and drunkenness. I haven't had time for much besides hauling people in."

"No problem. I'll find him," said Wallander. "I'll call you tomorrow morning at the latest."

Just after midday he set off for the hospital. His sister was waiting in reception. They took the lift up to the ward where their father had been moved after the first twenty four hours of observation.

By the time they arrived, he had already been discharged and was sitting in the corridor, waiting for them. He had his hat on, and the suitcase full of dirty underwear and tubes of paint was by his side. Wallander didn't recognise the suit he was wearing.

"I bought it for him," his sister said. "It must be thirty years since he bought himself a new suit."

"How are you, Dad?" asked Wallander.

His father looked him in the eye. Wallander could see that he had recovered.

"It'll be nice to get back home," he said curtly and stood up.

Wallander picked up the suitcase as his father leaned on Kristina's arm. She sat with him in the back seat on the drive to Löderup.

Wallander, who was in a hurry to get to Malmö, promised to come back around 6 p.m. His sister was going to stay the night, and she asked him to buy food for dinner. His father had immediately changed out of his suit and into his painting overalls. He was already at his easel, working on the unfinished painting.

"Do you think he'll be able to get by with home care?" asked Wallander.

"We'll have to wait and see," replied his sister.

It was almost 2 p.m. when Wallander pulled up in front of the county council's main building in Malmö. He parked his car and went into the large reception area.

"I'm looking for Erik Magnusson," he told the woman who shoved the glass window open.

"We have at least three Erik Magnussons working here," she said. "Which one are you looking for?"

Wallander took out his police identity card and showed it to her.

"I don't know," he said. "But he was born in the late 1950s."

The woman behind the glass knew at once who it was.

"Then it must be Erik Magnusson in central supply," she said. "The two other Erik Magnussons are much older. What did he do?"

Wallander smiled at her undisguised curiosity.

"Nothing," he said. "I just want to ask him some questions."

She told him how to get to central supply. He thanked her and returned to his car. The county council's supply warehouse was located on the northern outskirts, near the Oil Harbour. Wallander wandered around for a long time before he found the right place.

He went through a door marked *Office*. Through a big glass window he could see yellow forklift trucks driving back and forth between long rows of shelves.

The office was empty. He went down some stairs

and into the enormous warehouse. A young man with hair down to his shoulders was piling up big plastic sacks of toilet paper. Wallander went over to him.

"I'm looking for Erik Magnusson," he said.

The young man pointed to a yellow forklift which had stopped next to a loading dock where a van was being unloaded.

The man in the cab of the yellow forklift had fair hair. It seemed unlikely that Maria Lövgren would have thought about foreigners if this blond man was the one who put the noose around her neck. He pushed the thought away with annoyance. He was getting ahead of himself again.

"Erik Magnusson!" he shouted over the engine noise. The man gave him an inquiring look before he turned off the engine and jumped down.

"Erik Magnusson?" asked Wallander.

"Yes?"

"I'm a policeman. I'd like to have a word with you for a moment."

Wallander scrutinised his face. There was nothing unexpected about his reaction. He merely looked surprised. Quite naturally surprised.

"Why is that?" he asked.

Wallander looked around. "Is there somewhere we can sit down?" he asked.

Magnusson led the way to a corner with a coffee vending machine. There was a dirty wooden table and several makeshift benches. Wallander fed two one-krona coins into the machine and got a cup of coffee. Magnusson settled for a pinch of snuff.

"I'm from the police in Ystad," he began. "I have a few questions for you regarding a particularly nasty murder in a village called Lunnarp. Maybe you read about it in the papers?"

"I think so. But what does that have to do with me?"

Wallander was beginning to wonder the same thing. The man named Erik Magnusson seemed completely unruffled by a visit from the police at his place of work.

"I have to ask you for the name of your father."

The man frowned.

"My dad?" he said. "I don't have a dad."

"Everybody has one."

"Not one that I know about, at any rate."

"How can that be?"

"Mum wasn't married when I was born."

"And she never told you who your father was?"

"No."

"Did you ever ask her?"

"Of course I've asked her. I bugged her about it my whole childhood. Then I gave up."

"What did she say when you asked her about it?"

Magnusson stood up and pressed the button for a cup of coffee. "Why are you asking about my dad? Does he have something to do with the murder?"

"I'll get to that in a minute," said Wallander. "What did your mother say when you asked her about your father?"

"It varied."

"How do you mean?"

"Sometimes she would say that she didn't really know. Sometimes that it was a salesman she never saw again. Sometimes something else."

"And you were satisfied with that?"

"What the hell was I supposed to do? If she won't tell me, she won't tell me."

Wallander thought about the answers he was getting. Was it really possible to be so uninterested in who your father was?

"Do you get along well with your mother?" he asked.

"What do you mean by that?"

"Do you see each other often?"

"She calls me now and then. I drive over to Kristianstad once in a while. I got along better with my stepfather."

Wallander gave a start. Boman had said nothing about a stepfather.

"Is your mother remarried?"

"She lived with a man while I was growing up. They probably weren't ever married. But I still called him my dad. Then they split up when I was about fifteen. I moved to Malmö a year later."

"What's his name?"

"*Was* his name. He's dead. He was killed in a car crash."

"And you're sure that he wasn't your real father?"

"You'd have to look hard to find two people as unlike each other as we were."

Wallander tried a different tack. "The man who was murdered at Lunnarp was named Johannes Lövgren," he said. "Is it possible that he might have been your father?"

The man sitting across from Wallander gave him a look of surprise.

"How the hell would I know? You'll have to ask my mother."

"We've already done that. But she denies it."

"So ask her again. I'd like to know who my father is. Murdered or not."

Wallander believed him. He wrote down Magnusson's address and personal identity number and then stood up.

"You may hear from us again," he said.

The man climbed back into the cab of the forklift.

"That's fine with me," he said. "Say hello to my mum if you see her."

Wallander returned to Ystad. He parked near the square and headed down the street to buy some gauze bandages at the chemist. The salesman gazed sympathetically at his battered face. He bought food for dinner in the supermarket on the square. On his way back to the car he changed his mind and retraced his steps to the state liquor outlet. There he bought a bottle of whisky. Even though he couldn't really afford it, he chose malt.

By late afternoon Wallander was back at the station. Neither Rydberg nor Martinsson was there. He went over to the prosecutor's office. The girl at the reception desk smiled.

"She loved the flowers," she said.

"Is she in her office?"

"She's in district court."

Wallander headed back. In the corridor he ran into Svedberg.

"How's it going with Bergman?" asked Wallander.

"He's still not talking," said Svedberg. "But he'll soften up eventually. The evidence is piling up. The laboratory technicians think they can connect the weapon to the crime."

"What else have we got on this?"

"It looks as if Ström and Bergman were both active in a number of nationalist groups. But we don't know whether they were operating on their own or were acting under the instruction of an organisation."

"In other words, everybody is perfectly happy?"

"I'd hardly say that. Björk was saying how anxious he was to catch the murderer, but then it turned out to be a policeman. I suspect they're going to play down Bergman's importance and dump it all on Ström, who has nothing more to say about it. Personally, I think Bergman was equally up to his neck in the whole thing."

"I wonder whether Ström was the one who called me at home," said Wallander. "I never heard him say enough to tell for sure."

Svedberg gave him a searching look. "Which means?"

"That in the worst case, there are others who are prepared to take over the killing from Bergman and Ström."

"I'll tell Björk that we have to continue our patrols of the camps," said Svedberg. "By the way, we have a number of tip-offs indicating that it was a gang of youths who set the fire here in Ystad."

"Don't forget the old man who got a sack of turnips in the head," said Wallander.

"How's it going with Lunnarp?"

Wallander hesitated with his answer. "I'm not really sure," he said. "But we're doing some serious work on it again."

At 5:30 p.m. Martinsson and Rydberg were in Wallander's office. He thought that Rydberg still looked tired and worn-out. Martinsson was in a bad mood.

"It's a mystery how Lövgren got to Ystad and back again on Thursday the fourth of January," he said. "I talked to the bus driver on that route. He said that Johannes and Maria used to ride with him whenever they went into town. Either together or separately. He was absolutely certain that Johannes Lövgren did not ride in his bus anytime after New Year's. And no taxi had a fare to Lunnarp. According to Nyström, they took the bus whenever they had to go anywhere. And we know that Lövgren was tightfisted."

"They always drank coffee together," said Wallander.

"In the afternoon. The Nyströms must have noticed if Lövgren went off to Ystad or not."

"That's exactly what's such a mystery," said Martinsson. "Both of them claim that he didn't go into town that day. And yet we know that he went to two different banks between 11:30 a.m. and 1:15 p.m. He must have been gone from home at least three or four hours."

"Strange," said Wallander. "You'll have to keep working on it."

Martinsson referred to his notes. "At any rate, he doesn't have any other safe-deposit boxes in town."

"Good," said Wallander. "At least we know that much."

"But he might have one in Simrishamn," Martinsson said. "Or Trelleborg. Or Malmö."

"Let's concentrate on his trip to Ystad first," said Wallander, turning to Rydberg.

"Herdin stands by his story," he said after glancing at his worn notebook. "Quite by chance he ran into Lövgren and the woman in Kristianstad in the spring of 1979. And he says that it was from an anonymous letter that he found out they had a child together."

"Could he describe the woman?"

"Vaguely. In the worst case we could line up all the ladies and have him point out the right one. If she's one of them, that is," he added.

"You sound as though you have some doubt."

Rydberg closed his notebook with an irritable snap.

"I can't get anything to fit," he said. "You know that. Obviously we have to follow up the leads we have. But I'm not at all sure that we're on the right track. What bothers me is that I can't see an alternative path to take."

Wallander told them about his meeting with Erik Magnusson.

"Why didn't you ask him for an alibi for the night of the murder?" wondered Martinsson in surprise.

Wallander felt himself starting to blush behind his black and blue marks. It had slipped his mind. But he didn't tell them that.

"I decided to wait," he said. "I wanted to have an excuse to visit him again."

He could hear how lame that sounded. But neither Rydberg nor Martinsson appeared to react to his explanation. The conversation came to a halt. Each was wrapped up in his own thoughts. Wallander wondered how many times he had found himself in exactly this same situation. When an investigation suddenly ceases to breathe. Like a horse that refuses to budge. Now they would be forced to tug and pull at the horse until it started to move.

"How should we continue?" asked Wallander at last, when the silence became too oppressive.

He answered his own question. "For your part, Martinsson, it's a matter of finding out how Lövgren could go to Ystad and back without anyone noticing. We have to work that out as soon as possible."

"There was a jar full of receipts in one of the kitchen cupboards," said Rydberg. "He might have bought something in a shop on that Friday. Maybe a salesman would remember seeing him."

"Or maybe he had a flying carpet," said Martinsson. "I'll keep working on it."

"His relatives," said Wallander. "We have to go through all of them."

He pulled out a list of names and addresses from the thick folder and handed it to Rydberg.

"The funeral is on Wednesday," said Rydberg. "In Villie Church. I don't care much for funerals. But I think I'll go to this one."

"I'm going back to Kristianstad tomorrow," said Wallander. "Boman was suspicious of Ellen Magnusson. He didn't think she was telling the truth."

It was just before 6 p.m. when they finished their meeting. They decided to meet again on the following afternoon.

"If Näslund is feeling better, he can work on the stolen rental car," said Wallander. "By the way, did we ever find out what that Polish family is doing in Lunnarp?"

"The husband works at the sugar refinery in Jordberga," said Rydberg. "All his papers are in order. Even though he wasn't fully aware of it himself."

Wallander sat in his office for a while after Rydberg and Martinsson left. There was a stack of papers on his desk that he was supposed to go through, including all the material from the assault case he had been working on over New Year's. There were also reports pertaining to everything from missing bullocks to lorries that had tipped over during the last storm. At the bottom of the stack he found a note informing him that he had been given a pay raise. He worked out that he would be taking home an extra 39 kronor per month.

By the time he had made his way through the pile of papers, it was almost 7:30 p.m. He called Löderup and told his sister that he was on his way.

"We're starving," she said. "Do you always work this late?"

Wallander selected a cassette of a Puccini opera and went out to his car. He had wanted to make sure that Anette Brolin had put out of her mind what had happened the night before after all. But this would have to wait.

Kristina told him that the help for their father had turned out to be a solid woman in her fifties who would have no trouble taking care of him.

"He couldn't ask for anyone better," she said when she came out to the driveway and met him in the dark.

"What's Dad doing?"

"He's painting," she said.

While his sister made dinner, Wallander sat on the toboggan in the studio and watched the autumn motif emerge. His father seemed to have completely forgotten about what had happened.

I have to visit him more regularly, thought Wallander. At least three times a week, and preferably at specific times.

After dinner they played cards with their father for a couple of hours. At 11 p.m. he went to bed.

"I'm going home tomorrow," said Kristina. "I can't be away any longer."

"Thanks for coming," said Wallander.

They decided that he would pick her up at 8 a.m. the next morning and drive her to the airport.

"The plane was full out of Sturup," she said. "I'm leaving from Everöd."

That suited Wallander just fine, since he had to drive to Kristianstad anyway.

Just after midnight he walked into his apartment on Mariagatan. He poured himself a big glass of whisky and took it with him into the bathroom. He lay in the bath for a long time, thawing out his limbs in the hot water.

He tried to push them away, but Rune Bergman and Valfrid Ström kept popping into his thoughts. He was trying to understand. The only thing he came up with was the same idea he had had so many times before. A new world had emerged, and he hadn't even noticed it. As a policeman, he still lived in another, older world. How was he going to learn to live in the new? How would he deal with the great uneasiness he felt at these changes, at so much happening so fast?

The murder of the Somali had been a new kind of

murder. The double murder in Lunnarp, however, was an old-fashioned crime. Or was it really? He thought about the savagery, and the noose. He wasn't sure.

It was 1:30 a.m. when finally he crawled between the chilly sheets. He felt more lonely there than ever.

For the next three days nothing happened. Näslund came back to work and succeeded in solving the problem of the stolen car. A man and a woman went on a robbery spree and then left the car in Halmstad. On the night of the murder they had been staying in a boarding house in Båstad. The owner vouched for their alibi.

Göran Boman talked to Ellen Magnusson. She resolutely denied that Johannes Lövgren was the father of her son.

Wallander visited Erik Magnusson again and asked for the alibi he had forgotten to get during their first encounter. He had been with his fiancée. There was no reason to doubt him. Martinsson got nowhere with Lövgren's trip to Ystad. The Nyströms were quite sure about their story, as were the bus drivers and taxi companies. Rydberg went to the funeral, and talked to nineteen different relatives of the Lövgrens.

Nothing gave them any leads.

The temperature hovered around freezing point. One day there was no wind, the next day it was gusty. Wallander ran into Anette Brolin in the corridor. She thanked him for the flowers. But he couldn't be certain that she really had decided to forget about what had happened that night.

Bergman still refused to talk, even though the evidence against him was overwhelming. Various extreme nationalist movements tried to take credit for the crime. The press and the rest of the media became involved in a violent debate about Sweden's immigration policy. Although all was calm in Skåne, crosses burned in the night outside various refugee camps in other parts of the country.

Wallander and his colleagues on the investigative team shielded themselves from all of this. Only rarely were any opinions expressed that were not directly related to the deadlocked investigation. But Wallander realised that he was not alone in his feelings of uncertainty and confusion at the new society that was emerging.

We live as if we were in mourning for a lost paradise, he thought. As if we longed for the car thieves and safecrackers of the old days, who doffed their caps and behaved like gentlemen when we came to take them in. But those days have irretrievably vanished, and nor is it certain that they were as idyllic as we remember them.

Then on Friday, January 19, everything happened at once.

The day did not start off well for Wallander. At 7:30 a.m. he had his Peugeot checked out and barely managed to avoid having it declared unfit for the road. When he went through the inspection report, he saw that his car needed repairs that would cost thousands of kronor. Despondent, he drove to the police station.

He hadn't even taken off his overcoat when Martinsson came storming into his office.

"Damn it," he said. "I know how Johannes Lövgren got to Ystad and back home again."

Wallander forgot all about his car and felt himself instantly seized with excitement.

"It wasn't a flying carpet, after all," continued Martinsson. "The chimney sweep drove him."

Wallander sat down in his desk chair.

"What chimney sweep?"

"Master chimney sweep Arthur Lundin from Slimminge. Out of the blue Hanna Nyström has remembered that the chimney sweep had been there that Thursday, January 4. He cleaned the chimneys at both houses and then left. When she told me that he cleaned the Lövgrens' flues second and that he left around 10:30 a.m., bells started to go off in my head. I just talked to him. He was cleaning the hospital chimney in Rydsgård. It turned out that he never listens to the radio or watches TV or reads the papers. He cleans chimneys and spends the rest of his time drinking aquavit and looking after pet rabbits. He had no idea that the Lövgrens had been murdered. But he told me that he gave Johannes Lövgren a lift into Ystad. Since he has a van and Lövgren was sitting in the windowless back seat, it's not so strange that nobody saw him."

"But didn't the Nyströms see the car coming back?"

"No," replied Martinsson triumphantly. "That's just it. Lövgren asked Lundin to stop on Veberöds-vägen. From there you can walk along a dirt road right up to the back of Lövgren's house. It's about a kilo-metre. If the Nyströms were sitting in the window, it would have looked as if Lövgren were coming in from the stable."

Wallander frowned. "It still seems odd."

"Lundin was very frank. He said that Lövgren promised him a bottle of vodka if he would drive him home. He let Lövgren out in Ystad and then went on to a couple of houses north of town.

"He picked up him up at the agreed time, dropped him off on Veberödsvägen, and got his bottle of vodka."

"Good," said Wallander. "Do the times match up?"

"They fit perfectly."

"Did you ask him about the briefcase?"

"Lundin seemed to remember that he had a brief-case with him."

"Did he have anything else?"

"Lundin didn't think so."

"Did he see whether Lövgren met anybody in Ystad?"

"No."

"Had Lövgren said anything about what he was going to do in town?"

"No, nothing."

"And you don't think that this chimney sweep knew about Lövgren having 27,000 kronor in his briefcase?"

"Hardly. He seemed the least likely person to be a robber. I think he's just a solitary chimney sweep who lives contentedly with his rabbits and his aquavit. That's all."

Wallander thought for a moment. "Do you think Lövgren could have arranged a meeting with someone on that dirt road? Since the briefcase is gone."

"Maybe. I was thinking of taking a dog patrol out there."

"Do it right away," said Wallander. "Maybe we're at last getting somewhere."

Martinsson left the office. He almost collided with Hansson, who was on his way in.

"Do you have a minute?" he asked.

Wallander nodded. "How's it going?"

"He's not talking. But he's been linked to the crime. That bitch Brolin is going to remand him today."

Wallander didn't feel like commenting on Hansson's contemptuous opinion of Anette Brolin.

"What do you want?" he asked.

Hansson sat down on the wooden chair near the window, looking ill at ease.

"You probably know that I play the horses a bit," he began. "By the way, the horse you recommended came last by a street. Who gave you that tip?"

Wallander vaguely recalled a remark he had made

one time in Hansson's office. "It was just a joke," he said. "Go on."

"There's a chap named Erik Magnusson who often shows up at Jägersrö. He bets big time, loses a bundle, and I happen to know that he works for the county council."

Wallander was immediately interested.

"How old is he? What does he look like?"

Hansson described him. Wallander knew at once that it was the man he had met.

"There are rumours that he's in debt," said Hansson. "And gambling debts can be dangerous."

"Good," said Wallander. "That's exactly the kind of information we need."

Hansson stood up. "You never know," he said. "Gambling and drugs can sometimes have the same effect. Unless you're like me and just gamble for the fun of it."

Wallander thought about something Rydberg had said. About people who, because of a drug dependency, were capable of unlimited brutality.

"Good," he said to Hansson. "Excellent."

Hansson left the office. Wallander thought for a moment and then called Boman in Kristianstad. He was in luck and got hold of him at once.

"What do you want me to do?" he asked after Wallander had given him Hansson's news.

"Run the vacuum cleaner over him," said Wallander. "And keep an eye on her."

Boman promised to put Ellen Magnusson under surveillance.

Wallander got hold of Hansson just as he was on his way out of the station.

"Gambling debts," he said. "Who would he owe the money to?"

Hansson knew the answer. "There's a man from Tågarp who lends money," he said. "If Magnusson owes money to anybody, it would be him. He's a loan shark for a lot of the high rollers at Jägersrö. And as far as I know, he's got some really unpleasant types working for him that he sends out with reminders to people who are lax with their payments."

"Where can I get hold of him?"

"He's got a hardware shop in Tågarp. A short, hefty guy in his sixties."

"What's his name?"

"Larson. But people call him the Junkman."

Wallander went back to his office. He tried to find Rydberg. Ebba, who was on the switchboard, knew where he was. He wasn't due in until 10 a.m., because he was at the hospital.

"Is he ill?" wondered Wallander.

"It's probably his rheumatism," said Ebba. "Haven't you noticed how he's been limping this winter?"

Wallander decided not to wait for Rydberg. He put on his coat, went out to his car, and drove to Tågarp.

The hardware shop was in the middle of the town. It was advertising a sale on wheelbarrows. The man who came out of the back room when the bell rang was indeed short and hefty. Wallander was the only person in the shop; he decided to get right to the point. He took out his identity card. The Junkman studied it carefully but seemed totally unaffected.

"Ystad," he said. "What can the police from Ystad want with me?"

"Do you know a man named Erik Magnusson?"

The man behind the counter was much too experienced to lie.

"Could be. Why?"

"When did you first meet him?"

Wrong question, thought Wallander. It gives him the chance to retreat.

"I don't remember."

"But you do know him?"

"We have a few common interests."

"Such as betting on the horses?"

"That's possible."

Wallander felt provoked by the man's overbearing self-confidence.

"Listen," he said. "I know that you lend money to people who can't control their gambling. Right now I'm not thinking of asking about the interest rates you charge on your loans. I don't give a damn about your involvement in an illegal money-lending operation. I want to know about something else entirely."

The Junkman looked at him with curiosity.

"I want to know whether Erik Magnusson owes you money," he said. "And I want to know how much."

"Nothing," replied the man.

"Nothing?"

"Not a single öre."

Dead end, thought Wallander. Hansson's lead was a dead end.

"But if you want to know, he did owe me money," said the man.

"How much?"

"A lot. But he paid up 25,000 kronor."

"When?"

The man made a swift calculation. "A little over a week ago. The Thursday before last."

Thursday, January 11, thought Wallander. They were finally on the right track.

"How did he pay you?"

"He came over here."

"In what denominations?"

"Thousands. Five hundreds."

"Where did he have the money?"

"What do you mean?"

"In a bag? A briefcase?"

"In a plastic grocery bag. From I.C.A., I think."

"Was he late paying?"

"A little."

"What would have happened if he hadn't paid?"

"I would have had to send him a reminder."

"Do you know how he came up with the money?"

The Junkman shrugged. At that moment a customer came into the shop.

"That's none of my business," he said. "Will there
be anything else?"

"No, thanks. Not at the moment. But you may hear
from me again."

Wallander went out to his car. The wind had picked
up. OK, he thought. Now we've got him. Who would
have thought that something good would come out of
Hansson's lousy gambling? Wallander drove back to
Ystad feeling as if he had won the lottery. He was on
the scent of an answer.

Erik Magnusson, he thought. Here we come.

CHAPTER 14

After intensive work that dragged on until late into the night of Friday, January 19, Wallander and his colleagues were ready for battle. Björk had sat in on the long case meeting, and at Wallander's request he had let Hansson put aside work on the murder in Hageholm so he could join the Lunnarp group, as they now called themselves. Näslund was off ill again, but he rang in and said he'd be there the next day.

In spite of the weekend, the work had to continue with undiminished effort. Martinsson had returned with a dog patrol from a detailed inspection of the dirt road that led from Veberödsvägen to the back of Lövgren's stable. He had made a meticulous examination of the road, which ran for nearly two kilometres through a couple of copses, divided two pieces of pasture land as the boundary line, and then ran parallel to an almost dry creek bed. He hadn't found anything out of the ordinary, even though he came back to the station with a plastic bag full of bits and pieces. Among other things, there was a rusty wheel from a doll's pram, a greasy sheet of plastic, and an empty cigarette pack of a foreign brand. The objects would be examined, but Wallander didn't think they would produce anything of use to the investigation.

The most important decision during the meeting was that Magnusson would be placed under round-the-clock surveillance. He lived in a rented house in the old Rosengård district. Hansson reported that there were trotting races at Jägersrö on Sunday, and he was assigned the surveillance during the races.

"But I'm not authorising any bets," said Björk, in a half-hearted attempt at a joke.

"I propose that we all go in," replied Hansson. "There's good odds that this murder investigation could pay off."

But it was a serious mood that prevailed in Björk's office. There was a feeling that a decisive moment was approaching.

The question that aroused the longest discussion concerned whether Magnusson should be told that they were onto him. Both Rydberg and Björk were skeptical. But Wallander thought that they had nothing to lose if Magnusson discovered that he was the object of police interest. The surveillance would be discreet, of course. But beyond that, no measures would be taken to hide the fact that he was the subject of an investigation.

"Let him get nervous," said Wallander. "If he has anything to be nervous about, then I hope we discover what it is."

It took three hours to go through all the investigative material to look for threads that could be tied to Magnusson. They found nothing, but they also found nothing to contradict the possibility that it could have been Magnusson who was in Lunnarp that night, despite his fiancée's alibi.

Now and then Wallander felt vaguely uneasy; afraid that they were going down yet another blind alley. But it was mostly Rydberg who showed signs of doubt. Time after time he asked himself whether a lone individual could have carried out the murders.

"There was something that hinted at teamwork in that slaughterhouse," he said. "I can't get the idea out of my mind."

"There's nothing to say Magnusson didn't have an accomplice," replied Wallander. "We have to take one thing at a time."

"If he committed the murder to pay a gambling debt, he wouldn't want an accomplice," Rydberg objected.

"I know," said Wallander. "But we have to keep at it."

Thanks to some quick work by Martinsson, they obtained a photograph of Magnusson, which was dug up from the county council's archives. It was taken from a brochure in which the county council presented its activities to a populace that was clearly assumed to be ignorant. Björk was of the opinion that all national and municipal government bodies needed public relations teams, which when necessary could highlight the colossal significance of that institution. He thought the brochure was excellent. In any case, there was Magnusson, standing next to his yellow forklift truck, dressed in dazzling white overalls. He was smiling.

The police officers looked at his face and compared it with some black-and-white photos of Johannes Lövgren. One of the pictures showed Lövgren standing next to a tractor in a newly ploughed field.

Could they be father and son? The tractor driver and the forklift operator? Wallander had a hard time focusing on the pictures and making them blend together. The only thing he could see was the bloody face of an old man with his nose cut off.

By 11 p.m. on Friday they had completed their plan of attack. Björk had left them to go to a dinner organised by the local country club.

Wallander and Rydberg were going to spend Saturday paying a visit to Ellen Magnusson in Kristianstad. Martinsson, Näslund, and Hansson would split up the surveillance of Erik Magnusson and also confront his fiancée with the alibi. Sunday would be devoted to surveillance and an additional run-through of all the investigative material. On Monday Martinsson, who had been appointed computer expert in spite of his lack of any real interest in the subject, would examine Erik Magnusson's records. Did he have other debts? Had he ever been mixed up in any kind of criminal activity before?

Wallander asked Rydberg to go over all of the material. He wanted Rydberg to do what they called a treasure hunt. He would try to match up events and individuals who appeared to have nothing in common. Were there points of contact that they had previously missed? That was what he would try to discover.

Rydberg and Wallander walked out of the station together. Wallander was suddenly aware of Rydberg's fatigue and remembered that he had been to the hospital.

"How are you?" he asked.

Rydberg shrugged his shoulders and mumbled something unintelligible in reply.

"How's your leg, I mean," said Wallander.

"Same old thing," replied Rydberg, obviously not wanting to talk about his ailments.

Wallander drove home and poured himself a glass of whisky. But he left it untouched on the coffee table and went into the bedroom to lie down. His exhaustion got the upper hand. He fell asleep at once and escaped the thoughts that were whirling around in his head.

That night he dreamed about Sten Widén. Together they were attending an opera in which the performers were singing in an unfamiliar language. Later, when he awoke, Wallander couldn't remember which opera it had been.

As soon as he woke up the next day he remembered something they had talked about the day before. Johannes Lövgren's will. The missing will. Rydberg had spoken with the estate administrator who had been

engaged by the two surviving daughters, a lawyer who
was often called on by the farmers' organisations in the
area. No will existed. That meant that the two daughters would inherit all of Lövgren's hidden fortune.

Could Erik Magnusson have known that Lövgren
had huge assets? Or had Lövgren kept this secret from
everyone?

Wallander got out of bed intending not to let this
day pass before he knew definitively whether Ellen
Magnusson had given birth to Johannes Lövgren's
son.

He ate a hasty breakfast and met Rydberg at the station just after 9 a.m. Martinsson, who had spent the
night in a car outside Magnusson's flat in Rosengård
was relieved by Näslund, and reported that absolutely
nothing had happened during the night. Magnusson
was in his flat. All had been quiet.

The January day was hazy. Hoarfrost covered the
fields. Rydberg sat exhausted and uncommunicative in the front seat next to Wallander. They didn't
say a word to each other until they were approaching
Kristianstad.

At 10:30 a.m. they met Boman at the police station,
and went through the transcript of the initial interview with Ellen Magnusson, which Boman had conducted himself.

"We've got nothing on her," said Boman. "We
ran the vacuum cleaner over her and the people she
knows. Not a thing. Her whole story fits on one sheet

of paper. She has worked at the same chemist for thirty years. She belonged to a choral group for a few years but eventually quit. She takes a lot of books out of the library. She spends her holidays with a sister in Vemmenhög, never travels abroad, never buys new clothes. She's a person who, at least on the surface, lives a completely undramatic life. Her habits are regular almost to the point of pedantry. The most surprising thing is that she can stand to live this way."

Wallander thanked him for his work. "Now we'll take over," he said.

They drove to Ellen Magnusson's flat.

When she opened the door, Wallander thought that Erik looked a lot like his mother. He couldn't tell whether she had been expecting them. The look in her eyes was remote, as if she were somewhere else.

Wallander looked around the living room. She asked if they wanted a cup of coffee. Rydberg declined, but Wallander said yes.

Every time Wallander stepped into someone's home, he felt as though he were looking at the front cover of a book that he had just bought. The flat, the furniture, the pictures on the walls, and the smells were the title. Now he had to start reading. But Ellen Magnusson's flat was odourless, as if uninhabited. He breathed in the smell of hopelessness, resignation. Against a background of pale wallpaper hung coloured prints of abstract motifs. The furniture crammed into the room was heavy and old-fashioned. Doilies were decoratively arranged on several mahogany drop-leaf tables. On a little shelf stood a photograph of a child sitting in front of a rosebush. Wallander noticed that the only picture of her son on display was one from his childhood. The grown man was not present at all.

Next to the living room was a small dining room. Wallander nudged the half-open door with his foot. To his amazement, one of his father's paintings hung on the wall. It was the autumn landscape without the grouse. He stood looking at it until he heard the rattle of a tray behind him. It was as if he were looking at his father's painting for the first time.

Rydberg had sat down in a chair by the window. Someday Wallander would ask him why he always sat by a window.

Where do our habits come from? he wondered. What secret factory produces our habits, both good and bad? Ellen Magnusson served him coffee. He decided he'd better begin.

"Göran Boman from the Kristianstad police was here and asked you a number of questions," he said. "Please don't be surprised if we ask you some of the same ones."

"Just don't be surprised if you get the same answers," said Ellen Magnusson.

At that moment Wallander realised that the woman sitting across from him was the mystery woman with whom Johannes Lövgren had had a child. Wallander knew it without knowing how.

In a rash moment he decided to lie his way to the truth. If he wasn't mistaken, Ellen Magnusson had had very little experience with the police. She would assume that they searched for the truth by being honest themselves. She was the one who would lie, not the police.

"Mrs. Magnusson," said Wallander. "We know that Johannes Lövgren is the father of your son, Erik. There's no use denying it."

She looked at him, terrified. The absent look in her eyes was suddenly gone. Now she was with them again.

"That's not true," she said.

A lie that begs for mercy, thought Wallander. She's going to break soon.

"Of course it's true," he said. "You and I both know it's true. If Johannes Lövgren hadn't been murdered, we would never have had to worry about asking these questions. But now we have to know. And if we don't find out now, you'll be forced to answer these questions under oath in court."

It was easier than he thought. Suddenly she cracked.

"Why do you want to know?" she shrieked. "I haven't done anything. Why can't a person be allowed to keep her secrets?"

"No one is denying that right," said Wallander carefully. "But when people are murdered, we have to search for those responsible. This means we have to ask questions. And we have to get answers."

Rydberg sat motionless on his chair by the window. His tired eyes watched the woman. Together they listened to her story. Wallander thought it inexpressibly dreary. Her life, as it was laid out before him, was just as hopeless as the frosty landscape he had driven through that morning.

She had been born the daughter of an elderly farming couple in Yngsjö. She had torn herself free from the land and had eventually got a job in a chemist. Johannes Lövgren had come into her life as a customer there. She told Wallander and Rydberg that they first met when he was buying bicarbonate of soda. He had returned and started to court her.

He had described himself as a lonely farmer. Not until the baby was born did she find out that he was married. Her feelings had been resigned, never angry. He had bought her silence with money, which was paid to her several times a year. But she had raised the son alone. He was hers.

"What did you think when you found out that he had been murdered?" asked Wallander when she fell silent.

"I believe in God," she said. "I believe in righteous vengeance."

"Vengeance?"

"How many people did Johannes betray?" she asked. "He betrayed me, his son, his wife, and his daughters. He betrayed everyone."

And soon she will learn that her son is a murderer,

thought Wallander. Will she imagine that he was an archangel who was carrying out a divine decree for vengeance? Will she be able to bear it?

He continued asking his questions. Rydberg shifted his position on the chair by the window. A bell went off in the kitchen. When they finally left, Wallander felt that he had got all the answers he needed.

He had discovered who the mystery woman was. The secret son. He knew that she was expecting money from Lövgren. But he had never shown up.

One question, however, had an unexpected answer. Ellen Magnusson didn't give any of Lövgren's money to her son. She put it into a savings account. He wouldn't inherit the money until she was gone. Perhaps she was afraid that he would gamble it away.

But Erik Magnusson knew that Johannes Lövgren was his father. He had lied about that. Did he also know that his father had a huge fortune?

Rydberg was silent during the entire interview. Just as they were about to leave, he had asked her how often she saw her son. Whether they got along well with each other. Did she know about his fiancée?

Her reply was evasive. "He's grown now," she said. "He lives his own life. But he's good about coming to visit. And of course I know that he is engaged."

Now she's lying again, thought Wallander. She didn't know.

They stopped at an inn at Degeberga and ate. Rydberg seemed to have revived.

"Your interrogation was perfect," he said. "It should be used as a training exercise at the police academy."

"Still, I did lie," said Wallander. "And that's not considered kosher."

During the meal they discussed their strategy. Both of them agreed that they should wait for the report on Erik Magnusson's records to be compiled before they picked him up for questioning.

"Do you think he's the one?" asked Rydberg.

"Of course he is," replied Wallander. "Alone or with an accomplice. What do you think?"

"I hope you're right."

They arrived back at the police station in Ystad at 3:15 p.m. Näslund was sitting in his office, sneezing. He had been relieved by Hansson at midday. Erik Magnusson had spent the morning buying new shoes and turning in some betting slips at a tobacco shop. Then he had gone home.

"Does he seem on guard?" asked Wallander.

"I don't know," said Näslund. "Sometimes I think so. But then I think I'm imagining things."

Rydberg went home, and Wallander shut himself in his office. He leafed absentmindedly through a stack of papers that someone had put on his desk. He was having a hard time concentrating. Ellen Magnusson's story had made him uneasy. He imagined that his own life wasn't that different from hers. His own unstable life.

I'm going to take some time off when this is over,

he thought. With all my overtime I could probably be gone for a week. I'm going to devote seven whole days to myself. Seven days like seven lean years. Then I'll emerge a new man.

He pondered whether he ought to go to one of those health spas where he could get help losing weight. But the thought depressed him. He would rather get in his car and drive south. Maybe to Paris or Amsterdam. He knew a policeman in Arnhem whom he had met once at a narcotics seminar. Maybe he could visit him.

But first we have to solve these murders, he thought, We'll do that next week. Then I'll decide where I'm going to go.

On Thursday, January 25, Erik Magnusson was picked up by the police for questioning. Rydberg and Hansson nabbed him right outside the block of flats where he lived, while Wallander sat in the car and watched. Magnusson got into the squad car without protest. They had timed it for morning, when he was on his way to work. Since Wallander was anxious for the first interview to take place without notice, he let Magnusson call his work and give a reason for not coming in. Björk, Wallander, and Rydberg were present in the room when Magnusson was interviewed. Björk and Rydberg stayed in the background while Wallander asked the questions.

During the days before Magnusson was taken to Ystad, the police had grown even more certain that he was guilty of the murders. The investigations had shown that Magnusson had huge debts. On several occasions he had just avoided being beaten up for not paying his gambling debts. Hansson had watched Magnusson wagering large sums at Jägersrö. His financial situation was catastrophic.

The year before, he had been the suspect in a bank robbery at Eslöv, but it had not been possible to pin the crime on him. It was also conceivable that Magnusson was mixed up in narcotics smuggling. His fiancée, who was now unemployed, had been convicted of drug-related offences on several occasions and in one instance for postal fraud. Erik Magnusson had huge debts, but at times, however, he had enormous sums of money. And his salary from the county council was tiny.

Wallander had woken early on Thursday morning feeling great tension. This day would see the final breakthrough in the investigation. The murders in Lunnarp would be solved.

The next day, Friday, January 26, he realised that he was wrong.

The assumption that Erik Magnusson was the guilty party, or at least one of them, was completely obliterated. They had indeed gone down a blind alley. On Friday afternoon they realised that Magnusson was innocent.

His alibi for the night of the murder had been corroborated by his fiancée's mother, who was visiting. Her credibility was beyond reproach. She was an elderly lady who suffered from insomnia. Erik Magnusson had snored all night long the night that Johannes and Maria Lövgren were brutally murdered.

The money with which he had paid his debt to the Junkman came from the sale of a car. Magnusson was able to produce a receipt for the Chrysler he had sold. And the buyer, a cabinetmaker in Lomma, told them that he had paid cash, with 1,000-krona and 500-krona notes.

Magnusson was also able to give a satisfactory explanation for lying about Johannes Lövgren being his father. He had done it for his mother's sake, since he thought she would want it that way. When Wallander told him that Lövgren was a wealthy man, he had looked truly astonished.

In the end there was nothing left.

Björk asked whether anyone was opposed to sending Erik Magnusson home, dropping him from the case until further notice. No one had any objections. Wallander felt a crushing guilt at having steered the entire investigation in the wrong direction. Only Rydberg seemed unaffected. He was also the one who had been the most skeptical from the beginning.

They had run aground. All that was left was a wreck. There was nothing to do but start over again.

And then the snow arrived. In the early hours of Saturday, January 27, a violent snowstorm came in from the southwest. After a few hours, the E65 was closed. The snow fell steadily for six hours. The heavy wind made the efforts of the snowploughs futile. As fast as they scraped the snow off the roads, it would collect in drifts again. For twenty-four hours the police were busy preventing the mess from developing into chaos. Then the storm moved on, as quickly as it had come.

To Wallander's great delight, his daughter Linda called him a few days later. She was in Malmö and had decided to enroll at a college outside Stockholm. She promised to come and see him before she left.

Wallander arranged his schedule so that he could visit his father at least three times a week. He wrote a letter to his sister in Stockholm, telling her that the home help had done wonders with their father. The confusion that had driven him out on that desolate nighttime promenade towards Italy had gone. Having the woman come regularly to his house had been his salvation.

One evening, Wallander called up Anette Brolin and offered to show her around wintry Skåne. He apologised again for his behaviour. She thanked him and said yes, and the following Sunday, February 4, he took her out to see the ancient stones at Ales Stenar and the medieval castle of Glimmingehus. They had dinner in Hammenhög at the inn, and Wallander started to think that she really had decided that he was not the man who had pulled her down onto his knee.

The weeks passed with no new breakthrough in their investigation. Martinsson and Näslund were transferred to new assignments. Wallander and Rydberg, however, were allowed to concentrate exclusively on the murders for the time being.

One cold, clear, windless day in the middle of February, Wallander was visited in his office by the Lövgrens' daughter who lived and worked in Göteborg. She had come back to Skåne to oversee the placement of a headstone on her parents' grave in Villie cemetery. Wallander told her the truth—that the police were still fumbling around for a clue. The day after her visit, he drove out to the cemetery and stood there for a long while, staring at the black headstone with the gold inscription.

The month of February was spent in broadening and deepening the investigation.

Rydberg, who was uncommunicative and was suffering terribly from the pain in his leg, did most of his work by phone, while Wallander was often out in the field. They checked every single bank in Skåne, but found no more safe-deposit boxes. Wallander talked to more than two hundred people who were either relatives or acquaintances of Johannes and Maria Lövgren. He went over the bulging file of investigative material again and again, went back to points he had covered long ago, and tore apart reports, scrutinising them anew. But he found no opening.

One icy, windy day in February he picked up Sten Widén at his farm and they visited Lunnarp. Together they inspected the horse that might hold the answer, and watched the mare eat an armload of hay. Old

Nyström was at their heels wherever they went. He had been given the mare by the two daughters.

The property itself, which stood silent and closed up, had been turned over to an estate agent in Skurup for sale. Wallander stood in the wind looking at the smashed kitchen window, which had not been repaired, just boarded up with a piece of plywood. He tried to reestablish the bond with Widén that had been lost in the past years, but the racehorse trainer appeared uninterested. After Wallander had driven him home, he realised that their friendship was broken for good.

The investigation of the murder of the Somali refugee was concluded, and Rune Bergman was brought before the district court in Ystad. The courtroom was packed with people from the press. By now it had been established that it was Valfrid Ström who had fired the fatal shots. But Bergman was charged as an accessory to the murder, and the psychiatric evaluation declared him fit to be tried.

Wallander testified in court, and on several occasions he sat in and listened to Anette Brolin's submissions and cross-examination. Bergman said as little as possible. The court proceedings revealed a racist underground network in which political views similar to those of the Ku Klux Klan predominated. Bergman and Ström had acted on their own, but were connected to several racist organisations.

It again occurred to Wallander that a change was

taking place in Sweden. He sympathised with some of the arguments against immigration that arose in conversation and in the press while the trial was in progress. Did the government and the Immigration Service have any real control over which individuals sought asylum? Over who was a refugee and who was an opportunist? Was it possible to differentiate at all? How long could the current refugee policy operate without leading to chaos? Was there an upper limit?

Wallander had made half-hearted attempts at studying the issues thoroughly. He realised that he harboured the same vague apprehension that so many other people did. Anxiety at the unknown, at the future.

At the end of February Bergman was sentenced to a long prison term. To everyone's astonishment, he did not appeal the verdict, which took effect immediately.

No more snow fell on Skåne that winter. Early one morning at the beginning of March, Anette Brolin and Wallander took a long walk out on the Falsterbo Spit. Together they watched the flocks of birds returning from the distant lands of the Southern Cross. Wallander took her hand, and she didn't pull it away, at least not at once.

He managed to lose four kilos, but he realised that he would never get back to what he had weighed before Mona had left him. Occasionally they spoke on the telephone. Wallander noticed that his jealousy was gradually fading away. And the black woman no longer visited him in his dreams.

March began. Rydberg was admitted to the hospital for two weeks. At first everyone thought it was for his bad leg. But Ebba told Wallander in confidence that Rydberg was suffering from cancer. She didn't say how she knew, or what type of cancer it was. When Wallander visited Rydberg at the hospital, he told him it was only a routine checkup on his stomach. A shadow on an X-ray had revealed a possible lesion on his large intestine.

Wallander felt a burning pain inside him at the thought that Rydberg might be seriously ill. With a growing sense of hopelessness he trudged on with his investigation. One day, in a fit of rage, he threw the thick folders at the wall. The floor was covered with paper. For a long time he sat looking at the havoc. Then he crawled around sorting the material again and started from the beginning.

Somewhere there's something I'm not seeing, he thought. A connection, a detail, which is exactly the key I have to turn. But should I turn it to the right or the left?

He often called Boman in Kristianstad to complain about his plight. On his own authority, Boman had carried out intensive investigations of Nils Velander and other conceivable suspects. Nowhere did the rock crack. For two whole days Wallander sat with Lars Herdin without advancing an inch. But he still didn't want to believe that the crime would never be solved.

In the middle of March he managed to entice Anette

Brolin to go to Copenhagen with him to see an opera. They had spent the night together. But when he told her that he loved her, she shied away. It was what it was. Nothing more.

On the weekend of March 17 and 18, his daughter came to visit. She came alone, without the Kenyan medical student, and Wallander met her at the railway station. Ebba had sent a friend of hers over the day before to give his flat in Mariagatan a good clean.

Finally he felt that he had his daughter back. They took a long walk along the beach by Österleden, ate lunch at Lilla Vik, and then stayed up talking till 5 a.m. They visited Wallander's father, and he surprised them both by telling funny stories about Kurt as a child. On Monday morning he took her to the train. He seemed to have regained her trust a little.

He was back in his office, poring over the investigative material, when Rydberg came in. He sat down in the wooden chair by the window and told Wallander straight out that he had been diagnosed with prostate cancer. Now he was going in for radiation treatment and chemotherapy, which could last for a long time and might not do any good. He wouldn't allow sympathy. He had merely come to remind Wallander about Maria Lövgren's last words. And the noose. Then he stood up, shook Wallander's hand, and left.

Wallander was left alone with his pain and his investigation. Björk thought that for the time being he ought to work alone, since the police were swamped.

Nothing happened in March. Or in April either. The reports on the status of Rydberg's health varied. Ebba was the unflagging messenger.

Early in May, Wallander went into Björk's office and suggested that someone else take over the investigation. But Björk refused. Wallander would have to continue at least until the summer holiday period was over. Then they would reevaluate the situation.

Time after time Wallander started again. Retraced, prying and twisting at the material, trying to make it come alive. But the stones he was walking on remained cold.

At the beginning of June he traded in his Peugeot for a Nissan. On June 8 he went on holiday and drove up to Stockholm to see his daughter. Together they drove all the way to the North Cape. Herman Mboya was in Kenya but would be coming back in August.

On Monday, July 9, Wallander was back on duty. A memo from Björk informed him that he was to continue with his investigation until Björk returned in early August. Then they would decide what to do.

He also received a message from Ebba that Rydberg was much better. The doctors might be able to control the cancer after all.

Tuesday, July 10, was a beautiful day in Ystad. At lunch time Wallander went downtown and strolled around. He went into the electrical shop by the square and decided to buy a new stereo.

He remembered that he had some Norwegian notes

in his wallet that he had forgotten to exchange. He had been carrying them around since the trip to the North Cape. He went down to the Union Bank and stood in line for the only window that was open.

He didn't recognise the woman behind the counter. It wasn't Britta-Lena Bodén, the young woman with the good memory, or any of the other clerks he had met before. It must be a summer temp, he thought.

The man in front of him in line made a large withdrawal. Wallander wondered idly what he was going to use such a large amount of money for. While the man counted up the cash, Wallander absentmindedly read the name on the driver's licence that he had placed on the counter.

Then it was his turn, and he exchanged his Norwegian money. Behind him in the line he heard a tourist speaking Italian or Spanish.

As he emerged onto the street, an idea hit him. He stood there motionless, as if he were frozen solid by his inspiration. Then he went back inside the bank. He waited until the tourists had exchanged their money, and showed his identity card to the clerk.

"Britta-Lena Bodén," he said, smiling. "Is she on holiday?"

"She's probably with her parents in Simrishamn," said the teller. "She has two weeks of holiday left."

"Bodén," he said. "Is that her parents' name too?"

"Her father runs a petrol station in Simrishamn. I think it's the one called Statoil nowadays."

"Thank you," said Wallander. "I just have some routine questions to ask her."

"I remember you," said the clerk. "So you haven't been able to solve that awful crime yet?"

"No," said Wallander. "It's terrible, isn't it?"

He practically ran back to the station, jumped into his car, and drove to Simrishamn. From Britta-Lena Bodén's father he learned that she was spending the day with friends at the beach at Sandhammaren. He searched a long time before he found her, well hidden behind a sand dune. She was playing backgammon with her friends, and all of them gave Wallander an astonished look as he came trudging through the sand.

"I wouldn't bother you if it wasn't important," he said.

Britta-Lena Bodén seemed to grasp his serious mood and got up. She was dressed in a minuscule bathing suit, and Wallander averted his eyes. They sat down a little way from the others so they wouldn't be disturbed.

"That day in January," said Wallander. "I want to ask you about it again. I'd like you to think back, and try to remember whether there was anyone else in the bank when Johannes Lövgren made his large withdrawal."

Her memory was still excellent.

"No," she said. "He was alone."

He knew that what she said was true.

"Keep going," he continued. "Lövgren went out the door. The door closed behind him. What happened then?"

Her reply was quick and firm. "The door didn't close."

"Another customer came in?"

"Two of them."

"Did you know them?"

"No."

The next question was crucial.

"Because they were foreigners?"

She looked at him in astonishment.

"Yes. How did you know?"

"I didn't until now. Keep thinking."

"There were two men. Quite young."

"What did they want?"

"They wanted to change some money."

"Do you remember what currency?"

"Dollars."

"Did they speak English? Were they Americans?"

She shook her head. "Not English. I don't know what language they were speaking."

"Then what happened? Try to picture it in your mind."

"They came up to the counter."

"Both of them?"

She thought carefully before she answered. The warm wind was ruffling her hair.

"One of them came up and put the money on the

counter. I think it was 100 dollars. I asked him if he wanted to change it. He nodded."

"What was the other man doing?"

She thought again.

"He dropped something on the floor, which he bent over and picked up. A glove, I think."

He went back a step with his questions.

"Johannes Lövgren had just left," he said. "He had received a large amount of cash which he put into his briefcase. Did he receive anything else?"

"He got a receipt for his money."

"Which he put in the briefcase?"

For the first time she was hesitant.

"I think so."

"If he didn't put the receipt in his briefcase, then what happened to it?"

She thought again.

"There was nothing lying on the counter. I'm sure of that. Otherwise I would have picked it up."

"Could it have slipped onto the floor?"

"Possibly."

"And the man who bent over for the glove could have picked it up?"

"Perhaps."

"What was on the receipt?

"The amount. His name and address."

Wallander held his breath.

"All that was on it? Are you sure?"

"He filled out his withdrawal slip in big letters. I

know that he wrote down his address too, even though it wasn't required."

Wallander went back again. "Lövgren takes his money and leaves. In the doorway he runs into two unknown men. One of them bends down and picks up a glove, and maybe the withdrawal slip too. It says that Johannes Lövgren has just withdrawn 27,000 kronor. Is that correct?"

Suddenly she understood. "Are they the ones that did it?"

"I don't know. Think back again."

"I exchanged the money. He put the notes in his pocket. They left."

"How long did it take?"

"Three, four minutes. No more."

"The bank has a copy of their receipt, I suppose?"

She nodded.

"I exchanged money at the bank today. I had to give my name. Did they give an address?"

"Perhaps. I don't remember."

Kurt Wallander nodded. Now something was starting to spark. "Your memory is phenomenal," he said. "Did you ever see those two men again?"

"No. Never."

"Would you recognise them?"

"I think so. Maybe."

Wallander thought for a few moments. "You might have to interrupt your holiday for a few days," he said.

"We're supposed to drive to Öland tomorrow!"

Wallander made a decision on the spot. "I'm sorry, you can't," he said. "Maybe the next day. But not before then."

He stood up and brushed off the sand. "Be sure to tell your parents where we can reach you," he said.

She stood up and got ready to rejoin her friends.

"Can I tell them?" she asked.

"Invent something," he replied. "I'm sure you can do that."

Late that afternoon they found the exchange receipt in the Union Bank's files.

The signature was illegible. No address was given.

Wallander was not disappointed, because now at least he understood how the whole thing might have happened. From the bank he drove straight to Rydberg's place, where he was convalescing.

Rydberg was sitting on his balcony when Wallander rang the doorbell. He had grown thin and was very pale. Together they sat on the balcony, and Wallander told him about his discovery. Rydberg nodded thoughtfully.

"You're probably right," he said when Wallander finished. "That's probably how it happened."

"The question now is how to find them," said Wallander. "Some tourists who happened to be visiting Sweden more than six months ago.

"Maybe they're still here," said Rydberg. "As refugees, asylum seekers, immigrants."

"Where do I start?" asked Wallander.

"I don't know," said Rydberg. "But you'll figure out something."

They sat for a couple of hours on Rydberg's balcony. In the early evening Wallander went back to his car. The stones under his feet were no longer so cold.

CHAPTER 15

Wallander would always remember the following days as the time when the chart was drawn. He started with what Britta-Lena Bodén remembered and an illegible signature. A possible scenario existed, and the last word Maria Lövgren spoke before she died was a piece of the puzzle that had finally fallen into place. He also had the oddly knotted noose to consider.

He drew the chart. On the day he had talked with Britta-Lena Bodén in the warm sand dunes at Sandhammaren he had gone to Björk's house, interrupted his dinner, and extracted from him a promise there and then to assign Hansson and Martinsson back to the investigation, which was once again given top priority.

On Wednesday, July 11, before the bank opened for business, they reconstructed the scene. Britta-Lena Bodén took her place behind the window, Hansson assumed the role of Lövgren, and Martinsson and Björk played the two men who came in to change their money. Wallander insisted that everything should be exactly as it was on that day six months earlier. The anxious bank manager eventually agreed to allow Britta-Lena Bodén to hand over 27,000 kronor notes of mixed, large denominations to Hansson, who had borrowed an old briefcase from Ebba.

Wallander stood to one side, watching everything. Twice he ordered them to begin again when Britta-Lena Bodén remembered some detail that didn't seem right.

Wallander set up this reconstruction in order to trigger her memory. He was hoping that she could open a door to yet another room in her exceptional memory.

When it was over, she shook her head. She had told him everything she could remember. There was nothing more she could say. Wallander asked her to postpone her journey to Öland another couple of days and then left her in an office where she could look through photographs of foreign criminals who, for one reason or another, had been caught in the net of the Swedish police. When this produced no results, she was put on a flight to Norrköping to go through the extensive photo archives at the Immigration Service. After eighteen hours spent studying countless pictures, she returned to Sturup, where Wallander himself went to meet her. The results were negative.

The next step was to link up with Interpol. The scenario of how the crime might have occurred was fed into their computers, which then made comparative studies at European headquarters. Again, nothing turned up to change the situation significantly.

While Britta-Lena Bodén was sitting puzzling over the endless rows of photographs, Wallander conducted three long interviews with Arthur Lundin, the chimney sweep from Slimminge. The drives between Lunnarp and Ystad were reconstructed, clocked, and repeated. Wallander continued to draw up his chart.

Now and then he went to see Rydberg, who sat on his balcony, weak and pale, and went over the investigation with him. Rydberg insisted that these visits were not a burden for him. But Wallander left him each time with a nagging feeling of guilt.

Anette Brolin returned from her holiday, which she had spent with her husband and children in a summerhouse in Grebbestad on the west coast. Her family came back to Ystad with her, and Wallander adopted his most formal tone when he called to report his breakthrough in the hitherto stalled investigation.

After a week of intensive activity, everything came to a standstill. Wallander stared at his chart. They were stuck again.

"We'll just have to wait," said Björk. "Interpol's dough rises slowly."

Wallander winced at the strained metaphor, but realised that Björk was right.

When Britta-Lena Bodén came back from Öland, Wallander asked the bank to give her a few more days off. He took her to the refugee camps around

Ystad. They also visited the floating camps on ships in Malmö's Oil Harbour. But nowhere did she see a face that she recognised. Wallander arranged for a police artist to come down from Stockholm, but after countless sketches, Britta-Lena Bodén was not satisfied with any of the faces the artist produced.

Wallander began to have doubts. Björk forced him to give up Martinsson and make do with Hansson as his only colleague on the case.

On Friday, July 20, Wallander was once more ready to give up. Late in the evening he sat down and wrote a memo suggesting that the investigation be put on hold for the time being because no pertinent material that would move the case forwards could be found.

He put the paper on his desk and decided to leave the decision to Björk and Anette Brolin on Monday morning.

He spent Saturday and Sunday on the Danish island of Bornholm. It was windy and rainy, and something he ate on the ferry made him ill. He spent Sunday night in bed. At regular intervals he had to get up and vomit.

When he woke on Monday morning, he was feeling better, but he was still undecided about whether to stay in bed or not. At last he got up and left the flat. A few minutes before 9 a.m. he was at the station. Since it was Ebba's birthday, they all had cake in the canteen. It was almost 10 a.m. before Wallander finally had a chance to read through his memo to Björk. He was about to deliver it when the phone rang. It was Britta-Lena Bodén.

Her voice was barely a whisper.

"They've come back. Get here as fast as you can!"

"Who's come back?" asked Wallander.

"The men who changed the money. Don't you understand?"

In the corridor he ran into Norén, just come back from traffic duty.

"Come with me!" shouted Wallander.

"What the hell's going on?" said Norén, biting into a sandwich.

"Don't ask. Just come!"

When they reached the bank Norén was still clutching the half-eaten sandwich. On the way over, Wallander had gone through a red light and driven over a flower bed. He left the car right in the middle of some market stalls in the square by the town hall. But still they got there too late. The two men had disappeared. Britta-Lena Bodén had been so shaken to see them again that it hadn't occurred to her to ask anyone to follow them. But she had had the presence of mind to activate the security camera.

Wallander studied the signature on the receipt. The name was again illegible, but the signature was the same. No address was given this time either.

"Good," said Wallander to Britta-Lena Bodén, who was standing in the bank manager's office, shaking. "What did you say when you left to call me?"

"That I had to go and get a stamp."

"Do you think they suspected anything?"

She shook her head.

"Good," Wallander repeated. "You did exactly the right thing."

"Do you think you'll catch them now?" she asked.

"Yes," said Wallander. "This time we're going to get them."

The videotape from the camera showed two men who did not look particularly Mediterranean. One of them had short blond hair, the other was balding. The first was at once dubbed Lucia and the other Skinhead.

Britta-Lena Bodén listened to samples of recorded languages and finally decided that the men had spoken to each other in Czech or Bulgarian. The 50-dollar note they had exchanged was immediately sent to the laboratory for examination.

Björk called a meeting in his office.

"After six months they turn up again," said Wallander. "Why did they go back to the same small bank? First, because they live somewhere in the region. Second, they made a lucky catch after their earlier visit. This time they weren't so lucky. The man ahead of them in line was depositing money, not making a withdrawal. But he was an old man like Johannes Lövgren. Maybe they think that old men who look like farmers always make large cash withdrawals."

"Czechs?" asked Björk. "Or Bulgarians?"

"That's not positively confirmed," said Wallander.

"The girl could have been mistaken. But it fits with their appearance."

They watched the video four times and decided which pictures to copy and enlarge.

"Every Eastern European who lives in town and the surrounding area will have to be investigated," said Björk. "It's not going to be pleasant. It will be regarded as discrimination, but we'll have to say to hell with that. They've got to be here somewhere. I'll talk to the police chiefs in Malmö and Kristianstad and see what they think we should do on the county level."

"Show the video to every police officer," said Hansson. "They might turn up on the streets."

Wallander had a vision of the slaughterhouse that had been the Lövgren's farm.

"After what they did in Lunnarp," he said, "we have to treat them as dangerous."

"If they were the ones," said Björk. "We don't know that yet."

"That's true," said Wallander. "But even so."

"We're going to move into high gear now," said Björk. "Kurt is in charge and will divide up the work as he sees fit. Anything that doesn't have to be done straightaway should be put aside. I'll call the prosecutor; she'll be glad to hear that something's happening."

But nothing did happen. In spite of massive police effort and the relatively small size of the town, the men had vanished.

The next few days passed without result. The two county police chiefs gave the go-ahead to implement special measures in their districts. The videotape was distributed. Wallander had doubts as to whether the pictures should be released to the press. He was afraid that the men would make themselves even scarcer. He asked for Rydberg's advice.

"You have to drive foxes out into the open," he said. "Wait a few days. But then publish the pictures."

For a long time he sat staring at the copies that Wallander had brought along.

"There's no such thing as a murderer's face," he said. "You imagine something: a profile, a hairline, a set of the jaw. But it never matches up."

On Tuesday, July 31, ragged clouds raced across the sky, and the wind was gusting up to gale force. After waking at dawn, Wallander lay in bed for a long time and listened to the wind. When he stood on the scales in the bathroom, he saw that he had lost another kilo. This cheered him up so much that when he drove into the car park at the station he had shed the gloom he'd felt of late.

This investigation is turning into a personal defeat, he had been thinking. I'm driving my colleagues hard, we've fetched up in a dead end again. But those two men are out there, he thought angrily as he slammed the car door. Somewhere.

In reception he stopped to chat to Ebba. There was an old-fashioned music box next to the switchboard.

"I haven't seen one of those in ages," he said. "Where did you get it?"

"I bought it at a stall in the Sjöbo market," she replied. "Sometimes you can actually find something wonderful amongst all the junk."

Wallander smiled and moved on. On the way to his office he stopped to see Hansson and Martinsson and asked them to come along with him. Still no trace of Skinhead or Lucia.

"Two more days," said Wallander. "If we don't come up with something by Thursday, we'll call a press conference and release the pictures."

"We should have done that right away," said Hansson.

Wallander said nothing.

They went over the chart again. Martinsson would go on organising the search of camping grounds where the two men might be hiding out.

"Check the youth hostels," said Wallander. "And all the rooms rented in private homes for the summer."

"It was easier in the old days," said Martinsson. "People used to stay put in the summer. Now they scatter all over the place."

Hansson would go on to looking into a number of smaller, less particular building firms that were known to hire workers from various Eastern European countries without work permits. Wallander would go out to the strawberry fields. The two men might be hiding at one of the big fruit farms.

But their searches were in vain. When they gathered

again late in the afternoon, they had drawn only blanks.

"I found one Algerian pipe fitter," said Hansson, "two Kurdish bricklayers, and a huge number of Polish manual labourers. I feel like writing a note to Björk. If we hadn't had this damned double murder to solve, we could have cleaned up that shit. They're making the same wages as kids with summer jobs. They have no insurance. If there's an accident, the companies will say that the workers were living without permission at the sites."

Martinsson had no good news either.

"I found a bald Bulgarian," he said. "With a little luck he could have been Skinhead. But he's a doctor at the clinic in Mariestad and would have no trouble producing an alibi."

It was stuffy in the room. Wallander got up and opened the window. For some reason he thought of Ebba's music box. Though he hadn't heard its tune, the music box had been playing in his subconscious all day.

"The markets," he said, turning around. "We should look there. Which market is open next?"

Both Hansson and Martinsson knew the answer. The one in Kivik.

"It's open today and tomorrow," said Hansson.

"I'll go there tomorrow," said Wallander.

"It's a big one," said Hansson. "You should take somebody with you.

"I can go," said Martinsson.

Hansson looked relieved to be spared the assignment. Wallander thought that there probably were
races on Wednesday nights. The meeting over, they
said goodbye to one another, and Hansson and Martinsson left. Wallander remained at his desk and sorted
through a pile of phone messages. He arranged them
in order of priority for the following day and got ready
to leave. Then he caught sight of a note that had fallen
under the desk. He bent to pick it up and saw that it
was a message to call the director of a refugee camp.

He dialled the number. It rang ten times and he was
about to hang up when someone answered.

"This is Wallander at the Ystad police. I want to
speak to Mr. Modin."

"Speaking."

"I'm returning your call."

"I think I have something important to tell you."

Wallander held his breath.

"It's about the two men you're looking for. I came
back from holiday today. The photographs the police
sent were on my desk. I recognise those two men. They
lived at this camp for a while."

"I'm on my way," said Wallander. "Don't leave your
office before I get there."

The camp was outside Skurup, and Wallander was
there in nineteen minutes. It was housed in an old vic-
arage, and was only used as a temporary shelter when
all the permanent camps were full.

Modin, the director, was a short man, maybe sixty.

He was in the drive when Wallander's car skidded to a stop.

"The camp is empty at the moment," Modin said. "But we're expecting a number of Romanians next week."

They went into his small office.

"Start at the beginning," Wallander said.

"They were here from December of last year to the middle of February," said Modin, leafing through some papers. "Then they were transferred to Malmö. To Celsius House, to be exact."

Modin pointed to the photo of Skinhead. "That one is Lothar Kraftczyk. He's a Czech seeking political asylum on the grounds that he was persecuted as a member of an ethnic minority."

"Are there minorities in Czechoslovakia?" wondered Wallander.

"I think he claims he is a gypsy."

"Claims?"

Modin shrugged. "I don't believe he is. Refugees who know they don't have a strong enough case to be permitted to stay in Sweden quickly learn that one excellent way to improve their chances is to say that they're gypsies."

Modin picked up the photo of Lucia. "Andreas Haas. Also a Czech. I don't really know what his grounds for seeking asylum were. The paperwork went with them to Celsius House."

"And you're positive that they're the men in the photographs?"

"Yes. I'm sure of it."

"OK," said Wallander. "Tell me more."

"About what?"

"What were they like? Did anything unusual happen while they were here? Did they have plenty of money? Anything you can remember."

"I've been trying," said Modin. "By and large they kept to themselves. You should know that life in a refugee camp is extremely stressful. I do remember that they played chess. Day in, day out."

"Did they have money?"

"Not that I recall."

"What were they like?"

"They kept to themselves, but they weren't unfriendly."

"Anything else?"

Wallander noticed that Modin hesitated.

"What are you thinking?" he asked.

"This is a small camp," said Modin. "I'm not here at night, and neither is anyone else. On certain days it was also unstaffed. Except for a cook to prepare the meals. Usually we keep a car here. The keys are locked in my office. But sometimes when I got here in the morning I had the feeling that someone had been in my office, taken the keys, and used the car."

"And you suspected these two?"

Modin nodded. "I don't know why. It was just a feeling I had."

Wallander pondered this.

"So at night no one was here," he said. "Or on certain days either. Is that right?"

"Yes."

"January the fourth to January the sixth," said Wallander. "That's more than six months ago. Is there any way of knowing whether anyone was on duty those days?"

Modin paged through his desk calendar.

"I was at emergency meetings in Malmö," he said. "There was such a backlog of refugees that we had to find more temporary camps."

Wallander had goose bumps. The chart had come alive. Now it was speaking to him.

"So nobody was here on those days?"

"Only the cook. The kitchen is in the back so she might not have seen if anyone had driven away in the car."

"None of the refugees would have said anything?"

"Refugees don't get involved. They're scared. Even of each other."

Wallander stood up. Suddenly he was in a big hurry.

"Call your colleague at Celsius House and tell him I'm on my way," he said. "But don't say anything about these two men. Just make sure that the director is available."

Modin stared at him.

"Why are you looking for them?" he asked.

"They may have committed a crime. A serious crime."

"The murders in Lunnarp? Is that what you mean?"

Wallander saw no reason not to tell him. "Yes. I think they're the ones."

He reached Celsius House in central Malmö at a few minutes past 7 p.m. He parked on a side street and walked to the main entrance, where there was a security guard. After several minutes a man came to get him. His name was Larson, a retired seaman, and he smelled of beer.

"Haas and Kraftczyk," said Wallander when they were in Larson's office. "Two Czech asylum seekers."

"The chess players," he said. "Yes, they live here."

Damn it, thought Wallander. We've finally got them.

"Are they here, in the building?"

"Yes," said Larson. "I mean, no."

"No?"

"They live here. But they're not here."

"Where the hell are they?"

"I really don't know."

"But they do live here?"

"They ran away."

"Ran away?"

"It happens all the time—people running away."

"But aren't they trying to get asylum?"

"They still run away."

"What do you do then?"

"We report them, naturally."

"And then what happens?"

"Nothing, usually."

"Nothing? People run away who are waiting to hear whether they can stay in this country or whether they're going to be deported? And nobody cares?"

"I guess the police are supposed to look for them."

"This is bloody ridiculous. When did they disappear?"

"They left in May. Probably they expected that their applications would be turned down."

"Where do you think they went?"

Larson threw his hands wide. "If you only knew how many people lived here without residency permits. More than you can imagine. They live together, forge their papers, trade names with each other, work illegally. You can spend a lifetime in Sweden without anyone checking up on you. No one wants to believe it. But that's the way it is."

Wallander was speechless.

"This is crazy," he said. "This is fucking crazy."

"I agree with you. But that's the way of it."

Wallander groaned.

"I need all the documents you have on these two men."

"I am not at liberty to hand those over."

"These two men have committed murder," Wallander exploded. "Double murder."

"Nevertheless I can't release the papers."

Wallander stood up.

"Tomorrow you're going to hand over those papers. Even if I have to get the chief of the national police to come and get them himself."

"That's how it is. I can't change the regulations."

Wallander drove back to Ystad. At 8:45 p.m. he rang Björk's doorbell. Quickly he told him what had happened.

"Tomorrow we issue an APB for them," he said.

Björk nodded. "I'll call a press conference for 2 p.m. I have a meeting with the police chiefs in the morning, but I'll see to it that we get the papers from Celsius House."

Wallander went to see Rydberg. He was sitting in the dark on his balcony. Wallander looked at him and realised that he was in pain. Rydberg, who seemed to read his thoughts, said matter-of-factly, "I don't think I'm going to make it through this. I might live past Christmas; I might not."

Wallander didn't know what to say.

"One has to endure," said Rydberg. "Tell me why you're here."

Wallander told him. Dimly he could make out Rydberg's face in the darkness. They sat in silence. The night was cool. But Rydberg didn't seem to notice as he sat there in his old dressing gown and slippers.

"Maybe they've skipped the country," said Wallander. "Maybe we'll never catch them."

"In that case, we'll have to accept that at least we know the truth," said Rydberg. "Justice doesn't only mean that the people who commit crimes are punished. It also means that we can never give up seeking the truth."

With great effort he got to his feet and fetched a bottle of cognac, and with shaking hands poured two glasses.

"Some old police officers die worrying about ancient, unsolved puzzles," he said. "I suppose that I'm one of them."

"Have you ever regretted becoming a policeman?" asked Wallander.

"Never. Not once."

They drank their cognac. Talked some, or sat in silence. Not until midnight did Wallander get up to leave. He promised to return the following evening. He left Rydberg where he was, sitting on the balcony in the dark.

On Wednesday morning, August 1, Wallander briefed Hansson and Martinsson on what had happened the day before. The press conference would be in the afternoon, so they decided to check the Kivik market in the meantime. Hansson took on the job of writing the press release with Björk. Wallander said that he and Martinsson would be back no later than midday.

They went by way of Tomelilla and joined a long queue of cars just south of Kivik. They pulled in and parked in a field where an opportunistic farmer charged them 20 kronor.

It started to rain as they reached the market area, which stretched before them with a view of the sea. They stared in dismay at the mass of stalls and people. Loudspeakers were squawking, drunken youths were yelling, and they were shoved this way and that by the crowd.

"Let's try to meet somewhere in the middle," said Wallander.

"We should have brought walkie-talkies in case something happens," said Martinsson.

"Nothing's going to happen," said Wallander. "Let's meet one hour from now."

He watched Martinsson shamble off and be swallowed up by the crowd. He turned up the collar of his jacket and headed in the opposite direction.

After a little more than an hour they met again. They were soaked and exasperated with the crowds and the jostling.

"To hell with this," said Martinsson. "Let's go somewhere to have coffee."

Wallander pointed at a cabaret tent in front of them.

"Have you been in there?" he asked.

Martinsson grimaced. "Some tub of lard doing a striptease. The crowd screamed as if it were some kind of sexual revivalist meeting. Fuck!"

"Let's walk round the back of the tent," said Wallander. "I think there are a few stalls over there too. Then we can call it a day."

They trudged through the mud, pushing their way between a caravan and rusty tent pegs. The stalls were selling different goods, but each looked the same, their awnings pitched above red-painted metal poles.

Wallander and Martinsson saw the men at exactly the same moment. They were inside a stall, its counter covered with leather jackets. One price was displayed for all of them, and Wallander had time to think that the jackets were amazingly cheap.

The men behind the counter stared at the two police officers. Much too late Wallander realised that they had recognised him. His face had appeared so often in the newspapers and on television that it was known all over the country.

Everything happened very fast. Lucia stuck his hand under the leather jackets on the counter and pulled out a revolver. Martinsson and Wallander threw themselves to one side. Martinsson got tangled in the guy ropes of the tent. Wallander hit his head on the back end of the caravan. Lucia aimed at Wallander. The shot could hardly be heard above the commotion from the tent where "death riders" were hurtling around on roaring motorcycles. The bullet struck the caravan, inches from Wallander's head. In the next instant he saw that Martinsson was holding his revolver.

Martinsson fired. Wallander watched Lucia fly back and put his hand up to his shoulder. The gun fell from his hand and landed outside the counter. With a bellow Martinsson yanked himself free of the guy ropes and launched himself at the counter, straight at the wounded man. The counter collapsed, and Martinsson landed in a jumble of leather jackets.

Wallander lunged forwards and grabbed the gun from the mud. He saw Skinhead dash past him into the crowd. No one seemed to have noticed the shots. The traders in the surrounding stalls had watched in amazement as Martinsson made his ferocious tiger pounce.

"Get after him," Martinsson shouted from the heap of leather jackets. "I'll take care of this bastard."

Wallander ran. Terrified people shrank away as Wallander came running with mud on his face and the gun in his hand. He was afraid that he had lost Skinhead, when suddenly he caught sight of him again, in wild and reckless flight through the market crowds. He shoved aside an elderly woman who stepped in front of him and crashed into a stall selling cakes. Wallander ran through the mess, knocked over a sweet stand, and then took off after him.

Again the man disappeared.

Wallander swore and fought his way through the ambling crowd. Then he saw him again. He was running to the edge of the market, down to the cliff. Two security guards came running at him, but they leaped aside when he waved the gun and yelled at them to stay away. One fell back into a tent serving beer, while the other one knocked over a candlestick stall.

Wallander ran, his heart pounding like a piston.

The man vanished over the cliff edge. Wallander was about thirty metres behind him. When he reached the edge himself, he stumbled and fell headlong down the slope. He lost his grip on the gun. For a moment he hesitated, wondering whether he should stop and find it. Then he saw Skinhead running along the beach, and set off after him.

The chase ended when neither of them had any strength left to keep running. Skinhead leaned against the bottom of a black-tarred rowing boat. Wallander stood ten metres away, so out of breath that he thought he was going to fall over.

Skinhead had drawn a knife and was coming towards him. That's the knife he used to cut off Johannes Lövgren's nose, he thought. That's the knife he used to force Lövgren to tell him where the money was. He looked around for a weapon. A broken oar was all he could see. Skinhead made a lunge with the knife. Wallander parried with the heavy oar. The man jabbed again with the knife, and Wallander swung at him. The oar caught him on the collarbone. Wallander heard the bone crack. Skinhead stumbled, and Wallander dropped the oar and slammed his right fist into his chin. The pain in his knuckles was agonising, but Skinhead fell.

Wallander collapsed onto the wet sand. Seconds later Martinsson came running. The rain was pouring down.

"We got them," said Martinsson.

"Yes," said Wallander. "I guess we did."

He walked over to the water's edge and rinsed his face. In the distance he saw a tanker heading south. He thought how glad he was to be able to give Rydberg some good news to lighten his misery.

Two days later the man named Andreas Haas confessed to the murders, but he blamed it all on the other man. When Lothar Kraftczyk was confronted with the confession, he gave up too. The brutality, he insisted, was all Andreas Haas's doing.

It was exactly as Wallander had imagined it. On several occasions the two men had gone into banks to change money and to look for a customer who was withdrawing a large sum. They had followed Lövgren in the car from the refugee camp when Lundin, the chimney sweep, had driven him home. They had tailed him along the dirt road, and two nights later they had returned.

"There's one thing that puzzles me," said Wallander, who was leading the interrogation of Lothar Kraftczyk. "Why did you feed the horse?"

The man looked at him in surprise.

"The money was hidden in the hay net," he said. "Perhaps we threw some hay to the horse when we were looking for the briefcase."

Wallander nodded. The solution to the mystery was that simple.

"One more thing," said Wallander. "Why the noose?"

No answer. Neither man would confess to that insane violence. He repeated his question but never got an answer.

The Czech police sent word that Hass and Kraft-czyk had both done time for assault in Czechoslovakia.

When they had abandoned Celsius House, the two men had rented a dilapidated cottage outside of Höör. The jackets they were selling had been stolen from a leather shop in Tranås.

The detention hearing was over in a matter of minutes. No one doubted that the case would be airtight, even though the two men were still blaming each other for the violence.

Wallander sat in the courtroom and stared at the men he had been hunting for so long. He remembered that early morning in January when he stepped into the farmhouse in Lunnarp. The double murder had now been solved and the criminals would soon be sentenced; Wallander still wasn't happy. Why the noose around Maria Lövgren's neck? Why such violence?

He shuddered. He couldn't answer these questions, and that left him feeling unsatisfied.

Late on Saturday, August 11, Wallander took a bottle of whisky over to Rydberg's. On Sunday Anette Brolin was going to go with him to visit his father. Wallander thought of the question he had put to her. Would she consider getting a divorce for him? Of course she had said no, but he knew that she hadn't been offended by his asking.

As he was driving to see Rydberg, he listened to Maria Callas on the tape deck. He was taking the next week off, as time off in lieu of the extra hours he had worked. He was going to Lund to meet Herman Mboya, who had come back from Kenya, and then planned to spend the rest of the time repainting his flat. Maybe he would even treat himself to that new stereo. As he parked, he caught a glimpse of the yellow moon overhead. Autumn was on its way.

Rydberg was sitting as usual in the dark on his balcony. Wallander poured two glasses of whisky.

"Do you remember when we sat around worrying about Mrs. Lövgren's last words?" said Rydberg. "That we would be forced to search for some foreigners? Then, when Erik Magnusson came into the picture, we desperately wanted him to be the murderer. But he wasn't. So we got a pair of foreigners after all. And the wretched Somali died for no good reason."

"You knew all along," said Wallander. "Didn't you? You were sure that it was foreigners."

"I wasn't positive," said Rydberg. "But I thought so."

Slowly they went over the investigation, as if it were already a distant memory.

"We made lots of mistakes," said Wallander thoughtfully. "I made lots of mistakes."

"You're a good policeman," said Rydberg emphatically. "Maybe I never told you that. But I think you're a damned fine policeman."

"I made too many mistakes," replied Wallander.

"You kept at it," said Rydberg. "You never gave up. You wanted to catch whoever committed those murders in Lunnarp. That's the important thing."

The conversation gradually petered out. I'm sitting here with a dying man, thought Wallander in despair. I don't think I ever took in that Rydberg is actually going to die. He remembered the time he was stabbed. He also thought about the fact that a little less than six months ago he had driven his car while drunk. He should have been dismissed from the force.

Why don't I tell Rydberg about that? he wondered. Why don't I say anything? Or perhaps he already knows?

The incantation flashed through his mind. *A time to live, a time to die.*

"How are you?" he asked cautiously.

Rydberg's face was unreadable in the darkness.

"At the moment I don't have any pain," he said. "But tomorrow it'll be back. Or the next day."

It was almost 2 a.m. when Wallander left Rydberg sitting on his balcony. Wallander left his car where it was and walked home. The moon had disappeared behind a cloud. Now and then he skipped. The voice of Maria Callas resounded in his head.

Before he went to sleep, he lay in bed for a while in the darkness of his apartment with his eyes open. Again he thought about the violence. The new era, which demanded a different kind of policeman. We're living in the age of the noose, he thought. Fear will be on the rise.

He forced himself to push these thoughts aside and sought out the black woman of his dreams. The investigation was over. Now he could finally get some rest.

An excerpt from the new Kurt Wallander novel

The Troubled Man

by HENNING MANKELL

Coming from Knopf
March 2011

Håkan von Enke's birthday party was held in a rented party facility in Djursholm, the upmarket suburb of Stockholm. Wallander had never been there before. Linda assured him that a leisure suit would be appropriate—von Enke hated dinner jackets and tails, although he was very fond of the various uniforms he had worn during his long naval career. Wallander could have worn his police uniform if he'd wanted to; but he had taken his best suit with him. Under the circumstances, it didn't feel right for him to use his uniform.

Why on earth had he agreed to go to Stockholm, Wallander asked himself as the express train from Arlanda Airport came to a halt in the Central Station. Perhaps it would have been better to go somewhere else. He occasionally used to take short trips to Skagen in Denmark, where he liked to stroll along the beaches, visit the art gallery, and lounge around in one of the guesthouses he had been using for the past thirty years. It was to Skagen that he had retreated many years ago when he had toyed with the idea of resigning from the police force. But here he was in Stockholm to attend Linda's future father-in-law's birthday party.

When everyone had finished eating, Wallander went out into a conservatory to stretch his legs. The restaurant was surrounded by spacious grounds—the estate had previously been the home of one of Sweden's first and richest industrialists.

He gave a start when Håkan von Enke appeared by his side out of nowhere, clutching something as un-PC as an old-fashioned pipe and a pack of tobacco. Wallander recognized the brand: Hamilton's Blend. For a short period in his late teens he had been a pipe smoker himself, and used the same tobacco.

"Winter," said von Enke. "And we're in for a snow-storm, according to the forecast."

Von Enke paused for a moment and gazed out at the dark sky.

"When you're on board a submarine at a sufficient depth, the climate and weather conditions are totally irrelevant. Everything is calm; you're in a sort of ocean basement. In the Baltic Sea, twenty-five meters is deep enough if there isn't too much wind. It's more difficult in the North Sea. I remember once leaving Scotland in stormy conditions. We were listing fifteen degrees at a depth of thirty meters. It wasn't exactly pleasant."

He lit his pipe and eyed Wallander keenly.

"Is that too poetic a thought for a police officer?"

"No, but a submarine is a different world as far as I'm concerned. A scary one, I should add."

The commander sucked eagerly at his pipe.

"Let's be honest," he said. "This party is boring both of us stiff. Everybody knows that I arranged it. I did it because a lot of my friends wanted me to. But now we can hide ourselves away in one of the little side rooms. Sooner or later my wife will come looking for me, but we can talk in peace until then."

"But you're the star of this show," said Wallander.

"It's like in a good play," said von Enke. "In order to increase the excitement, the main character doesn't need to be onstage all the time. It can be advantageous if some of the most important parts of the plot take place in the wings."

He fell silent. Too abruptly, far too abruptly, Wallander thought. Von Enke was staring at something behind Wallander's back. Wallander turned around. He could see the garden, and beyond it one of the minor roads that eventually joined the main Djursholm-Stockholm highway. Wallander caught a glimpse of a man on the other side of the fence, standing under a lamppost. Next to him was a parked car, with the engine running. The exhaust fumes rose and slowly dispersed in the yellow light.

Wallander could tell that von Enke was worried.

"Let's get our coffee and then shut ourselves away," he said.

Before leaving the conservatory, Wallander turned

around again; the car had vanished, and so had the man by the lamppost. Perhaps it was someone von Enke had forgotten to invite to the party, Wallander thought. It couldn't have been anyone looking for me, surely—some journalist wanting to talk to me about the gun I left in the restaurant.

After they picked up their coffee, von Enke led Wallander into a little room with brown wooden paneling and leather easy chairs. Wallander noticed that the room had no windows. Von Enke had been watching him.

"There's a reason for this room being a sort of bunker," he said. "In the 1930s the house was owned for a few years by a man who owned a lot of Stockholm nightclubs, most of them illegal. Every night his armed couriers would drive around and collect all the takings, which were brought back here. In those days this room contained a big safe. His accountants would sit here, adding up the cash, doing the books, and then stash the money away in the safe. When the owner was arrested for his shady dealings, the safe was cut up. The man was called Göransson, if I remember correctly. He was given a long sentence that he couldn't handle. He hanged himself in his cell at Långholmen Prison."

He fell silent, took a sip of coffee and sucked at his pipe, which had gone out. And that was the moment, in that insulated little room, where the only sound was a faint hum from the party guests outside, that Wallander realized Håkan von Enke was scared. He had seen this many times before in his life: a person frightened of something, real or imagined. He was certain he wasn't mistaken.

The conversation started awkwardly, with von Enke reminiscing about the years when he was still on active duty as a naval officer.

"The fall of 1980," he said. "That's a long time ago now, a generation back, twenty-eight long years. What were you doing then?"

"I was working as a police officer in Ystad. Linda was very young. I'd decided to move there in order to be closer to my elderly father. I also thought it would be a better environment for Linda to grow up in. Or at least, that was one of the reasons why we left Malmö. What happened next is a different story altogether."

Von Enke didn't seem to be listening to what Wallander said. He continued along his own line.

"I was working at the East Coast naval base that fall. Two years before I had stepped down as officer in charge of one of our best submarines, one of the Water Snake class. We submariners always called it simply the Snake. My posting at the marine base was only temporary. I wanted to go back to sea, but the powers that be wanted me to become part of the operations command of the whole Swedish naval defense forces. In September the Warsaw Pact countries were conducting an exercise along the East German coast. MILOBALT, they called it. I can still remember that. It was nothing remarkable; they generally had their fall exercises at about the same time as we had ours. But an unusually large number of vessels was involved, since they were practicing landings and submarine recovery. We had succeeded in finding out the details without too much effort. We heard from the National Defense Radio Center that there was an awful lot of radio communication traffic between Russian vessels and their home base near Leningrad, but everything seemed to be routine; we kept an eye on what they were doing and made a note of anything we thought important in our logbooks. But then came that Thursday—it was September 18, a date that will be the very last thing I forget. We had a call from the duty officer on one of the fleet's tugs, HMS *Ajax*, saying that they had just discovered a foreign submarine in Swedish territorial waters. I was in one of the map rooms at the naval base, looking for a more detailed chart of the East German coast, when an agitated national serviceman burst into the room. He never managed to explain exactly what had happened, but I went back to the command center and spoke to the duty officer on the *Ajax*. He said he'd been scanning the sea with his telescope and suddenly noticed the submarine's aerials some three hundred yards away. Fifteen seconds later the submarine surfaced. The officer was on the ball, and figured out that the submarine had probably been at periscope depth but had then started to dive when they saw the tug. The *Ajax* was just south of Huvudskär when the incident happened, and the submarine was heading southwest, which meant that she was parallel with the border of Swedish waters but definitely on the Swedish side of the line. It didn't take long for me to find out if there were any Swedish submarines in the area: there were not. I requested radio contact with the *Ajax* again, and asked the duty officer if he could describe the conning tower or the periscope he had seen. From what he said I realized immediately that it was one of the submarines of the class NATO called Whiskey. And at the time they were used only by the Russians and the Poles. I'm sure you'll understand that my heart started beating faster when I established that. But I had two other questions."

Von Enke paused, as if he expected Wallander to ask what the two questions were. Some peals of laughter could be heard on the other side of the door, but they soon faded away.

"I suppose you wanted to know if the submarine was in Swedish territorial waters by mistake," said Wallander. "As was claimed when that other Russian submarine ran aground off Karlskrona?"

"I had already answered that question. There is no naval vessel as meticulous with its navigation as a submarine. That goes without saying. The submarine the *Ajax* had come across intended to be where it was. The question was what exactly it was up to. Why was it reconnoitering and surfacing, apparently not expecting to be discovered? It could have been a sign that the crew was being careless. But, of course, there was also another possibility."

"That the submarine wanted to be discovered?"

Von Enke nodded, and made another attempt to light his reluctant pipe.

"In that case," he said, "to encounter a tugboat would be ideal. A vessel like that probably wouldn't even have a catapult to attack you with. Nor would the crew be trained for confrontation. Since I was in charge at the base, I contacted the supreme commander, and he agreed with me that we should immediately send in a helicopter equipped for tracking down submarines. It made sonar contact with a moving object we decided was a submarine. For the first time in my life I gave an order to open fire in circumstances other than training exercises. The helicopter fired a depth charge to warn the submarine. Then it vanished, and we lost contact."

"How could it simply disappear?"

"Submarines have many ways of making themselves invisible. They can descend into deep troughs, hugging the cliff walls, and thus confuse anybody trying to trace them with echo sounders. We sent out several helicopters, but we never found any further trace of it."

"But couldn't it have been damaged?"

"That's not the way it goes. According to international law, the first depth charge must be a warning. It's only later that you can force a submarine up to the surface for identification."

"What happened next?"

"Nothing, really. There was an inquiry, and they decided that I'd done the right thing. Maybe this was the overture for what was to follow a couple of years later, when Swedish territorial waters were crawling with foreign submarines, mainly in the Stockholm archipelago. I suppose the most important result was that we had confirmation of the fact that Russian interest in our navigational channels was as great as ever. This happened at a time when nobody thought the Berlin Wall would fall or the Soviet Union collapse. It's easy to forget that. The Cold War wasn't over. After that incident, the Swedish navy was granted a big increase in funding. But that was all."

Von Enke drained the rest of his coffee. Wallander was about to stand up when his host started speaking again.

"I'm not done yet. Two years later, off we went again. By then I'd been promoted to the very top of the Swedish naval defense staff. Our HQ was in Berga, and there was a combat command on duty around the clock. On October 1 we had an alarm call that we could never have imagined, even in our wildest dreams. There were indications that a submarine, or even several, was in the Hårsfjärden channel, very close to our base on Muskö. So it was no longer just a case of trespassing in Swedish territorial waters; there were foreign submarines in a restricted area. No doubt you remember all the fuss?"

"The newspapers were full of it, and television reporters were clambering around on slippery rocks."

"I don't know what you could compare it to. Perhaps a foreign helicopter landing in a courtyard at the heart of the royal palace. That's what it felt like, having submarines close to our top secret military installations."

"That was when I'd just received confirmation that I could start working in Ystad."

Suddenly the door opened. Von Enke gave a start. Wallander noted that his right hand was on its way to the breast pocket of his jacket. Then he let it fall back onto his knee again. The door had been opened by a semi-inebriated woman who was looking for a bathroom. She withdrew, and they were alone again.

"It was in October," von Enke resumed once the door had closed. "It sometimes felt as if the whole Swedish coast was under siege by unidentified foreign submarines. I was glad I wasn't the one responsible for talking to all the journalists who had gathered out at Berga. We had to convert a few barrack rooms into press rooms. I was extremely busy all the time, trying to find one of those submarines. We'd lose all our credibility if we couldn't manage to force a single one to the surface. And then, at last, came the evening when we had trapped a submarine in the Hårsfjärden channel. There was no doubt about it; the command team was convinced this was it. I was the one responsible for giving the order to open fire. During those hectic hours I spoke several times to the supreme commander and the new minister of defense. His name was Andersson, if you recall—a man from Borlänge."

"I have a vague memory of him being called 'Red Börje.'"

"That's right. But he wasn't up to the job. He no doubt thought the submarines were pure hell. He went back home to Dalarna and we got Anders Thunborg as minister of defense. One of Palme's blue-eyed boys. A lot of my colleagues didn't trust him, but the contact I had with him was good. He didn't interfere; he asked questions. If he got an answer, he was satisfied. But once when he called me I had the distinct impression that Palme was in the room with him, standing by his side. I don't know if that was true. But the feeling was very strong."

"Anyway, what happened?"

Von Enke's face twitched, as if he was annoyed by Wallander interrupting him. But when he continued there was no sign of that.

"We had cornered the submarine in such a way that it couldn't move without our permission. I spoke to the supreme commander and told him that we were about to fire depth charges and force the sub up to the surface. We needed another hour to prepare for the operation, and then we would be able to reveal to the world the identity of this submarine that had invaded Swedish territorial waters. Half an hour passed. The hands on the wall clock seemed to be moving unbearably slowly. The whole time, I was in touch with the helicopters and the surface vessels surrounding the submarine. Forty-five minutes passed. And then it happened."

Von Enke broke off abruptly, then stood up and left the room. Wallander wondered if he had been taken ill. But after a few moments the commander returned, carrying two glasses of cognac.

"It's a chilly winter evening," he said. "We need something to warm us up. Nobody seems to have missed us, so we can carry on chatting in this bunker."

Wallander waited for the rest of the story. Even if it wasn't perhaps totally engrossing, listening to old stories about submarines, he preferred von Enke's company to having to talk to people he didn't know.

"That's when it happened," repeated von Enke. "Four minutes before the attack was due to take place, the phone rang—the direct line to Defense Command Sweden. As far as I know it was one of the few lines guaranteed to be safe from bugging, and it was also fitted with an automatic scrambler. I was given an order that I would never have expected in a thousand years. Can you guess what it was?"

Wallander shook his head, and wrapped his hand around the brandy glass to warm up the brandy.

"We were ordered to abort the depth charge attack. Naturally, I was dumbstruck and demanded an explanation. But I didn't receive one—not then, at least. Just the specific order that on no account should any depth charges be fired. Obviously, I had no choice but to obey. There were only two minutes left when the helicopters were informed of the decision. None of us at Berga could understand what was going on. It was exactly ten minutes before we received our next order. If possible, it was even more incomprehensible. Our superiors seemed to have taken leave of their senses. We were ordered to back off."

Wallander was becoming more interested.

"So you were told to let the submarine get away?"

"Nobody actually said that, of course. Not in so many words, at least. We were ordered to concentrate our attention on a different part of the Hårsfjärden channel, at its very edge, south of the Danzig straits. A helicopter had made contact with another submarine. Why was that one more important than the one we had encircled and were just about to force up to the surface? My colleagues and I were at a loss. I asked to speak to the supreme commander in person, but he was busy and couldn't be interrupted. Which was very odd, because he was the one who had authorized the operation not long before. I even tried to speak to the minister of defense or his private secretary, but everyone seemed to have vanished, unplugged their phones, or been instructed to say nothing. The supreme commander and the minister of defense instructed to say nothing? By whom? The government could have done it, of course, or the prime minister. I had agonizing stomach pains for several hours. I didn't understand the orders I'd been given. Aborting the operation went against my experience and instincts. I came very close to refusing to obey. That would have been the end of my military career. But I still had a grain of common sense left. And so we moved all our helicopters and two surface vessels to the Danzig straits. I asked for permission to keep at least one helicopter hovering over the place where we knew the submarine was hiding, but that was not granted. We should leave the area, and do so immediately. Which we did. With the expected result."

"Which was?"

"Needless to say, we didn't find a submarine near the Danzig straits. We continued searching for the rest of the night. I still wonder how many thousand liters of fuel the helicopters used up."

"What happened to the submarine you had encircled?"

"It disappeared. Without a trace."

Wallander thought over what he had heard. Once, in the far distant past, he had completed his national military service with a tank regiment in Skövde. He had unpleasant memories of that period of his life. On being called up he had tried to join the navy, but he had been sent to Västergötland. He had never had any trouble accepting discipline, but he did find it difficult to understand a lot of the orders they were given. It often seemed that chaos ruled, despite the fact that they were supposed to imagine themselves in a potentially lethal confrontation with an enemy.

Von Enke emptied his cognac glass.

"I started asking questions about what had happened. I shouldn't have. I soon noticed that it was not a particularly popular thing to do. Even some of my colleagues whom I had regarded as my best friends objected to my curiosity. But all I wanted to know was why these counterorders had been issued. I'm convinced that we were closer than we'd ever been before, or have been since, to finally making a submarine surface and identify itself. Two minutes away, no more than that. At first I wasn't the only one to be upset about the situation. Another commander, Arosenius, and an analyst from Defense Command Sweden were part of the top-level team that day. But after a few weeks they both started keeping me at arm's length. They didn't want to be associated with the way I was stirring things up and asking questions. And eventually I gave up as well."

Von Enke put his glass down on the table and leaned forward toward Wallander.

"But I haven't forgotten it, of course. I still keep trying to understand what happened—not just on that day when we allowed a submarine to give us the slip. I keep rehashing everything that happened during those years. And I think that now, at long last, I'm beginning to get some idea of what was really going on."

"You mean, why you weren't allowed to force that submarine to surface?"

He nodded slowly, lit his pipe again, but said nothing. Wallander wondered if the story he had heard was destined to remain unfinished.

"I'm curious, of course. What was the explanation?"

Von Enke made a dismissive gesture.

"It's too early for me to say anything about it. I still haven't come to the end of the road. So right now I have nothing more to say. Perhaps we'd better go and join the other guests."

They stood up and left the room. Wallander went back to the conservatory, and bumped into the woman who had disturbed them. Only now did he reflect on the way von Enke had moved his right hand when she had burst into the room—at first very decisively, but then slowing down and eventually dropping it back onto his knee.

Even if it seemed almost inconceivable, Wallander could only think of one explanation. Von Enke was carrying a gun. Was that really possible, he thought as he stared out through the window at the deserted garden. A retired naval commander carrying a gun at his seventy-fifth birthday party?

Wallander simply couldn't believe it. He dismissed the thought. He must have been imagining things. One bewildering experience must have led to another. First the idea that von Enke was scared, and then that he was carrying a gun. Wallander wondered if his intuition was fading, just as he was beginning to grow more forgetful.

Linda came into the conservatory.

"I thought you must have left."

"Not yet. But soon."

"I'm sure both Håkan and Louise are glad that you came."

"He's been telling me about the submarines."

Linda raised an eyebrow.

"Really? That surprises me."

"Why?"

"I've tried to get him to tell me about that lots of times. But he always refuses, says he doesn't want to. He seems to get annoyed."

Hans shouted for her, and Linda left. Wallander thought about what she had said. Why had Håkan von Enke chosen to tell him his story?

Three months later—on April 11 to be more precise—something happened that forced Wallander to think back yet again to that evening in January.

It happened without warning and was totally unexpected by everyone involved. Håkan von Enke disappeared without a trace from his home in the Östermalm district of Stockholm.

ALSO BY HENNING MANKELL

THE DOGS OF RIGA

On Sweden's coast, two bodies, victims of torture and execution, are discovered in a raft. After they are traced to the Baltic state of Latvia, Wallander is called to Riga and plunged into a world where old regimes do anything to stay alive.

Crime Fiction/978-1-4000-3152-8

THE WHITE LIONESS

When Wallander investigates the execution-style murder of a Swedish housewife, he uncovers a suspicious stalker. But when the suspect's alibi is airtight, he must look deeper, and what he discovers is far more complex than he ever imagined.

Crime Fiction/978-1-4000-3155-9

THE MAN WHO SMILED

A lawyer stops to examine an effigy in the middle of the highway and is hit over the head and dies. Within a week his son is also killed. Wallander's prime suspect is a corporate mogul with a gleaming smile that seems to hide the evil glee of a killer.

Crime Fiction/978-1-4000-9583-4

SIDETRACKED

A teenage girl sets herself aflame just as Wallander arrives on scene. Next he's called to a beach where Sweden's former minister of justice has been axed to death and scalped. The murder has the obvious markings of a demented serial killer, and Wallander is frantic to find him before he strikes again.

Crime Fiction/978-1-4000-3156-6

THE FIFTH WOMAN

In Africa, four nuns and a unidentified fifth woman are murdered. A year later, a retired car dealer and bird-watcher is impaled on bamboo poles, and the body of a missing florist is discovered—tied to a tree. Wallander will need to uncover the elusive connection between all these cases to solve them.

Crime Fiction/978-1-4000-3154-2

ONE STEP BEHIND

Three role-playing teens dressed in eighteenth-century garb are shot in a Swedish meadow. When one of Wallander's most trusted colleagues also turns up dead, he knows the murders are related. But with his only clue a picture of a woman no one in Sweden seems to know, he can't begin to imagine how.

Crime Fiction/978-1-4000-3151-1

FIREWALL

A body is found at an ATM, the apparent victim of a heart attack. Then two teenage girls are arrested for the brutal murder of a cab driver. At first these two incidents seem to have nothing in common, but as Wallander delves deeper into the mystery, he begins to unravel a wide-ranging conspiracy.

Crime Fiction/978-1-4000-3153-5

THE PYRAMID
The First Wallander Cases

Here, we see Wallander on his first homicide case as a 21-year-old patrolman, as a young father facing danger on Christmas Eve, as a middle-aged detective with his marriage on the brink, as a newly separated investigator solving the murder of a local photographer, and finally as a veteran detective.

Crime Fiction/978-1-4000-9582-7

BEFORE THE FROST

Having just graduated from the police academy, Linda Wallander returns to Skåne to join the police force, and she already shows all the hallmarks of her father—the maverick approach, the flaring temper. And before she even starts work, she takes on the case of a missing childhood friend.

Crime Fiction/978-1-4000-9581-0

ALSO AVAILABLE

Chronicler of the Winds • Depths • The Eye of the Leopard
Kennedy's Brain • The Return of the Dancing Master
Italian Shoes

Available at your local bookstore, or visit
www.randomhouse.com

New from

Henning Mankell

THE TROUBLED MAN

The first Kurt Wallander novel in more than a decade. A high-ranking naval officer disappears during his daily walk, and Wallander reacts in his inimitable way: interfering in matters that are not his responsibility, making promises he has no intention of keeping, paying little attention to the law—and getting results.

"Henning Mankell is a master of Swedish noir." —*The New York Times*

Available March 2011 in hardcover from Knopf
$25.95 • 384 pages • 978-0-307-59349-8

Please visit aaknopf.com